Death of a Queen

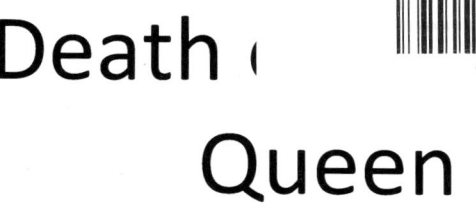

Queen

A Wes and Oz Mystery

By

S.B. Biddinger

Saying a special "Thanks"

I learned it took a team to help me write "Death of a Trailer Queen." The following people make it possible to bring my story to you. I would like to show my heartfelt thanks and appreciation to these ladies for helping me by giving their time, guidance and words of wisdom to make this a fun mystery to read.

To my friend Phyllis, without your thoughts, direction and educational background I would have never been able to bring my story to life.

To my friend Dallas, who struggled through my rough draft and saw potential for me to continue on, by offering her encouragement.

And to the most important person, my loving wife, Robin to who I owe a very special "Thanks" as she worked tirelessly by my side with re-write after re-write.

I appreciate these wonderful ladies for taking their time and energy for helping bring Wes and Oz to life in their first adventure "Death of a Trailer Queen."

I hope you enjoy the story.

Chapter 1

The night air was thick with humidity for this time of year causing my clothes to stick to my body. Sweat was rolling down my forehead. We were following up a lead on the Jackson murder case which had led us to this dark alley. Chuck was my partner and we worked out of the City Homicide Division. Currently we were waiting for uniforms to show for backup. I had only been Chuck's partner for a couple of months and he called me "The Rook." I had been a patrol officer for two years when I passed my detectives grade. Chuck had been a detective for over sixteen years. He had a no nonsense, take no crap from anyone attitude. He was as straight as they came. He stood about six feet tall, all muscle with salt and pepper hair. Everyone in the division had placed bets on how long I would last. Chuck's last partner only lasted about a month before she requested to be transferred. Prior to her, the two previous partners went back on patrol after three months. There had been a couple of days which I had thought the same but decided to stick it out.

Chuck looked around and still no uniforms. His patience was at the end, "Where in the hell are they. I hate waiting for these guys, let's go."

I knew we were going in alone. I had learned he hated to wait. I nodded and we started our long walk down the dark alley to the door at the end. There was a single 40-watt bulb above the door lighting our way. With my first steps, I felt the wet hairs on my back rise. I knew this wasn't going to be a good idea but with Chuck, being my senior and impulsive, what was I to do? My job was to back up my partner.

"Are you sure this is a good idea?" He turned back and gave me one of his keep your mouth shut looks and kept on walking.

My senses of the unknown and fear were working overtime as my eyes slowly adjusted to the darkness of the alley. My nose picked up very strange, pungent and offensive smells. My ears strained for sounds trying to pick up anything out of place. Yes, being the newbie, fear filled my body with anticipation that something bad was coming my way. "Do you think this guy is going be behind that door and how good was your tip?"

He just nodded and put his finger to his mouth, "Shhhhh." I needed to learn when to keep my mouth shut, like now.

With each slow step forward my eyes adjusted to the darkness. I saw what looked like lights from cigarettes burning about knee high. We were not alone in this alley. Great! I could smell urine, puke, sweat, bad body odor and everything else you could imagine. I heard faint whispers as we kept moving closer toward the door at end of this long smelly darkness. Where in the hell was our back up I kept asking myself?

The alley was full of street people trying to get shelter for the night. Some were trying to sleep and others were passed out from too much booze. There were a few sitting, smoking and watching us. My stomach was tied up in at least twenty knots as we kept moving forward. As I took my next step, my foot stumbled against something and I caught myself before crashing into the back of Chuck. That would not have been a good thing.

"Watch it," he whispered. I could feel Chuck's eyes glaring at me even although I couldn't see them.

We still had a ways to go and I felt as if I was going to throw up. The smells were getting to me. It was bad. I couldn't understand how people lived this way. I just wanted to leave and get back in our air conditioned squad car. I needed to get some fresh air. My legs each felt like a hundred pounds with every step.

Just then I felt something slam into my chest and before I could react I was flat on my back. I couldn't move from the weight on top of me. There was ringing in my ears and through my closed eyes could see flashes of light. I just laid there for a moment trying to gather my composer and get a bearing of my surroundings. I couldn't understand a word I was hearing and the weight on my chest pressed my back hard into the ground. It was like I was frozen in time and not able to move. The ringing in my ears kept getting louder and louder and I was starting to become aware of what was happening when it hit me. "Shit!"

"Oz, would you please get your big, fat body off of me! Damn it dog, you're not a dainty Yorkie! Now get off!"

I struggled to turn over and shut off the alarm. The morning light was coming through the windows as the sun peaked over the mountains. "It was going to be another beautiful day in paradise," I thought to myself. Before I could bury my face under the covers, Oz was all over me trying to get my attention. Each morning as soon as he would hear the voice coming from my alarm clock I was attacked. This was our routine and you would think I would've gotten used to it by now. But no, that would never happen. "Oz, give me a couple more minutes and I will be happy to give you some attention."

He continued to bounce around the bed. This was his way of saying, "Get up, get up, the sun is up and I need my morning doggie treat."

After a couple of minutes of wrestling with him on the bed I knew I wasn't going to be able to get any more sleep so I reluctantly put my feet on the floor, stood up and looked back at Oz. He had claimed the bed for himself. It was only when I opened the living room patio door to let the fresh air in that he got off the bed. The birds were chirping "Good morning" as if I gave a damn. Oz now danced around my feet waiting for his morning treat. As soon as I opened his treat canister he sat. I gave him one and after a quick gulp he ran out the doggie door to chase the birds out in the back yard.

I chose to climb back into bed in an attempt to get a few more minutes of shut eye but Oz had other plans. He came running into the bedroom and jumped on the bed and began to lick my face. His body was full of energy and wanted to play. He worked hard to get me up and play with him but I wasn't quite ready to start my day. I reached out and grabbed him by the collar and he quickly laid his body next to mine and rolled onto his back hoping for a belly rub. His tail thumped against my leg at least 90 beats a minute. He loved having his belly rubbed. This was my few minutes of calm before he would start jumping around the bed again trying to get me up to feed him. My phone's alarm broke the stillness in the room with music and I knew my time of additional shut eye was not going to happen. Before I climbed out Oz had bounded off the bed and was in the kitchen barking letting me know to hurry up. He was hungry and wanted to be fed. By the time I entered the kitchen he was sitting and staring at his dish waiting for his breakfast.

You see, Oz was my shadow, buddy, self-appointed bodyguard and overall ball of hair. He weighed at least eighty plus pounds and stood twenty-seven inches tall at his shoulders. He was a tri color smooth collie which is a short hair collie but you would think he was ninety percent hair. I told everyone who came over to visit at my house that it was decorated in early collie. It was the way his hair covered the entire house: on the furniture, my clothes, in the air and mostly on the hardwood floors. I called it Oz's special touch and when our friends left they always took a bit of Oz with them. Watching him sit there as I prepared his breakfast reminded me of the first day we had met. He was just a puppy. I had stopped by to visit a friend and to see the litter of puppies their collie had. Tanya, my friend, put this little fur ball in my arms and said, "You need a buddy, he is yours."

How I could resist those eyes? Ever since that day, four years ago we had been best buds. I put his dish in front of him and he just sat there, first staring at the dish and then back at me.

"Okay, so I forgot your special doggie treat which goes on top." Just the word doggie treat and he started dancing and prancing. After devouring his treat, he buried his face in the dish.

My name is Wesley Johns or Wes to those who are close to me. Whenever the state of Idaho Insurance Department and or various insurance companies felt they had a possible fraudulent workman's comp claim they called me to investigate. I have been an independent private investigator for ten years and I am good at what I do.

While Oz scoffed down his food, I took a long hot shower letting the room fill with steam as I planned out my day. This being Saturday meant only one thing, a car show at the park. I did a quick washing of the thinning patch of hair on my head. I could make a bottle of shampoo last almost six months since now most of my head hair had relocated to my ears and nose. Combing and drying was always a cinch. I quickly dressed and went to the garage to pack the Bird. Yes, I have a nineteen fifty eight Ford Thunderbird, it is my pride and joy.

Once Oz saw me packing the Bird he knew we were going to a car show with a stop at Betty's for a treat. During the summer months our Saturday's routine were car shows which always included a stop at Betty's. We had been doing this ever since he was a puppy.

I fired up the engine and loved the sound it made. Engines on today's cars just don't have that magic, the deep rumble sound coming out the exhaust. The thrill of driving a Detroit made American classic always made my heart race. The chrome and the original white paint of my Ford Thunderbird shined bright as the sun danced along the body. I nicknamed it "the Bird". It was in good condition, not great, but then I was no mechanic.

Today's car show was one of my yearly favorites. A local car club put it on for a local veteran's charity. Last year they raised a couple of thousand dollars. With the windows down and Oz's head out the passenger side window we cruised to Betty's. I sang along with the classic fifties and sixties tunes on the radio and it didn't take us long before we pulled into the parking lot of our favorite donut shop. It was named the "Whole Experience Bakery," but I called it Betty's since that was the name of the owner. The good thing or maybe bad if you talked to my doctor, was the Betty's shop was very close to my home. Both Oz and I had checked out all the donut shops in the valley and I do mean all of them and this was our favorite by far. Betty knew her donuts and she made the best apple fritters for miles around.

I pulled into two parking spaces making sure no one parked to close to ding my steel treasure when they opened their car doors. I am sure if that were to ever happen Oz would give them an earful. People coming out and going into the donut shop noticed the Bird and nodded in approval. "Cool car" a man commented as I walked into the shop. I gave him a "Thanks" reply.

"Morning, Wes. The usual?" Betty called out from behind the counter.

"You know me. Let's go with the usual. Oz doesn't like surprises."

Betty was the queen of the donuts and other enticing baked goods. It showed as I had to stand in line to get our fried deliciousness. Betty had owned this shop for at least thirty years and she knew all her loyal customer's names and greeted them each time they walked in. You could tell she loved her work and her product. Her body showed she was good at quality control. Our usual was two apple fritters for me and two of Betty's famous doggie donuts for Oz. Betty was also a pet lover. She had pictures of her two Basset Hounds covering the walls of her shop. One of her pet friendly specialties was the dog bone shaped donut. They were baked just for her four legged customers. I tried one once and it was not for human consumption. Oz loved them and she sold a lot of her special donuts.

Grabbing a bottle of orange juice I paid my tab and I waved goodbye to Betty as I walked out the door. She was busy helping another customer. Oz did his oh boy, oh boy I love my donut dance as I got back into the Bird. "You are going to have to wait until we get the show. I didn't spend all last night getting the Bird ready for the show to have you get crumbs and slobber all over the inside." It was bad enough with all his hair!

As we got closer to the park we came across more and more classic cars heading to the show. By the time we arrived there must have been at least sixty to seventy cars already parked and on display. I located where quite a few cars from of our little group were parked and headed that way. As we slowly creped past a row of parked cars I chuckled, I get the most enjoyment at these shows watching the guys and some ladies fussing over their pride and joy's making sure their baby was "The Bell of the Show."

Mike, a member of our little car group was signaling us where he had saved us a spot. We always had one person who would get to the show early enough to save spots for everyone. They knew that would never be me because Oz and I always had to first pay a visit to Betty's. It was no fun arriving late and having to park away from the group. Oz barked with excitement seeing Mike who was his car show bud. I backed in next to Mike's nineteen fortyish tan Dodge. I could never remember what year it was. He must have spent all night working on it because it looked great. I walked over to say hi but he was already busy petting Oz who had jumped out the passenger side window. Oz was not going to miss a chance at getting his ears scratched by his friend. Mike was close to my age and married to a cutie named Marsha. He worked for a large manufacturing company and traveled a lot. We talked for a few minutes and then I had to get to work cleaning someone's slobber off the passenger door. I looked down at Oz and said, "I wonder who did this?" He just sat and gave me a returned look of "What's the problem? You know and I know dogs like to slobber out car windows."

I counted eight cars which included me from our little group. I became friends with Mike about three years ago when he had asked me to join this group of car aficionados. Our little group included an eclectic collection of American made cars ranging from various years, makes and models, which were unlike most car clubs here. Other clubs were more make or model specific. We considered ourselves more of a social group who all own and love any America classic.

Now let me set the record straight. As I said earlier, I am not a car enthusiast like most of the people here today. I love my Thunderbird and I enjoy the shows and to cruise the streets, but besides filling it with gas, checking the oil and tires my knowledge of the working of my car stops there. My mechanic knows my car from bumper to bumper. When I first started using him as the Bird's mechanic I had no trouble getting it in to have some work done on it. But recently I had noticed he and his wife had been taking a lot of vacations. I am sure I helped fund parts of those trips. Now unlike most classic car junkies here at the show, after cleaning up after Oz and registering my car I just pull out my chair and cooler and sat to relax. Occasionally, from time to time, I would get up and run a duster lightly over the Bird but as I said occasionally. I was here to socialize, watch people, take some pictures and just have fun. After all, it was the weekend.

Oz took his usual place at the front of the Bird, standing guard making sure everyone who passed by knew this was his baby but most of all he was trying to impress the ladies. He got his picture taken more times than the Bird and many of them were with the ladies. He was one smart guy. I walked over to Mike and asked, "I noticed you are saving one more spot. Who's missing?"

I started to munch on my fritter when he said, "Hey, watch where you're eating that! I just finished lightly waxing my car. I'm saving it for Ed. It's strange he is still not here, you know Ed always the first one to arrive. It's what he lives for and especially since this is one of his favorite shows. For some reason he's running late."

I nodded my head in agreement, "Yea, knowing Ed I think he's here at these shows before the sun comes up. He always wants to make sure everything looks perfect on his Cadillac."

Mike gave out a chuckle, but I knew he was not much different than Ed. I think it was a competition between the two of them to see who would be the first one at a car show. Mike loved his wife and kids, but we all knew his first love was his Dodge. Mike was one of those true car guys. When he was not working or traveling he spent a lot of his time out in the garage with his steel bodied baby. He had purchased the car about 15 years prior and when he got it, it was a mess. Piece by piece he took it apart: cleaned, painted and fixed each part and then put it back together. Now it almost looked as if it had just come off the show room floor.

Just then an arm wrapped around mine and it was Marsha, Mike's wife, "Hey stud, I see Oz is playing to the crowd as usual."

I turned and there were three young ladies petting and talking to him. They were each taking turns of having their picture taken with him. He was in heaven. He had a smile on his face and was eating this moment up. "Yep, he loves the ladies."

Pretty soon we were joined by the rest of our group. Doug and Doris have a sixty-three Ford Thunderbird. They were an older retired couple and traveled a lot in their camper when not at car shows. Dave and his sister Jane were there and they share ownership of a royal blue fifty-seven Chevy Nomad. Dave worked for a local supply company and Jane at a grocery store. They also were close to my age and neither one had yet to find that someone special to settle down with. Bruce and Sue were owners of the Ford midnight black Falcon. They were also an older couple who just recently moved to our fair city and joined the group. Jeff was here with his beautiful silver Buick Regal that he called "The Silver Bullet." Jeff was like Doug and Doris, retired and traveled a lot. We all said the usual hellos and played catch up on what had happened in our lives since the last time we had gotten together. Usually there was nothing to exciting going on.

It didn't take long before the topic came up of where in the hell was Ed. Jeff said that he'd tried calling him a couple of days ago but he'd never answered or returned his call. We all thought it was strange since in all the years we had known him he had never missed a show. I commented that maybe he had gotten held up and would be here soon and the others agreed.

After sitting and chatting for a while it was time for Oz and me to walk around and check out the other cars. We had seen about half of them when Oz picked up a scent in the air, his nose busy sniffing. Yes, I picked up the same scent of meat cooking on the flattop. We looked at each other and it was off to the burger stand with Oz in the lead.

We were greeted by Bill the owner of the stand. Both Oz and I were one of his loyal car show customers. His menu was very basic, hamburger or cheeseburger. You added the fixings the way you liked it and grabbed a bag of chips. During the summer months this helped Bill make some extra money to put his kids through college. He was starting to get a crowd, but he must've seen us coming because before I could place our order, his daughter Julia handed me our burgers. Oz and I had never changed up our routine even when it came to Bill's burgers. Mine was with cheese and Oz's without. I handed Julie a ten and waved goodbye.

I grabbed my chair and joined the group where hot gossip was being passed around. I started to un-wrap Oz's burger but before I could do it he snatched it out my hand and wolfed it down. He then turned his attention to mine. I asked him, "Did you even taste it?" He just tilted his head from side to side drooling with the thought that I should share mine with him. Figuring out he was not going to enjoy a second burger he walked over to the ladies hoping for a handout or two. He knew who the softies were.

The afternoon temperatures were warming up and I spent the rest of the day making small talk with my car group buddies and talking to a few people who stopped by and showed some interest in the Bird. Oz was happy to just stand and guard the Bird. He always kept an eye on me and made sure I was always within range if I were to need his protection.

With the sun now moving to the horizon it was trophy time. I was always amazed to see how many lived to receive a trophy for their hard work: Mike, Ed, Dave and even Jane. It was a competition between them to see who would end up with the most trophies at the end of the car show season. As for me, in all the years of coming to these events, I think I won one or maybe two. I always thought I won those because the judges felt sorry for me. As the awards were being given out to the winners I noticed Oz was acting strange. He was staring at this one person and I could see the hairs on his back where standing up. This was an odd behavior for Oz. I looked over at the person he was focused on and the guy was acting a little weird. Oz let out a slight growl and everyone turned to look at him. When I looked up the guy was gone. That was strange.

Well, as usual, Mike and even Jeff took home a trophy. I was happy for Jeff because I think this was his first one. He sported a smile from ear to ear.

Another favorite part of a car show was to watch how fast people were able to take down their displays, put away their chairs, tents and other items and try to be one of the first ones to leave. There was usually only one exit and all two hundred cars tried to leave at once. It was kind of comical to watch, so I sat back and enjoyed the circus. I liked watching people and maybe that was why I was so good at my job as an investigator. Oz crashed on the blanket next to my chair and waited with me. It had been a long day for him of hanging out with the ladies and standing guard.

As I enjoyed watching the three ring chaos around me Jane walked over and commented, "It's strange not having Ed here today. I hope he's okay?"

"If it will make you feel any better, Oz and I will stop by his place on our way home and check on him. I'm sure he is fine and who knows, maybe the reason he didn't show today was a work thing." I assured her I would call later and let her know what I found out.

The park was almost empty except for a few of us who waited for the others to leave so I started to pack up my stuff. Oz started growling and was staring at that same man he was focused on at the trophy presentation. I had never seen him act this way at any of the shows. I didn't know what this person had done to get his attention but he kept a watchful eye on him. "Oz let's go," I said and Oz reluctantly got in the Bird all the while keeping his eyes on the man as he walked out of the park.

Chapter 2

While driving over to check on Ed I asked Oz if he had
gotten any new phone numbers from his admirers during
the show and he just looked at me. I had met Ed through
our little car group and had known him for around three
years. He lived alone and was about forty give or take a
year or two. He was a loan officer at a branch office on
Broadway for a regional bank. He loved anything classic,
old classic movies and classic cars made before the
seventies. He owned a beauty of a nineteen forty two
convertible, baby blue Cadillac. It was his pride and joy.
Besides showing his car at shows Ed also enjoyed being in
parades. Some local celebrity lady would sit on the top of
the back seat waving her hand to the crowd. Since I had
known him, the only lady in his life was Annabelle, an
eight-year-old black and white border collie. He had
rescued her from the local shelter. I called her Annie.

Ed lived about twenty minutes from the car show we had
just left. His home was located in one of those high-end
living communities on the west side of town. The homes
looked to be in the four hundred thousand plus range. Oz
and I had been to Ed's home a couple of times mostly
after a car show for a group barbeque. As we pulled up
front Oz started to get excited. He knew he was going to
get to play with his girlfriend, Annie. By the time I got out

of the car, Oz had already jumped out the window and had his nose to the ground. I looked around the quiet neighborhood and that was when I noticed Ed's neighbor lady from across the street staring at me out her front window. I could still feel her eyes on me as I walked up Ed's driveway. I turned around and yep, she was still staring at me, but now she was actually glaring. "Yikes," I wondered what her issue was. I rang the doorbell and there was a strange silence. Annie wasn't barking at the door like she usually did and Oz started pacing back and forth occasionally putting his nose to the door. I knocked on the door a couple more times and still no response. Oz was sniffing around the front of the house after getting something was not right. I pulled out my phone and dialed Ed's number. I heard his cell phone ringing on the other side of the door but no one answered. Maybe he was out in his backyard so both Oz and I started walking toward the side gate when I heard Annie barking. The barking was not coming from inside the house or back yard. She came running toward us from down the street. Oz ran over to greet her, but instead of joy, they both looked at each other and started barking. Annie and Oz both came running to me still barking and then the two of them ran off toward the side gate and disappeared into the backyard. It was odd the side gate had been left open so Annie could get out. Ed must be out visiting some friends in the neighborhood and unintentionally left it open. I went back to the Bird and grabbed a cold bottle of water. I would let the guys play in the backyard while I sat on the patio and waited for him to return. As I walked into the backyard I thought to myself again, what was so important for Ed not to make to the car show today? That wasn't like him?

When I got around to the back of the house the guys were nowhere in sight, they must had gone inside through the doggie door. I must say I loved having a doggie door. That was until Oz would go out in the middle of the night barking. I assumed he was letting the neighbors know he was on duty protecting his turf. There was some serious barking coming from inside, followed by both Oz and Annie running out into the backyard barking and prancing back and forth and then running back inside. This was Oz's serious bark and he was trying to tell me something was not right. I looked through the patio door window and both dogs shot through the doggie door again and continued to bark inside the house. I pulled on the patio door, it opened and I stepped inside. I was immediately confronted with a strange odor which filled the house. I left the door open to help clear out the smell. It smelled like the trash had not been taken out for a few days but that was unlike Ed since he was such a clean freak.

I called out his name but there was no response. I walked into the front hall where the dogs were barking and there on the floor was Ed's lifeless body in a puddle of dark red blood. I stood there in shock and stared. It took a couple of minutes for me to regain my composure. I checked to see if there was a pulse, but unfortunately there was none. His brown eyes just stared at the ceiling. There was a big red stain that had soaked his white shirt from a hole in the middle of his chest. He must have been like this for at least a couple of days due to the smell. Standing there, looking down at Ed's body and the blood, my body told me it was time to get out of there because I was about to lose my lunch. I walked back outside to get some fresh air and to calm down my stomach. I was in shock as to what I had just witnessed. This was a first for me. Out in the backyard and having taken a couple of deep breaths I dialed 911. Both Oz and Annie were sitting at my feet. Annie was whimpering so I bent down and petted her behind her ears. Oz was in alert mode scanning the backyard ready to pounce at anything that moved.

My senses came back to me and I decided to go back inside to look around. Having the door open for the short time had helped dissipate some of the unpleasant odor. In the living room the first thing I saw was a gun on the floor and I knew best not touch it. There were cases and cases of movies and music discs covering most of the floor and it was obvious this room had been trashed. Someone had been looking for something. I continued on into Ed's office and it was also a mess. Papers were scattered all over the floor and desk drawers pulled all the way out. I continued through the rest of house with both Oz and Annie close by my side. I was not sure who was protecting who. Making sure not to touch anything I continued to search the house. The bedroom had been trashed. The drawers pulled out from the dresser, bed sheets ripped off the bed and clothes tossed about. The closet hangers were empty and clothes cluttered the floor. I walked into the kitchen followed closely by my two bodyguards. It was the only room in the house which hadn't been touched. When I opened the door to the garage I saw Ed's Trailer Queen was missing. This whole house had been turned upside down as if someone was looking for something and now the Cadillac was gone. The hairs on my neck stood straight up and a jolt of panic went throughout my body when a voice called out "Hello." It was a female's voice.

Both Oz and Annie started barking and quickly moved toward the patio door. Once Annie saw the lady, she then started wagging her tail and rubbing up against the ladies leg. Oz stood there watching and put himself between the lady and me.

"Ed, your dog's barking keeps waking up Lyle. This is the third day this has been going on and it has to stop! Ed are you listening to me?" She hadn't noticed me or Oz and when I stepped out from the kitchen and back into the hallway, she jumped, "Who in the hell are you and where is Ed?"

"I am a friend of Ed's, and we'd better step outside," I said.

She looked to be in her late twenties with long blonde hair pulled back in a ponytail. She had dark brown eyes and was about five foot six inches. I figured she worked out a lot after looking at her body. She was wearing tight denim shorts the kind you had to peel off. She had on a light pink tank top leaving nothing to the imagination of what was underneath. I turned her from looking into the house and escorted her out into the backyard. There was no need exposing her to Ed's body in the hall. I heard the sirens off in the distance and as they got louder and closer she had a very puzzled look on her face.

"Hi, I'm Wes. I'm a friend of Ed's. There has been an accident."

Her face went blank and she just stared me. "An annn accident. What happened? Is Ed okay?" I guided her to a chair on the patio. She looked as if she was about to collapse. I gave her my unopened bottle of water. She was going to need it. The barking had increased and she jumped out of the chair and said, "See what I mean about the barking? Annie is going to wake up my son from his nap. Wait, where did that other dog come from and who the hell are you?"

"That is Oz and he is my traveling buddy and I am Wes."

A police officer walked through the side gate and I pointed him in the direction of the patio door and he walked inside.

"What are the police doing here? What is going on? Where is Ed?" There was horror in her eyes and tears running down her cheeks, "Where is Ed, what is happening, is he alright?" she asked with a whimper then her body started to give out on her and I helped her back down in the chair.

Oz and Annie had calmed down for the moment and both were lying on the grass watching the chaos start to unfold as more and more police officers began to swarm onto the property. To the neighbors it must've looked like a used car lot with a lot of flashing lights. I bet everyone, including that crazy lady from across the street was getting an eye full about now.

I looked down at Ed's neighbor. Her body was shaking and tears were flowing down her cheek and her lips were trembling, "I've got to get home. I have a child in the house."

"You've been here all this time, and you left your child alone?"

"No, no nothing like that. What I meant to say was that my sister is there with him, but she's not good with the little one. I really need to get out of here."

"You and me both," I said.

A voice from behind said, "Well, well if it's not Wes and look here is Oz. Hey fella, how is it going?"

I turned and there behind me was Detective Rodney Miller. Our paths had crossed before. Rod walked over and shook my hand and then introduced himself to Ed's next door neighbor. "Hi, I'm Detective Miller with the Homicide Division and you are Miss?"

"I'm Mrs. Jackson. Please call me Ronnie. I'm Ed's next door neighbor." She replied as she pointed to her house.

"Okay, Ronnie. Were you the one who found the body?"

"Body! No, I just came over to complain to Ed about Annabelle's constant barking. The side gate was open so I came into the backyard and the patio door was open. I started to go into the house when I saw this guy. He was just coming out of the kitchen and into the hall. He startled me."

"So then Wes, it must have been you who found the body and called the police. Who is Annabelle?"

I pointed at the dog and said, "Guilty as charged."

A voice from within the house called out Detective Miller's name. "You both have a seat. You are going to be here for a while." He turned and disappeared inside the house. By this time there must have been at least twenty police, detectives and emergency personnel inside the house and more were coming though the side gate.

Ronnie was in sheer panic mode, her eyes twitching back and forth. She was constantly rubbing her hands like she was washing them. Her large breast heaved with each short breath and her whole body shook. "Oh, crap, I have company coming over for dinner tonight and I haven't finished cleaning the house. I need to get to my son and start dinner. This is a freaking nightmare! I wished I had never ever come over here."

I took a seat next to hers since there was no use standing. It sounded like we were going to be here for a while. Annie came over and crashed at the bottom of my feet while Oz sat close by keeping a watchful eye on the comings and goings inside the house. Oz made sure he was between me and Ronnie because he was my personal bodyguard and his meal ticket.

Ronnie looked at me for a second and asked, "How can you be so calm at a time like this? I'm a nervous wreck."

On the outside I must have looked like a cool cucumber on a hot summer's day but on the inside I was just like her, a nervous wreck. I too wished I was not living this nightmare. My friend was dead! At this time there was really nothing to do but sit and wait as Detective Miller had instructed.

She asked, "So what is going on? No one has really said what has happened to Ed."

"When I came over this afternoon, I found Ed. He was lying in the front hallway, dead."

Tears flowed freely down her cheeks, "What did you just say? Ed's dead? Oh God, No! This can't be happening! Ed's dead? How? Did he fall or something?"

"Yes, it was something like that I'm afraid." I didn't want to be the one to tell her Ed had been shot.

Ronnie wrapped her arms around herself and sat there quietly mumbling with an occasional whimper, rocking back and forth. The chair she was sitting in was not a rocker. After a few minutes I felt it was best to change the subject.

"So how old is your little one at home? I think you mentioned his name, Lyle?"

Ronnie stopped rocking and looked at me, "What did you say?"

"How old is Lyle?"

"Oh, what a mess. Do you think we will be here long? Linda will wonder what is taking me so long and I know she's wondering about all the police!"

She hadn't heard a word I said. "It's hard to say. These things take a while to sort out. Linda must be your sister. So have you known Ed for very long?"

She gazed off into the distance, "We have been neighbors for about three years I think. Yes, about two or three years. I don't know. What is happening inside? I've got to get home."

"So did you guys get along as neighbors?"

"What? Yes, of course. We became good friends. Ed would watch my son, Lyle, once and a while when my husband and I would have a date night. Ed and Nick, that's my husband, would help each other from time to time with house projects. Nick really liked Ed and would visit with him whenever Ed had his car out of the garage."

"It sounds like you all were pretty good friends."

Ronnie looked around the yard very nervously. She had the look on her face of a trapped animal looking for a way to escape. "I guess you would say that. Occasionally Ed would even join us for dinner. He and my sister Linda dated for a while, but it didn't work out."

What! Ed had been dating? This was news to me. Ed at one time had a girlfriend? "How long did they go together?"

"Um, I would say maybe six months, but it didn't end well. Ever since the split up there had been tense moments between to two of them. Whenever Linda would come over to visit us she would obsess about him. I think maybe she wanted the relationship to go on longer but Ed didn't."

A voice disrupted our conversation and called out my name. "Wes, could I see you for a moment?" Rod requested.

I looked at Ronnie and told her I would be right back. I told Oz and Annie to stay and keep her company. Sometimes the stay command worked and other times, like when there was a pizza on the counter, it didn't. Oz had very selective hearing.

Detective Miller and I had known each other for about ten years. Because of my line of work he had helped me on a couple of my cases. I wouldn't say we were good friends, but we had a good working relationship.

"So what is up?"

He started off in his official police tone, "Did you touch anything in the house when you went inside?"

"Well, let me think, there's the patio door, the garage door and I did check to see if Ed was alive."

"Okay, what's the reason you decided to stop over at your friend's house today?"

I took a deep breath and explained that Ed hadn't shown up earlier for the car show at the Valley City Park. I told him that whenever we tried calling there was no answer so I volunteered to stop by and checkup on him.

"So walk me through everything you did when you first arrived."

"When I first showed up I thought it was strange that Annie was out front running around and barking frantically. I rang the doorbell several times and then called his cell. I could hear it ringing inside the house but it went to voicemail. The side gate was open so I assumed Ed was visiting one of the neighbors and so I thought I'd wait for him in the backyard. But when both dogs were barking and making a ruckus running back and forth through the doggie door I wanted to go in and to see what was causing all this commotion. The patio door was unlocked so I went inside and that's when I found Ed on the floor. I saw all the blood and realized he'd been shot and there was a bullet hole in his chest."

Rod looked at me and paused, "Did you happen to go into any of the other rooms?"

"I just peeked into the garage and noticed the Cadillac was missing." I didn't want to tell Rod I had checked out the rest of the house. I knew better.

I heard loud voices behind me and I turned and saw a couple of officers questioning Ronnie. The fear on her face said a lot.

"Wes, I know you saw a gun on the floor in the living room, did you touch it?"

"No! Nada! No way! Not in a million years! What do you take me for like one of those idiots you see on those television mysteries?"

A grin came over Rod's face, and he just waved and walked away.

"Hey, just asking but is there a chance Oz and I can get out of here soon? You know he becomes a bear when he doesn't get his dinner on time."

Rod turned and looked at Oz who was asleep. He just smiled and walked away. The other officers had left

Ronnie alone, so I walked back out and sat down next to her. We both just sat there in silence.

A police officer escorted a man and a lady carrying a little boy through the side gate. Ronnie looked up and ran over to them. I figured they must be her husband, sister and son. I watched as Ronnie explained what had happened and why all the police. Being a trained people watcher, I observed their body language and they were sending mixed signals. From the looks of it, Ronnie's sister was a basket case. Her body was shaking and she couldn't make eye contact as she put her face in her hands and tears flowed down her cheeks. Her body was semi limp and was being held up by the man. Ronnie looked to be a couple years older than her sister but it would be hard to tell them apart from a distance. As for the man, his demeanor was cold like a rock not showing one bit of emotion on his face or body and his eyes were glassed over as if he was on something. He stood there intently watching the police with his cold, blue, steel eyes while he had his arm wrapped around Ronnie's sister. Maybe he was not Ronnie's husband but a new boyfriend of Linda. He and Ronnie both kept their distance from each other. He stood about six feet five and broad in the shoulders, thick black hair. I bet he was in his early thirties. His body was very muscular I assume from lifting weights. He weighed close to three hundred pounds and looked to be someone you didn't want to meet in a dark alley late at night. Both Oz and Annie were focused on him. There was something about him they were wary of. Oz looked as if he was about to pounce. Ronnie brought the group over to where I was sitting.

I was the first to speak, "You must be Ronnie's sister," I guessed while I shook her hand.

"Why, yes, I am Linda and this is Ronnie's son Lyle," she struggled to get the words out.

Lyle's eyes lit up, and he said, "I'm three."

"It's nice to meet you, Lyle."

I then turned to the gentleman with my hand out to greet him and asked, "You are?"

"What the hell happened? What's with all the cops and who the hell are you again?" he questioned.

I started to answer but he was so focused on what was happening inside the house that he didn't hear a word I said. I paused and in a harsh tone I asked him again, "You are?" Ronnie spoke, "This is Nick, my husband." I pulled away my hand since he was not going to shake it.

I stood there in shock, why did he have his arm around Linda and not Ronnie. Those two were still keeping their distance from each other. There must be trouble in paradise. We all stood looking at each other and not saying a word. It was an awkward meeting at an unpleasant time.

I finally broke the ice, "So Nick, what you do for a living?"

He looked stunned at my question, "I manage a grocery store in town. What do you think they are doing inside?" His eyes had never left the opening of the patio door ever since he had arrived.

Ronnie took Linda and Lyle over to the patio and they sat on the loveseat holding each other while Lyle played with Annie. Oz stood by my side keeping a keen eye on Nick. For some reason he didn't trust him. I could tell he was about to attack if Nick made any sudden moves. I tried to hold a conversation with him, but he wasn't having any part of it. He walked to the back of the yard to get away from me. "I better brush up on my people skills," I thought. I sat next to the ladies and continued to watch Ronnie and her family. Linda had her head in Ronnie's lap and they both were silent.

Lyle ran around the yard with Annie chasing after him. Oz sat close by my side. Rod came out of the house and walked over to Ronnie and Linda. Nick quickly joined them.

Ronnie introduced her family to Detective Miller and explained they lived next door to Ed. Rod said to Ronnie, "You and your family can leave now. Officers will be stopping by in the morning to speak with each one of you."

Rod and I both watched as they left and then he turned to me, "Did you happen to notice in your investigation of the house that many of the rooms had been trashed by whoever did this?"

I gave him my innocent look, he just smiled and I knew I was busted. Having worked together in the past on some of my cases Rod knew me all too well. "Okay, I did do a little looking around, but I didn't touch anything."

"Did you move or touch anything on the body?"

"No, I used my mystic powers of deduction to see that poor Ed had been shot in the chest."

"Well, sit tight and I'll be right back."

Rod went back inside the house and I stood there with both Oz and Annie at my feet. He soon returned with a bag of dog food.

"I figure since we are going to be here all night Annabelle should go home with you. It looks like she and Oz are good buddies."

I looked down at her brown eyes. How could I refuse?

"I have dogs and I know it messes up their system when eating new food. I don't want a cowboy like you having to clean up after her." Rod smiled as he handed me her food.

He also handed me her leash, bent down to pet them both on the head and walked away. "See you tomorrow, Wes. Let's say about ten a.m. at the diner on Market." He waved goodbye and went back inside.

"Okay you two let's go home." I put the leash on Annie and at first she started walking fine but once she passed the gate she started to pull back. I could tell she didn't want to leave her home or Ed. Oz was a big help though in getting her into the Bird. As I fired it up Annie started to whimper. Oz already had his head out the car's back window and soon Annie started to calm down. She put her head out the other side back window, too. Just before I headed home I looked around at all the vehicles parked in the street. That's when I saw Ed's neighbor lady across the street still watching me out her front window. The hairs on the back of my neck were standing up again. There was something eerie about that lady.

The drive home was a blur. The radio played in the background and my mind was just numb. I parked the Bird in the garage and decided to clean it out in the morning. It had been a very long day and I was ready for a hot shower. First I had to feed the dogs and play referee since Oz wanted Annie's dinner and Annie wanted Oz's. After they had eaten it was time for me. I stood there with the water running off my body thinking about Ed and why someone would want to murder him. I couldn't think of one reason why. I must have been in the shower for over an hour since the water was getting colder. I dressed in shorts and a t-shirt and then went to forage for something to eat. I grabbed some cheese and crackers. I was ready to relax and try to put this day behind me. Both Oz and Annie were sacked out on the floor in front of the fireplace like best buddies. I looked down at the two of them and thought that as long as Annie was staying with us for a while it would be easier to nickname them "the guys" instead of saying, Oz and Annie all the time. "So what do you think about being called the guys?" Annie let out a little snort and Oz didn't even look up at me. Okay the "guys" it is. Just as I turned on the television my phone rang. The caller ID said it was Bruce.

"Hey Wes, I just saw the news about something going on at Ed's house. It showed the police at his house and your car was parked out front. Is Ed okay?"

"Oh crap," I thought, things had happened so fast I's forgotten to inform our little car group about Ed. I just stared at the television before replying, "No, he is not."

There was a long awkward silence when Bruce finally spoke, "Okay buddy, so what happened?"

I tried to think the best way to break the news to him but there wasn't an easy way. "He's dead." I didn't want to tell him Ed was lying there with a bullet hole in his chest.

"Jesus! What do you mean Ed's dead? Did he have a heart attack or some kind of accident or what?"

"You could say that. Bruce, I'm in as much shock about this as you are so what you say we talk about it tomorrow. Could you please call everyone and let them know I will be in touch. We'll get together soon."

"Yea sure, you sound pretty shook up. I understand and will let you go. If you need anything you know where to find me."

An old Charles Bronson movie played in the background but I wasn't paying any attention to it. My mind was running through all the events of the afternoon. I got up and walked into my office to make some notes. The guys were right behind me. I liked the sound of that, "the guys."

I found it was best to put my mental notes in writing. It always had helped me with my fraud cases. I knew I would want to help find out what had happened to my friend. I knew the police would investigate his murder but it wouldn't hurt if I did a little digging around myself. An hour past when I finished and my stomach alarm was going off. I made up a couple of PB & J's and poured a large glass of milk, dinner of champions.

I walked back into the family room and the Charles Bronson movie had ended and a Henry Fonda western was playing. I sat down to watch and eat. There staring at me were four sad eyes watching each and every bite. At first I held firm, I was not going to share but soon gave up and I caved. First, they just got the crust but towards the last bite they each got a taste of the peanut butter and jelly. It was just what the doctor ordered. I chuckled as I watched them try to get the peanut butter off the roof to their mouths. The three of us finished off the first sandwich and I saved the second one for later. I put the plate on the side table away from busy noses trying to get at it.

Chapter 3

I turned my attention to the movie as the guys slept at my feet. Annie was snoring so loudly that I had to turn up the volume. Concentrating on the movie was difficult. My mind kept playing over and over what I had witnessed this afternoon and knowing my friend was dead. The dog alarm shattered the silence of the house when the doorbell rang. Both guys jumped up and ran to the front door barking and warning. The doorbell rang again and this set off another frenzy. I pushed past the guys and pulled the door open. There was Marti with her hands full. She had a bottle of wine in one hand and an overnight bag in the other. She just smiled.

Marti was the most beautiful lady I had ever met. She had long, flowing auburn hair, brown seductive eyes, a killer looking figure and a smile that would melt an iceberg. She stood about five foot six and her body was one most actresses and models would love to have. She was the sexiest lady on the planet in my eyes.

Once Oz saw who it was, he went from barking mode to a dancing and prancing mode. The guys finally calmed down and I pushed them aside so Marti could come in.

"Well, what a welcoming committee." She put the wine and her bag down. She bent down and grabbed Oz's face and gave him a kiss on his nose. He loved receiving attention from Marti. Then she turned and looked at Annie, "Hmm, it looks like we have company. How are you today, Annabelle?"

She petted Annie for a moment then it was my turn. We embraced and kissed. It felt good to have her in my arms, just the therapy I needed after what I had experienced at Ed's today. We looked into each other's eyes and kissed again. Marti could tell that something was wrong so she pulled me in close and gave me a hug. "What's going on?" She whispered in my ear.

I heard a crash coming from the living room and by the time I got there the guys were gone and so was my other peanut butter and jelly sandwich. The empty plate sat on the floor, luckily it didn't break. We watched out the back window as they tried hard to get the peanut butter off the roof of their mouths. We stood there laughing at the funny faces they made. "It serves you right," I said.

I felt Marti's hand on my shoulder and turned to see she had tears running down her cheeks. She was laughing so hard she was having a hard time catching her breath. I wrapped her in my arms and gave her a big hug, "It's so good have you here in my arms. You are what the doctor ordered tonight!"

We kissed and just stood there embraced in each other's warmth not saying a word. Suddenly the silence was broken by the thundering flapping noise from the flap on the doggie door. Once again the room was filled with the clicking sounds of their toenails on the hard wood floors. I looked into her eyes and smiled.

"I'll open the wine and get out some snacks, while you get into something more comfortable."

Marti kissed me on the cheek and disappeared into the bedroom. By the time I had opened the wine and put together a plate filled with crackers, cheese, and some fruit, she returned wearing boxers and a tank top.

I looked into her eyes, "I really missed you."

She kissed me and indicated the same. We hugged each other tightly for a long period before we sat on the sofa. I guarded the plate full of food from probing noses as we sat together. I turned off the T.V. and the room became quiet.

Marti closed her eyes, sunk deep into the sofa and took another sipped of wine. I could tell from the moment she walked through the door she had had a very long day. Marti was a flight attendant for an airline and our town was one of her overnight stops. She would spend the time with Oz and me instead joining her crew at a hotel.

We had been doing this for years. It was our special time together.

"You should've called and I would've met you at the airport."

"Thought I would surprise you and by the look on your face apparently I did." The smirk on her face was adorable.

"Yes, you did."

Marti picked up a piece of cheese and a cracker and Annie placed her chin on Marti's leg with a "please feed me" look. Marti couldn't refuse and gave them each a cracker.

Retrieving the bottle of wine from the kitchen, I refilled Marti's glass.

"So why is Annabelle here? Is Ed out of town on a business trip again?"

"No, Annie will be staying here for quite a while."

I took a drink of water and then I explained the events of my day. By the time I finished Marti's eyes were full of tears and she had buried her body deep into mine for comfort. Both dogs sensed there would be no more snacks coming their way and found a spot on the floor to sleep. We sat there in silence for quite a while just staring off into space, the room had become very strangely quiet.

Marti asked in a soft voice still trying to get her composure back, "Has anyone contacted his sister?"

"I'm not sure but I'm betting Rod will. Ed's parents were both deceased and he had just one sister. Her name was Joy and she lived in a neighboring city about thirty miles west of here. It might be a good idea to ask Rod tomorrow if he had contacted her." It was getting late and we both had had a very long day. I suggested maybe it was time to go to bed.

"My feet are tired and sore. I want to soak them in the hot tub for a while," she replied.

I went out to the patio and took the cover off the hot tub and before I knew it Marti had already stripped off the shorts and shirt and was sliding into the water.

"Oh, that feels so good. Aren't you going to join me? It's no fun with just one in here." There was this devilish look on her face.

Who am I to refuse such a request from a beautiful sexy lady and with that off came my shirt and shorts. The boxers stayed on for the time being as I settled in the warm swirling water. Ah, it felt so good.

The night air was calm and the stars slowly started to appear as the sun set for the night. Both the guys were asleep out on the grass butt to butt. The neighborhood was quiet except for the crickets in the grass and an occasional car moving down the street. It was so peaceful and relaxing. We laid there with our eyes closed allowing the warm, swirling water to ease the strains of the day.

Marti slid her body between my legs and pressed her back against my chest. I bent over and kissed her on the ear not once but twice. She tilted her head to allow me better access and hinted to keep it up. I wrapped my arms around her and pulled her soft silky body into mine. This was the therapy we both needed. I ran my fingers up and down her body caressing each and every part. She let out soft moans and her body tensed up with each caress. She pulled away, turned around and wrapped her arms around my neck. Her lips locked onto mine and her warm, soft kisses became more and more passionate. She straddled my body, and we embraced as one into each other's arms. Our bodies locked into passion and desire.

"Shall we finish this in the bedroom?" I whispered in her ear.

She nibbled on my ear and replied, "I have a better idea." She stood up and got out of the hot tub taking me with her. Then she pulled the cover over the tub and lay down on top on it. "Take me now you sexy man," and we made love under the stars.

We laid there regaining our strength from our passionate moment. The cool night breeze suddenly created a chill across our wet bodies. I grabbed a couple of towels that were stored in a cabinet next to the hot tub and we took turns drying each other off.

I escorted her to the bedroom where we snuggled into each other's arms and soon fell asleep. I was awaken to a strange noise which I soon figured out was Annie snoring at the base of the bed.

Before I knew it, the sun was in my eyes, the birds were chirping outside and the guys were clicking their nails on the hardwood floor ready for breakfast. I rolled over and noticed I was the only one in the bed. I wondered where Marti had gone when the guys hopped up on the bed to wish me good morning. I covered my face with the sheets as they were my only defense from the pair of fast acting tongues. "Who wants a doggie treat?" and with that Oz jumped off the bed with Annie in tow and headed to the kitchen.

I smelled the fresh brewed coffee as I made my way towards the kitchen. Coffee was one of Marti's vices, she drank about five or six cups a day. She must have gotten up early to brew a pot. I gave the guys their treats and noticed a note on the counter that she had left.

"I had an early flight and didn't want to wake you. Last night was great! Please keep me updated about what you find out concerning Ed. I'll be back in town Thursday and have a week's layover. You got any ideas of what we can do? Love you my sexy man, love Marti."

I looked down at Oz and Annie both staring at me and wondering if I was going to get my act together and feed them breakfast any time soon. I just sighed and thought to myself, "Boy, life's a bitch when you are married to a flight attendant."

"Okay guys, who's in the mood pancakes?"

They started prancing and dancing with anticipation of something good coming their way. I gathered the ingredients to make my world famous blueberry pancakes. I looked down at Annie and was reminded of the tragic loss of my friend. Tears welled up in my eyes. I then thought of Ed's sister and wondered if she would let us keep Annie? Annie and Oz were such close buddies now. Maybe I could make a deal with her and offer to buy Annie.

Making meals in the kitchen was like a dance. With one dog you had to choreograph each move, but now with two I was learning it was a hot mess trying to move around. The guys were at my feet so when I moved to the fridge we all moved to the fridge. When I moved to the stove, we all moved to the stove. Get the picture? I had two shadows and many times my toes as well as theirs got stepped on. I was going to have to learn to wear my slippers to soften the blow from their nails.

I always gave Oz what I called the test pancakes loaded with butter and syrup. I put a couple of pancakes in each of their doggie dishes but Annie got hers plain not sure how the butter and syrup would affect her system. It didn't take them long before both dishes were empty and they were looking up at me with "is that all we get" look. I plated my pancakes with a couple stripes of bacon and we all moved outside to the patio. After eating, I cleaned up my mess and went back out to patio to read the paper. I read the article about Ed's death a couple of times and it was still hard to believe that he was gone. Interestingly the paper didn't say anything about it being a murder.

The guys were asleep on the grass and being warmed by the sun. I wondered if they were dreaming of my great pancakes. Looking out into the back yard I saw it needed some major attention. Maybe after meeting with Rod I should get out there and do some work.

Chapter 4

Since I had time before I had to meet with him I decided to get some work done and review the information on my newest case for the state. The best part of being an independent private investigator was being able to set my own schedule. There were no real deadlines given by either the state or the insurance companies, but occasionally there might be a rush. Reviewing this new case, the state was sure they were being defrauded by a woman who claimed her medical conditions had kept her from working. Her bio revealed she was twenty years old and had been working for the state for just a few months when she had slipped on a wet floor at work and injured her back. She claimed it was too painful to sit for long hours at her desk and was not able to stand for long periods. Filing was a requirement of her job and she insisted she could not preform the tasks. The doctor's reports showed no conclusive findings of any injury and the state had been paying her workman's compensation for the past three months.

The state felt this case needed some additional investigating and that's why they had requested my assistance. I had been doing this kind of work for fifteen years and I must admit I was pretty good at what I did. Due to budget cuts however, the state had found it to be more cost effective to contract out this type of investigation. Out of the five different investigators they started with, I was the only one now who did case work for them and it kept me pretty busy. What I liked most about my job was being able to set my hours around Marti's schedule. This allowed us to spend as much time as possible together when she was home. Our time together was precious to each of us since her schedule was so unpredictable. I preferred working for insurance companies rather than state jobs because they paid a lot better, but a paycheck is a paycheck.

I continued to read the report on this suspect and decided with some online research I could come up with a plan to either prove or disapprove her claim. The report read she had to walk with a cane and was unable to sit for more than an hour at a time. It also said she didn't have the strength to do her weekly shopping or chores around the house. Supposedly she had to rely on friends and family to do those things for her. She reported she spent ninety percent of her time in bed. Funny thing though, last month one of her previous co-workers thought they saw her at one of the dance bars in town on a Saturday night. She told a friend who worked in the State Insurance Department that my suspect was dancing up a storm. The co-worker knew about her claim and thought she should mention it to someone.

My plan was to put on my best Peter Seller's Pink Panther disguise and go to work tomorrow. I made sure the battery in my camera was fully charged and I had a blank photo card inside. I was ready to investigate. I looked up at the clock and there was just enough time to take a shower before I had to meet up with Rod.

As I backed out of the drive, Vern our lawn boy rode up on his bike. "Hey Wes," he called as he parked his bike next to the garage. He was a typical high school kid who lived down the street from us and during the summer made extra money doing yard maintenance in his neighborhood. I hired him a couple summers ago when he went door to door marketing his business. He was a tall bean pole of a kid and there was not a lot of meat on his body. I always thought he would be a good basketball player but it didn't seem like sports was his thing.

"Vern, how's summer been treating you so far? I bet you're glad to be out of school for a while," I said.

"Mom is making me take summer school. She wasn't too impressed with my English grades," he said as he started for the side gate.

"Well, at least it's not all day. Your payment is on the patio table. Keep smiling and thanks," I said as I pull out onto the street.

One of the luxuries I afforded myself was hiring Vern to cut the grass and pick up after Oz. I figured I was helping a young entrepreneur and I had gotten him a few more jobs in the neighborhood. This gave him some extra money and the side benefit for us was that he and Oz got along great.

"Hey Wes, there's another dog in the back yard with Oz," he shouted at me.

"Her name is Annabelle. I call her Annie, and she will be staying with us for a while," I shouted back to him.

He waved and disappeared behind the gate and I made a mental note to increase his pay now that he was cleaning up after two dogs.

I usually didn't go out to eat on Sundays because it seemed like everyone else did. Often you had a long wait for a table and the service was usually not that great. They seemed to push you to eat your meal and push you out the door to make room for the next customer. But this was where Rod wanted to meet and who was I to argue.

He was waiting for me in the back of the diner and knew how to butter me up. He'd ordered me a slice of coconut cream pie which was one of my favorites and had it waiting for me. Rod looked like he was just having coffee. I took a seat across from him, "Man, it must have been a long night. Did you get the license number of the truck that ran you over? You look like hell," I commented.

"Shut up and eat your pie. I haven't even gone to bed yet so stop giving me a bad time." he snapped with a grimace.

Detective Rodney Miller was about six foot two and about two hundred pounds which was mostly muscle. His skin had the look of leather from being out in the sun most of his life. In college he was on the school's tennis team and did construction work during the summer months to help pay his way. He had a full head of dark brown hair, which made me jealous. He was married once, but it didn't last. I think it was because he was married more to the job instead of his wife. We were now business acquaintances since the only time our paths crossed was when I needed some of his expertise help on one of my cases.

I took a couple of bites of my pie and looked up, "You're not eating?" I asked jokingly.

He just shook his head no and took a sip of coffee and then started off with small talk. "How's Marti?"

"She stopped by last night for a little action and is back in the air today. She'll be home on Thursday for a week but you didn't ask me here about my personal life. So was the gun in the living room the one used to kill Ed?"

"That gun had never been fired. We're tracking down the registration to see who owned it. So there's another gun out there somewhere. We were able to recover the bullet from Ed's body and it's in pretty good shape so when we find the gun, we'll be able to match them. We think he was shot sometime around noon on Friday."

He took another sip of his coffee and grimaced as he swallowed. He signaled the waitress for a refill and after a long pause he continued, "I visited with his sister and wow, is she a jewel. Talking to her I got the feeling they were not on good terms and it even sounded as if she hated him. The only time she smiled was when she asked, "Does this mean I get his house, cars, and his money? The entire hour I spent with her she did nothing but complained about Ed, how and he wouldn't give her money when she needed it. I asked if she owned a gun and she said no, but with the attitude I was getting I couldn't tell if she was lying or telling the truth."

I took a bite of my pie and asked, "So do you think she killed Ed?"

"At this time we are just gathering the facts. When I talked to her I got this feeling there was something else but I'm just not sure what she's hiding." He took a long drink of the fresh hot coffee, "So now you know everything I know."

The waitress returned again and refilled his cup, Rod nodded thanks and took a sip, "Okay, it's your turn to spill the beans. I know you walked around the house before we got there. What did you see?"

I just about choked on the bite I had just taken, "Okay, you caught me. I did take a stroll around the house and saw someone was on a quest looking for something. The rooms had been trashed and the strangest thing was the Trailer Queen was not in the garage where Ed always kept it. It was his baby."

Rod interrupted me, "The Trailer Queen?"

I smiled, "Yes, that's the nickname our little car group gave Ed's Cadillac. You see most of the time when he went to a car show he trailered the Cadillac instead of driving it. He was afraid of getting it rock chipped or that someone might wreck into him while driving." I allowed that information to soak in for a minute and continued. "The office was the biggest mess with all the desk drawers pulled out and all the papers littered on the floor. Someone was definitely looking for something. The bedroom and living rooms were not far behind in being trashed. Ed was always such a neat freak. I knew this was none of his doing."

Rod just nodded as the waitress came by and took my plate and refilled his cup of coffee again. From my count since I had arrived he was working on his fourth cup. He looked into the full cup of hot steaming black liquid for a moment before asking, "Wes, could you do me a favor? Could you check some of the local auto shops where Ed might have taken his so called Trailer Queen, since you know those shops better than I do. Maybe he was having it serviced. I would really appreciate it"

I could tell by the amount of coffee Rod must have drunk this morning and the previous night working at the murder scene, he was about to collapse. His body was running on empty and he needed to get some rest. His hands were shaking from all the caffeine he had consumed and was having a hard time not spilling any of the coffee on the table.

"You got it," I said and with that we both got up. He paid the bill, I left a tip and we parted ways.

Since the rest of my day was free I decided it would be a good time to stop at the store. I picked up a steak along with a potato and some veggies for my dinner. I also needed to replenish my stash of doggie treats now that Annie was staying with us. I made my way to the check out and watched a young lady ahead of me paying for her groceries. She wore very tight shorts leaving nothing to the imagination. A butterfly tattoo was on the back of her left leg. She had on a neon pink bikini top which didn't cover up much and her long blonde hair was tied back in a ponytail. Her shopping cart was full of beer and ice. I joking said, "So where's the party?"

She turned and lifted up her sunglasses. Her eyes were dark brown and gave me the once over, "At the lake. You want to join us old man?" she replied jokingly. She paid for her groceries and left the store swaying her hips and laughing all the way out the door.

"Hey, who are you calling an old man?" I said but by then she was long gone. The lady cashier looked at me and laughed as she started ringing up my groceries. With my ego deflated I left the store, muttering to myself, "Who was she to call me an old man?"

Back home with the groceries put away I settled in to watch NASCAR and by three in the afternoon I was sound asleep on the sofa. The guys were on the floor doing the same. I was awakened by my cell pinging. It was a text from Marti that read, "I'm in Los Angeles and done for the day. My crew and I are going to check out some of the local sights. Love you."

I texted a reply, "Have a great time! Please send pictures and bring me back something. Love you, too." I looked at the clock and it was close to six. I had slept almost three hours and didn't have a clue who had won the race.

I fed the guys and started grilling up my steak, veggies and zapped the potato for dinner. The guys, as usual, wolfed down their dinner and then had their noses working overtime from the smell of the steak cooking on the grill. They were thinking they were having steak tonight too. While I ate I did shared a hand out to each of them but I don't think they even chewed it. With the dishes cleaned and all of us fed I went into my office. I wanted to make notes from my conversation with Rod this morning.

It was hard to concentrate on updating my file about Ed's murder because Marti kept sending texts and pictures from their afternoon adventure. My favorite picture was one of her holding a small box. The text read, "Guess what I got my favorite stud?" I really loved that lady!

I texted back a couple of guesses but struck out with each one. I completed my notes and texted her, "Good night and love you." Marti replied with a sleepy smiley face and a heart.

With the house locked up for the night and the guys asleep I climbed into bed. I turn out the lights and laid there thinking about Ed and what Rod and I had talked about this morning. Tomorrow I would make a list of auto mechanics to call.

Chapter 5

I was up early and ready to start my next investigation. Not wanting to stand out like a rotten apple in my suspect's neighborhood, I chose to use my Kelley Surveyor's disguise. I loaded the equipment in my truck and put the magnetic decals on the truck's front doors. Making sure the guys had plenty of water I grabbed my paperwork and headed out the front door. Looking back I saw both Oz and Annie were staring at me with their sad eyes as if to say, "You're going without us?" Sorry guys, not today. You'll have to stay here and guard the house.

I wanted to get an early start on the case because I never knew what my suspects daily routines would be until after a few days of surveillance. I hadn't taken the time to eat breakfast so what better way to start my day than with a quick stop at Betty's. When I opened the shop's front door the smells triggered my taste buds, sending rumbles throughout my stomach.

"Morning Wes, I don't usually see you on Mondays."

"I know, this is going to be a treat. A couple of fritters please."

The gentleman Betty had just finished helping smiled and agreed with me as he walked out carrying boxes containing three dozen donuts. He must have been getting them for his co-workers. Betty put my two usual fritters in a bag and a special treat. I told her that Oz wasn't with me, but she said it's one of her new creations and wanted me to try it and give her my opinion. Who was I to argue? I paid my bill and turned around to see a long line of people waiting to get their sugar fix. While driving to my investigation site, I sampled Betty's new donut which was stuffed with peanut butter and jelly. It was pretty good, but her fritters were still my favorite.

I parked a couple of houses down the street from my suspect's house which gave me a good view of her front yard and the front door. I set up my surveying equipment and walked up and down the street with my notebook giving the appearance that I was working. I stopped in front of my suspect's house and looked in the front window but couldn't see anyone inside so I walked back to the truck.

Being an investigator for insurance fraud cases takes a lot of patience and time. There had been cases where I was able to collect evidence within a couple of hours and other times when it took days and sometimes even weeks to determine if they were committing fraud or not. In some cases suspects had been prosecuted and had even done jail time. Once in a blue moon I would have to go to court and testify on the behalf of my clients but most often the case was settled without my expertise. They had to make full monetary restitution with either the state or insurance companies.

Back in my truck I kept an eye on the suspect's house. While munching on one of Betty's fritters, I started thinking about Ed and who and why someone wanted to kill him? Where was the Trailer Queen? This reminded me to call around to the auto repair shops later for Rod. I wondered who would inherit the car and his house. Maybe Ed's sister would be the beneficiary but from what Rod had said there was no love loss between the two of them. As far as I knew there were no other living relatives, but Ed had kept his family life close to him so who knew. He had been a pretty sharp businessman so he must have had a will. Maybe it would give us clues to possibly any additional family members.

Returning to the task at hand, I pulled out my file on this lady. As I re-read the report and looked at her picture I noticed there was something very familiar about her as if I had met her before. Just then there was a knock on the truck's window that scared the crap out of me and I must have jumped a mile. "Hey," a guy shouted to me through the glass.

"Yep, neighborhood watch was out early this morning walking his dog," I thought to myself. I lowered the window and gave him my innocent smile and responded with a "Good morning, what a beautiful day."

He looked to be in his seventies. He had silver hair, glasses with his shorts pulled up to his chest showing off his pure white, bony legs. If he walked his dog a couple times a day he'd likely kept up with all the coming and goings on his street. He might be a good source of information.

"What are you surveying? Are they planning to tear up our street again?" He inquired.

"They're thinking about it. A couple of utility companies are checking out the street to make some improvements for their customers," I replied with a big smile.

During my past experiences over the years of investigating I found it best to give vague information so people were less inclined to check up on me.

He looked up and down the street and shook his head in disgust, "Someone is always tearing up this street for one reason or another. It sure makes it hard on us. The goddamn noise starts early in the morning and doesn't end until late at night and most of the time you can barely get out of your drive."

I tried to ask him a few questions but his dog kept pulling on his leash which at one point almost caused the old man to fall over. He reached out and grabbed on to the truck's mirror to regain his balance. The dog won and I watched as it dragged him down the street. I chuckled watching this little toy poodle drag his owner away looking for a place to do his business.

I placed a small movie camera on the dash and pointed it so I would be able to record as soon as I saw any activity. I took one more look at my suspect's photo in the file but I couldn't place where I had seen her and it was starting to bug me.

Since there had been no activity and I needed to stretch, I got out of my truck and made it look as if I was actually working. I walked past my suspect's home and down the street stopping from time to time to make some fake notes and take some measurements along the sidewalk and street. This helped with keeping other neighborhood watchers from coming up and asking questions. As I was returning to my truck I stopped again in front of my suspect's home and looked in the front window. All I could see was the light coming from a television which meant someone was now up.

Back in my truck I decided this would be a good time to make a couple of calls and try to locate the Trailer Queen. Knowing Rod, he would soon be calling to see what progress I had made. I went old school and started calling auto repair shops listed in the phone book. Every year I would get two or three of these books tossed on my driveway and I'd throw one in the truck just for this reason. I knew Ed had done most of his own work on his Cadillac but when it came to major service he talked about a mechanic he trusted. He never mentioned the shops name so I started with the first listing and worked my way through the two pages of repair shops but with no luck. I still had half the automotive repair section to go through but I needed to take a break. Keeping an eye on my suspect's house and munching on a fritter I received a text from Marti telling me she was in Chicago. I replied telling her about my stake out.

I was about to dial another shop when the front door opened at my suspect's house. I quickly pushed the button on my camera when a young man came out and climbed into the blue Jeep which was parked in the driveway and drove past me. "Rats," I said and turned off the camera. I wasn't interested in him so I continued making calls trying to locate the Trailer Queen but I was still coming up with nothing. Rod would be calling soon and I had no information to give him. He was a man who wanted results and wanted them now.

My butt was getting sore and it was letting me know it was time to take another walk along the street. As I looked again in the front window the television was still on but I couldn't tell who was watching it. My concentration on this case was low. After Rod had asked me to try and locate the Trailer Queen all I wanted to do was spend my time and energy on locating it. I also wanted to know where it was. Walking down the street I tried to think of the name of the shop where Ed once mentioned he had taken it to be worked on. That had been a long time ago. I decided to call Doug, a member of our little car group thinking he might know.

I was almost back to my truck when my cell rang and it was Bruce. "Wes, this morning I have been talking to the others in our car group, we thought it would be a good idea if we all drive our cars to Ed's funeral service. What do you think?"

"I like it. Keep me informed when you find out when it will be. Hey do you have any idea where Ed might have taken the Queen to be serviced? It wasn't in his garage."

"No, not a clue. Why do you want to know?" He paused, "Have you heard any more about what happened to him?"

"Just curious and I don't know anymore. The police have been pretty tight lipped about it," I replied.

"You know, you could do some snooping around. Ed was our friend and you're an investigator."

"Whoa there cowboy. I just check out simple fraud cases, nothing like murder."

"So you think it was murder?"

Crap! I just let the cat out of the bag. Bruce paused to let my comment soak in and then continued, "You should try to find out who killed him. You are an investigator. If you need some help let me know. Talk to you later." And before I could say another word Bruce hung up.

I stood there thinking about our conversation when the jeep, which had pulled out of the driveway of my suspect's house, returned. I quickly got back in my truck and turned the dash camera back on as the young man with a tray of coffee and a bag of something got out of the car. A female walked out the front door to greet him. "Bingo!" She was the lady at the grocery store yesterday and she was the one going up to the lake to party. The one who called me an old man and laughed. She gave the guy a big kiss and they went inside. I re-read her file and I had not seen a cane yesterday or today.

The rest of the morning passed by quickly as I talked to the neighbors who showed interest in my surveying and I was even able to ask a few questions about my suspect. Most of them didn't know her, but they commented that there were always people coming and going. I was also able to make a few more calls on the Trailer Queen, still no luck. I changed the battery and disc in my camera and got out of the truck. I walked up and down the street a couple more times passing her house hoping to see what was going on inside. This time the television was off and music was blaring out of the house. It was so loud out here I hated to think what it was like inside.

I was standing by the truck when my cell rang and it was Jeff, "Hey buddy, you aren't going to believe what I just saw?"

"Let me guess and don't tell me. Nope, I don't have a clue. What did you just see?" I jokingly replied.

"The Trailer Queen! I saw the Trailer Queen parked at that classic car lot on Victory Street and it has a price tag on it. I didn't know Ed was selling his caddy. Wait until the others hear about this."

"Wow, are you sure? I would have never guessed he'd sell it. He never mentioned anything to me about selling his car," I said.

"I know, it's really strange. I talked to Bruce to tell him about it and he said you were going to do some investigating into Ed's murder. I am right? Ed was murdered wasn't he? Bruce told me to tell you about the Queen since you had asked him where Ed might have taken it to be repaired. He thought it might help you with the case. I mean after all you own an investigation agency."

"Oh yea, I have a large office of employees at my disposal, me, myself, and I with occasional assistance from Oz. I have a back log of cases sitting on my desk. In fact, I'm working on a case as we speak. Where will I find the time to work on Ed's case?"

He just chuckled and said, "Maybe now it's time to move up to the big leagues."

"No thanks. I like it just fine here in the minors."

"I know you. You are as curious as a cat and you'll have to stop at the car lot and check it out."

"Okay, tell you what, when I'm finished working here, I might go by and check it out but we should let the police do their job."

Jeff ended our conversation with "Let me know what you find out Mr. Investigator." I sat there wondering why in the world Ed would want to sell his baby. He loved that car.

A car pulled up to the front of my suspect's house and I started the camera again. A couple of young ladies got out and walked inside. They were wearing very skimpy bikinis and my great investigating skills told me they were going to the lake again today. Although I wanted to skip out on this surveillance and check out the story about the Trailer Queen, I thought better of it and continued with my investigation. I got out of the truck and walked past the house with my note pad in hand just in case someone came out and asked questions. Music was louder as the front door was partially open. I could see they were all sitting around and not doing much. Since it was almost noon, I needed to take a break. It looked as if my suspect and friends had settled in for the time being so I packed up my equipment and decided to go home and check on the guys. Taking the long way, I drove by the car lot where Jeff had spotted Ed's car. Yep, there was the Trailer Queen parked in the back like Jeff had mentioned. Unfortunately the shop had a closed sign on the office door. Darn, that Jeff was right. I needed to know more about why the Trailer Queen was on this lot for sale before I told Rod where to find it. I would be back.

The welcoming committee greeted me at the front door, toes tapping on the floor, tails bouncing back and forth and smiles on the guy's faces. I loved coming home to such fanfare. "Would you guys like a doggie treat?"

They followed me into the kitchen and I give them each a treat. I made a fried egg sandwich and ate my lunch on the patio. The guys looked up at me as if they hadn't eaten for months, but it didn't work. I was hungry and I ate every last bite. I grabbed a couple bottles of cold water out of the fridge and a large bag of peanuts as I walked out the door. It was back to work to continue my investigation.

This time instead of parking down the street I decided to set up across from my suspect's house and see if curiosity would bring her out. No blue jeep was parked in her driveway and the car with the bikini clad ladies was gone. I still heard music coming from the house and hoped my suspect was home and not the boyfriend. I just sat watching and waiting. While at home I replaced the battery and disc in my camera and it was good for a couple more of hours of video recording.

It had been over an hour that I had been sitting there and it was time to get out and stretch. I pressed the start button on my camera and decided to make some measurements of the sidewalk out front of her house. I hoped this would spark some curiosity and as luck would have it the front door opened and my suspect walked out.

"Hey, what are you doing?" She shouted.

"Well, good afternoon. I'm surveying the street for a utility project," I said with an innocent smile. I didn't think she remembered me from the store the other day. "They want me to get some specs on the sidewalk, so they know where to dig."

She took the bait and walked over to talk to me. "So what kind of work?" she asked.

"They don't tell me much. My boss hands me a work ticket and says go do it. I couldn't help but notice you have a great looking front yard with all these flowers. Are you the person with the green thumb?"

"No, they were here when I moved in a couple of months ago. I'm sure they'll all die soon because I don't like working in the yard. I'm just renting this place anyway. I'm thinking of moving to Alaska with my boyfriend," she said.

"Alaska, why do you want to move there?" I questioned. It was good having her talk.

"I'm just looking for a change and my boyfriend might be working on one of those fishing boats."

"Well, that would be an adventure. I'd like to keep talking but I have to get back to work so I can get out of this hot sun. I hope you don't think I'm out of place but could you give me a hand for a minute?" I asked.

"Sure, I have a little time. I'm going up to the lake in about an hour with some friends. What can I do?" she replied and smiled.

"Just take this end of the tape measure and put it on the ground where the driveway and sidewalk meet?" I made sure she was in full view of my camera.

Over the next 15 minutes, I had her move from here to there, bending over while I made fake notes on my pad. Once I made it look like I made a mistake and accidently retracted the tape measure. She ran after it and bent down to pick it up. This was some good stuff. This was the proof she had been faking her injury. Little did she know she was being video recorded and all this evidence was going to be used against her by the state. I thanked her and packed up my equipment. I sat in my truck and waited around since she said she was going up to the lake. I replaced my battery and disc and set my camera back on the dash, making sure it was still facing the front of her house.

It was getting late and I was getting hungry, so I call Vinnies Deli and placed an order for one of their famous Roast Beef Subs and a couple of pickles. They had the best pickles in town. The car from earlier pulled up front loaded with the same two ladies I had seen earlier this morning. The horn honked a couple of times and my suspect opened her front door waved and disappeared back inside. A few moments later out she came out dressed for the lake in the same outfit as I had seen her the day before. She ran to the car and hopped in the backseat. They drove off toward the lake and I drove off to get my sandwich. At the deli I quickly grabbed my meal and removed the magnetic signs off the truck. I also changed my shirt and then proceeded to the lake. I was betting that on their way they would stop at the store to stock up on beer and ice like they had done the previous day.

There was only one road to get into the lake's recreation area and once there you had your choice of a couple of picnic sites and four boat ramps to choose from. I parked off to the side and waited. I got lucky and soon the ladies drove past me. I followed them into the picnic area and parked where I could keep an eye on them. They met up with more friends and it looked as if they were getting ready to go out on the lake. Down at the dock was a boat with the same guy that I had seen at her house earlier this morning. I got some great shots of her carrying the cooler and her dancing with her friends. I had the feeling this was her boyfriend's boat since he was the same person I saw this morning with the coffee. I bet the state had helped pay for some of it.

I sat and watched as they took turns skiing. When it was my suspect's turn, I walked to the edge of the boat ramp where I was able to get closer and take better pictures. Fifteen minutes later it was time to go home. I had enough evidence to close this case. Tonight I would finish my report, collate all the pictures and videos and turn it into the state tomorrow. "Not too bad for this old man," I chuckled and smiled all the way home.

I was greeted by another round of fan fair barking as I opened the front door. They were saying "Where have you been? We missed you so much. We are starving and is that roast beef we smell?" I gave them each good butt scribbles and they danced with happiness. They followed me out to the truck while I unloaded my gear. I think they were hoping for a ride and their faces showed disappointment when we walked back inside the house. We all needed to blow off steam so I grabbed their leashes and struggled to put them on. They were excited to get out and explore the neighborhood.

I was hoping for a nice stroll in the park kind of walk, but unfortunately for me it turned into a power walk. They were in competition to see whose nose could be the one out front. Now and then there would be a smell and we would come to an abrupt stop to check it out. Then it was back to my nose is in front of yours contest. We made it around a couple of blocks and back home in record time. It definitely was not the stroll I was hoping for. Boy, were my dogs barking and I don't mean the four legged kind. I couldn't wait to get inside and take my shoes off. I placed their dinner in front of them and they raced to see who could finish theirs first. This time I didn't have to referee.

I reached for a bottle of water in the fridge and walked into my office. I wanted to finish my report while I still had everything fresh in my mind. I turned on my computer and took out the collection of discs from today's investigation and settled in for a couple hours of report writing. The guys came into the office to keep me company and found a spot to crash. Before I had typed my first word Annie's snoring broke the silence of the room. I looked down at her and smiled. She would be a good fit to this family.

I had been so involved with my report I hadn't noticed it was dark outside. The state had a strong case against this lady and once they showed her these videos and pictures she would think twice before calling me an old man again. I loaded my report on a thumb drive and was ready to call it a night.

I started to get up when I remember Rod hadn't called. Maybe he found the Trailer Queen and didn't think to mention it to me. I'll drive by the lot first thing tomorrow and check it out.

I made my rounds making sure the house was locked up, not that it really mattered with Oz around. It would be foolish for someone to make an uninvited visit during the night. Oz would greet them with his pearly whites and the growl of a wolf. I was in bed reading when I received a call from Marti. We talked about our day and how we missed each other. We concluded by saying our "love yous." I was out of energy. I turned off the light and I was asleep as soon as my head hit the pillow.

Chapter 6

The humidity was sitting heavy in the air and I was sweating profusely. We were still waiting for backup when Chuck made the call, "We're going in."

The alley was dark, smelled, and was littered with homeless people and drunks. I didn't have a good feeling about this but Chuck was the lead detective on the case and whatever he said went. I checked my gun for a second time when we started down the long, dark alley taking one small step at a time. We were in the middle of it and I was about to lose my lunch from the putrid smell when our backup arrived. "Great, I thought. If we had just waited a few minutes longer we could have sent them on this miserable journey and we could have stayed by the car. I stumbled but regained my balance as we approached the door at the end of the alley. The light above the door illuminated the measly surroundings of the stoop. From what I could make out it was not a pretty picture. There were three steps to climb to reach the landing and just enough room for the two of us. Chuck stepped up on the landing and I choose to remain two steps back.

I would give a week's paid time off not to be in this mess right now. My stomach's churned like a violent thunderstorm from fear and the stench of this place. I was doing everything possible to keep my lunch down and constantly wiping the sweat out of my eyes. My legs felt like rubber bands. Chuck rapped on the door four times. The sound filled the air as it echoed down the alley. Moans of discontentment followed with muttering of "Hey, keep it down, I'm trying to sleep."

Again Chuck rapped on the door but this time much louder and harder. The door suddenly swung open and a cheery female's voice broke the night silence. "It's seven thirty in the morning. Time for you sleepy heads to get up, it's going to be another great sunny day in our city. Don't forget to check out the Tuesday Night Summer Festival in the heart of downtown. Festivities start around five p.m."

The guys jumped on the bed and made sure I was awake as soon as they heard the DJ's voice from the radio. I covered up doing everything possible to avoid their licks. After a struggle I finally got them to settle down on the bed. I laid there listening to the radio covered in doggie slobber. I thought to myself I was going to have to stop watching Charles Bronson movies just before bed because they really messed with my sleep.

I started organizing my day with my first stop to submit my report to the state followed by a visit to the classic car lot where Trailer Queen was parked. I hoped Rod had not been there first. I would try to pry information from whoever was working the lot. I would then call Rod and tell him where he could find the queen and ask him if he would give me Ed's sister's phone number. I would like to talk to her myself and possibly, since I wasn't the police, she might be more open to talk to me. It was time to get a move on as John Wayne would say, "We're burning daylight."

With the guys having been fed I started to walk out of the house but there sat two sets of sad brown eyes by the front door looking up at me as if to say, "Please take us with you." How could I refuse? I grabbed their leashes and they pranced around in circles excited to be going on a road trip. The back windows of the truck were rolled down and they hung their heads out letting the wind flow across their faces. Their tongues were flapping in the wind and their drool was all over the outside of my truck. The radio station played my favorite classic rock and I occasionally joined in as the lead singer of the band. It was a good thing it was just me and the guys because anyone else would have plugged their ears. I admit I'm not the best person to carry a tune but enjoy singing along.

I found an empty parking space at the State Insurance office under the watchful eyes of security by the front entrance. I made sure to roll the windows up half way knowing Oz would stay in the truck but I wasn't too sure about Annie. It would only take but a few minutes to drop off my paperwork. I needed to go to the fourth floor and being lazy I rode the elevator up. I was in no mood to get my exercise by climbing all those stairs this early. On my ride up I thought about how best to approach whoever was working at the classic car lot this morning. I didn't want to just walk on the lot and start asking questions about the Trailer Queen. I would need to ease into it. The elevator door opened and I walked through the investigation department door and there at the front desk sat Lucy. Ever since I began working for the state we'd gotten to know each other quite well. Lucy was in her late fifties. She always had a smile for me whenever I stopped by to either pick up or drop off a case. Her desk was littered with photos of her grandchildren and Cooper her beloved German Shepard. Every time I visited she made it a point to show me her latest pictures.

"Hey Wes, you've finish that case already? I just gave it to you a couple of days ago," she said.

I placed the information on her desk, "You know me, when I smell fraud I don't rest until I have caught my criminal type person." We both chuckled.

Just then her phone rang, she smiled and handed me two more cases. I waved goodbye and returned to the truck where I found the guys had moved to the front seats. I had to push them aside to get in and I noticed the front seat was covered in their hair. My truck was a mess and when I looked down so were my pants. I hadn't noticed all the hair before I had walked into the office building. Good thing the only person that saw me was Lucy and since she owned Cooper she would understand. This would be a good time to drop them off at the groomers. I called Angie, who had been Oz's stylist ever since he was a pup. I was in luck and she would be able to squeeze them in this morning. Within fifteen minutes we walked into Angie's place which was located in the middle of a strip mall. Oz was excited to see her again but as for Annie that was another story. It took some convincing to get her inside and in the end I had to carry her.

"Oz, who's your lady friend?" Angie asked.

"This is Annabelle. I call her Annie. She will be staying with us for a while."

"She is a cutie." Angie sat on the floor to greet Annie. Oz was very jealous of all the attention Annie was getting and tried to push in between them. Angie turned to Oz, "Are we a little jealous, big boy?"

As I was almost out the door Angie yelled, "I will call you when they are ready to be picked up, most likely in about four hours."

My phone pinged twice and I had two texts. One was from Rod and he wanted to know what I had found out on the Trailer Queen. "I was in luck he hadn't found it before me," I thought to myself. My reply to his text would have to wait until I was able to question the person at the lot. I didn't want him to come and interrupt me when I was trying to get some information. The other text was from Marti. She was on her way to the Big Apple. I replied back that both Oz and Annie were at the groomers and I was off to do some detective work.

As I opened the door to the truck I realized it also needed to be washed and vacuumed.   The carwash was just down the street so I pulled in line. This must have been my lucky day because there were only a few cars ahead of me. When it was my turn I stepped out of the truck and handed the guy my keys and he looked inside.

"What the hell? Where's the dog? Did it explode? There is hair all over this place," he said in disgust.

I looked at him and smiled, "You should see my house."

I turned to walk into the lobby when, "Wait! I'm not going bust my chops to clean up this mess and have you dirty it up. Stand right there and don't move." He started vacuuming me from top to bottom. The other drivers in line who were waiting their turn were laughing at the situation. I stood there and smiled and appreciated the extra effort. This kid was going to get a good tip.

With both the truck and me cleaned and vacuumed, I drove across town to the classic car lot. I pulled onto the lot where there must have been at least fifty cars ranging from the twenties era to the eighties. They were all American made.   My plan was simple, I was shopping for a classic. As soon as I got out of my truck I saw a 1960 Ford Thunderbird and saw it was the only Thunderbird on the lot. I looked in the driver's window and there stood the "shark." I mean the salesman.

"Good morning. She is sure a beauty. My name is Maclyne J. Harris but my friends call me Mac and so can you."

We shook hands, "I agree, it's a good looking ride." Mac looked to be in his late sixties, his weathered face showed he had spent most of his life out in the sun. By the smell he was a smoker and his clothes and breath reeked of it. The hard chomping and chewing of gum did nothing to mask the odor.

I stepped back to get some fresh air, " So Mac, are you the owner of this lot?"

"Yes sir, I have been in the car business all my life and I know my cars. I will make sure you are happy when you drive one of these beauties off the lot."

The sales pitch had started and I needed to control the conversation, "What can you tell me about the T-Bird?"

I expected a story of the little old lady who drove it to and from church each week. He patted the hood of the car and started in with his sales pitch, "It's had four owners, all parts mostly original except for the motor which was replaced about two years ago. It drives like a dream and the ladies love it." He opened the driver's door and was trying to get me to sit inside. "Take a look how pristine the interior is, almost as if it just had come off the showroom floor."

I thought to myself, it was true the ladies did love a man with a classic car. My mind had begun to wander. I had owned "The Bird" for ten years and my first date with Marti was in it. She was hooked the moment I opened the door for her. I stood there dreaming of our first date. I must've had a smile on my face, Mac put his hand on my shoulder to regain my attention.

This startled me and brought me back to reality, "Oh, I was just thinking how great it would be driving one of these around town with my lady."

Mac just nodded and gave me a smirk. I wanted him to think I was interested in purchasing a classic car to gain his confidence. I hoped I could pry some information out of him. I looked down at the price of the Thunderbird and was sent immediately into sticker shock. It was way overpriced! I looked up to see the Trailer Queen was parked in the back of the lot and I needed to work my way closer to it. As I walked toward it, I stopped and looked at various makes and models of American made classic cars with Mac closely on my tail. He kept pointing out various cars and trying to steer me in their direction. I bet they were the ones with bigger commission pay outs.

I stopped in front of a 1949 four door Pontiac Chieftain. I had always loved this style of car. It had a drab brown paint job and looked as if it had spent most of its life in the military. The body was in fair condition but then what could you expect from the military. The interior appeared to be in pretty decent shape, the seats weren't torn and it had a column shift. I bet there was a flathead under the hood. Look at me acting like "Mister Car Guy". I had done my research on this particular model of car and if one of these had been around when I purchased the Bird it would had been my first choice. I looked again at the Chieftain and my dreams of owning it crashed hard. Wow, it was way over priced too but then so were most of the cars on this lot.

Mac could see my interest in this car and his eyes lit up. He started throwing out his best lines one after another trying to get me to purchase this baby. He opened the driver's door enticing me to have a seat. I didn't have time for this. I needed to focus on finding out more information about the Trailer Queen. As I started to back away I felt a little nudge and before I knew it I was sitting in the driver's seat.

Mac pulled down the visor and the keys fell into my lap, "What do you say we take her for drive?"

Wow! This guy was good. He had totally thrown me off my game. How could I resist such an offer? The motor came to life as I turned the ignition key and my heart thumped with excitement. Mac hopped in the passenger seat and away we went. The car drove like a dream, with the window down and my arm on the door jam, I cruised in style. People stared and waved as we drove past them. Mac kept working on me giving me his best sales pitch and setting the hook in deeper and deeper into my pocketbook.

Then he said the one thing which brought me back to reality and to the task at hand, "Just think when you drive this beauty home and impress the little lady. You will be one lucky guy tonight."

Yes, what would Marti say when she saw this car parked in the garage and hers parked out on the driveway? It was time to get back to reality and look out for Ed by trying to find the person who killed him.

We returned to the lot and I got out and walk around the car a couple of times to gather my thoughts. "You know Mac I must admit I can see myself driving this beauty but its way out of my price range." He was about to respond to my comment when I dropped a "Wow, Mac, is that a fifty-six Cadillac?"

Mac looked shocked at the question and I quickly walked over to the Trailer Queen before he knew what had hit him. I was betting he had already spent his commission check from selling me the Pontiac. I walked around the caddy making sure it was Ed's. The price was much lower than the other cars on the lot, well below the market value. I remembered the small scratch on the passenger side rear fender, Ed had complained about it when it happened. Yes, there it was, confirmation this was Ed's Trailer Queen.

"Hey Mac, how long has this beauty been on your lot? Now this is what I call a ride. My honey would like to cruise in this car for sure. What do you say we take her for a ride?" I tried the driver's door and it was locked.

"Sorry pal, I already have a down payment. An elderly couple took one look at it and fell in love. They said it reminded them of the one they had when they first got married. They're moving to Arizona soon and are going to tour the desert. We just need to get some paperwork cleaned up before they take ownership. So let's go back to the Chieftain and talk about you taking it home tonight. I could tell you're very interested." Mac steered me back to the Chieftain.

As we walked back to the Pontiac it was now my turn to start throwing out the lures and get my hooks into Mac, "I am just curious about the person who brought in the caddy. I mean who would want part with such a treasure? I bet it is a young guy. Maybe he was looking to get into one of the new sports cars or needed some cash."

Mac took the bait and opened up. "It was a young lady who brought it in. She told me it was her father's and since he'd passed away she wanted to sell it and buy her husband a new fishing boat. She begged me to buy it outright, but I don't work that way. Every car you see on this lot is on consignment and the owners set the price."

I put my hand on the Pontiac and felt my heart starting to race again. Whoever brought in the Trailer Queen was looking to get some cash and quickly. I turned to Mac, little did he know the car was hot and the police soon would be taking ownership of it. Once I got off this lot I was going to call Rod and tell him all about it. I was bothered though about Mac saying it was a lady trying to sell Ed's car. Ed was not married. It could have been his sister since Rod did say she was always looking for money.

"Mac, if I purchase the Pontiac from you, do you have the title?"

His eyes lit up and he smiled, "Why yes! Why don't we go into the office and see about you taking the baby home to the little lady tonight. I'm sure we can work out some kind of deal."

If he had the Pontiac title then I bet he had the title to the Cadillac as well. That should help the police track down Ed's murderer. I smiled and walked around the Pontiac giving it one more look. After Ed was murdered the killer must have been looking for the title to the car. That's why his office had been trashed.

"Mac, I love this car but you know I'm going to have to bring my sweetie around. She is going to want to drive it. It's also quite a bit out of my price range plus I'd also like to have a buddy of mine take a look at it. He's a good mechanic."

"Yea, sure bring the little lady and your buddy by but don't let the price scare you. I'll make you a great deal on this baby. Just don't wait too long." He handed me a business card knowing the sale had gone cold and walked back to his office.

As I walked back to my truck I thought to myself that I'd sure like to see the look on Mac's face when Rod showed up to impound the car. I parked in the shopping center lot down the street and called Rod. I told him where to find the Trailer Queen and that he'd better hurry since it had been sold and it would soon be on its way to Arizona. I asked him for Joy's address and her phone number and gave him a story about wanting to talk to her about Annie. I knew however as soon as I asked him he saw through my story about Annie. He still reluctantly gave me her information. I sat there for a few moments thinking about the Trailer Queen. If a lady brought the car into be sold and the title had Ed's name on it, then how did she ever expect to sell it? Ed would have had to sign it. I was betting that wasn't Ed's signature on the title or maybe he had been forced to sign it before he was murdered?

While trying to figure out the best way to approach Ed's sister my thoughts quickly switched to food. Where was the smell of meat cooking coming from? It had set off my stomach alarm. I looked around and saw I had parked next a burger joint without knowing it. It was perfect timing so I walked inside and placed my order.

Chapter 7

It was strange walking into my house and not being greeted at the door. Angie hadn't called yet to let me know the guys were ready from their day at the spa so I went to work in my office. I had a small stack of case files from the state and I grabbed the top one and started reading the person they wanted me to investigate. He claimed due to a back injury from a fall on the job he was unable to work. The majority of cases the state had me investigate had to do with various kinds of back injury. I was having a hard time concentrating on this case because my mind kept flashing back to my meeting with Mac this morning.

My cell rang and before I could say hello, Bruce started talking, "Hey, Doris just called me. She and one of her friends were driving down Wilson Street and they saw Ed's car on the back of a police tow truck."

I wasn't about to tell Bruce it was me who informed the police of its location. "Maybe finding the car will help them solve the case," I replied.

"I sure hope so. Are you going to the car show this Saturday? Some of us are thinking about meeting at Donavon's Pizza afterwards and have a small private memorial for Ed."

"I mentioned it to Marti and she'll be in town, but she hasn't given me an answer about whether she'll be able to join us or not. I'll be there for sure." The conversation ended with me assuring him I would get back to him about our plans.

Just as I started back into reading the case for the state my phone rang again and this time it was Angie letting me know the guys were ready to be picked up. I told her I would be there in an hour or so and she said that wouldn't be a problem. I had lost my concentration on the state's case so I placed the file back on the stack of cases waiting to be investigated. I decided my time would be best spent updating Ed's murder file. I added what I had learned from my meeting with Mac especially the fact that it was a lady who wanted to sell Ed's Cadillac. That made my female suspect consist of: Joy, Ed's sister, his ex-girlfriend Linda and the neighbor Ronnie. I put an asterisk next to each of their names and then drew a couple more lines below just in case more suspects needed to be added.

I reviewed what I had written so far and hoped it would start to make some sense. First, there was Annie. She was running freely throughout the neighborhood and someone should have tried to let Ed know his dog was running loose. Ronnie said Annie was constantly barking so that should have gotten someone's attention. Why did it take her so long say something? Maybe she already knew what had happened to Ed. If Annie was making that much noise I'm sure someone would have said something. Maybe they did but since Ed didn't answer the door they just let it go. That raised another question. Ed's front door had partial frosted glass so if someone looked in closely enough they would have spotted his body lying on the floor. Come to think of it, I didn't notice him lying there when I showed up and rang the doorbell. Then there was the fact that the house had been trashed as if someone was looking for something. I bet they were looking for the car title or maybe something else, but what? Maybe one of Ed's neighbors saw who drove the caddy away or the killer might have taken it late at night or early in the morning before anyone had a chance to notice. I bet the police had already been around the neighborhood asking that very question. I made a mental note to ask if Ronnie, Linda or Nick had seen anything since they were his next door neighbors and seemed somewhat close. Another theory was that this could have been a robbery gone wrong and since the killer couldn't find any cash or valuables in the house he or she took the car. When I arrived the other day there were no signs that the house had been broken into and the patio door was unlocked. I didn't even think to check the front door.

I did recall when I walked into the house a gun was lying on the living room floor. My first thought was it had been the murder weapon but after speaking with Rod, apparently it wasn't. Was it Ed's gun? Did he even own a gun? Rod hadn't said who the gun belonged to. The gun in the living room hadn't been fired which meant there were two guns. Whoever invaded Ed's home intentionally brought the murder weapon with them to rob him or worse, murder him. I needed to find out who the gun on the living room floor belonged to. By now the police should have run the ballistics on the bullet and maybe they even had a suspect in mind.

Okay, the suspect or suspects must have wanted something from Ed. Was it the car or was it something else? Why steal the car? It was a classic and would stand out and it would be hard to sell. But still there it was on the car lot and it seemed that no questions were asked. I had a feeling this was not a robbery that had gone bad. There was something more to this case that I was not seeing.

I thought back when I first met Ed's neighbor, Nick. He was pretty cold and distant and was always focused more on the police than comforting his family. However that could have been because he had just lost a friend. But it was strange he had his arm around Linda and not his wife.

Then there was Linda and per Ronnie, she and Ed had dated. I should focus on Ed's and Linda's past relationship and how it had ended. Maybe Linda still harbored some issues and those unresolved issues might have caused her to kill Ed. I didn't get much from Mac or the description of the lady who had brought the Trailer Queen in to sell. Maybe it was not one of the three ladies already on my list. It could be a co-worker, someone from our car group or maybe even a complete stranger. Considering the car club ladies and even the men, I couldn't believe any of them had a motive to kill Ed. To be safe thought I'd add their names to my list of suspects. There was also a chance that it could be a bank co-worker or someone else completely out of the blue who had a grudge against him. It was going to be a daunting task to find whoever the killer was and then again prove it. I figured the next place to look was at the branch office on Willow. Tomorrow I'd stop by and talk to the employees.

I also needed to take another look inside Ed's place and try to find a clue or two to help me tie up some of these loose ends and find a clue or two the police had missed. I'd call Rod in the morning and see if he'd give me access. I needed a good reason to get back inside the house. I would tell him I needed to get the rest of Annie's food and toys.

My office was quiet except the ticking of the clock and when I looked up I saw it was almost five. I had forgotten all about the guys. I phoned Angie and told her I was on my way and as soon as I walked into her shop there came the guys both looking great and excited to see me. Each was wearing a bandana. Oz's was blue and Annie's pink. Angie told me how well behaved they had been and advised me not to wait so long before their next grooming. I paid the bill and looked down at the guys, "I bet you're hungry." What was I saying? Oz was always hungry! They both looked up at me and wagged their tails.

We arrived home and the first thing they did was to run out back. Soon they came crashing through the doggie door and started jumping and chasing each other around the house. We went for a pre-dinner walk around the block since I could tell we all needed rid of some pent up energy. I'm not one to do a lot of exercising but I'm not in too bad of shape for my age, or so that's what I kept telling myself. After sitting all afternoon it was good to get out and stretch my legs and clear my mind. Our walk was enjoyable and Annie gave Oz the lead and she walked by my side. We stopped and visited with neighbors who were out in their front yards and the guys received plenty of attention. Everyone commented how nice they looked wearing their new bandanas. We were just about to head up our driveway when Dolly, our next door neighbor's dog, came over to check out Oz and Annie. At first she was not sure about Annie but after a few sniffs and dances in circles, she decided Annie was okay.

Carrie, Dolly's owner walked over and asked, "So who is this cute little lady?"

"This is Annabelle but I call her Annie. She's going be staying with us for a while."

Carrie had been my next door neighbor ever since I purchased my home. That was about eight years ago when I was single. A couple of years later Oz moved in and shortly after that Marti joined the family. A couple days after I had moved in I was out in the garage unpacking when I heard a commotion next door. I peeked out the garage door to see Carrie having an argument with a man who looked to be her same age. She told me many times afterward she was glad to be rid of her no good, cheating worthless scumbag of a husband. She has been single ever since. She was one of those physical fitness types who looked great even for someone in their late sixties. She had short silver hair and wore her glasses around her neck. She was always dressed in a jogging suit and today it was lime green. She must have had a different one for each day of the week. Whenever Marti was in town, the two of them either jogged or biked trying to stay in shape. Marti told me she used their time together to get caught up on the local gossip. I also was suspicious Marti had asked Carrie keep an eye on me when she was out of town.

"So with a male and female under one roof are you worried about some hanky panky between the two of them?" Carrie asked with a smirk.

"Not with Oz. He can never be a father and as for Annie, I'm not sure."

We chatted for about another ten minutes when Carrie picked up Dolly and started for her house. "Got to go, 'Wheel of Fortune' is about to start. Dolly and I try to solve the puzzles before the contestants. Boy, some of those people are so dumb."

I was fixing the guy's dinner when Marti called to tell me she and her crew were in New York and they were currently having dinner at a famous television chef's restaurant. She went into great detail about the amazing food the chef had prepared and described each and every bite. My stomach was now grumbling listening to Marti go on and on. She ended the call with, "Honey, you should see this dessert! OMG! It looks scrumptious! I gotta go," and she quickly hung up the phone.

I gave the guys their dinner and went to the freezer to take out a frozen pizza. I added my special touch with some additional toppings and put it in the oven to bake. I had just set the timer when my phone pinged and Marti had sent me pictures. I texted her back, "You really know how to hit below the belt."

I decided while I was waiting for my pizza to cook it would be a good time to try and reach out to Ed's sister. She surprisingly answered on the first ring.

"Hi, my name is Wes. I'm a friend of your brother. We were in a car group together and I just wanted to call and offer my condolences."

There was a long silent period before she replied, "Yea, thanks, shit happens."

"I was hoping we could meet tomorrow. The car group would like to help with his funeral arrangements and I was hoping you could give us some information and answer some questions I have about him."

"Who said anything about me planning his dumb funeral? Hey look pal, I can't talk right now. Try calling me back in the morning," she abruptly ended the call and hung up.

Rod was right. She was some piece of work. I would have thought she would have shown some regrets about the loss of her brother but maybe she knew more about his murder than she was letting on. "Joy, you have just moved to the top of my suspect list," I said out loud.

The oven timer went off and dinner was served. I took a picture of my culinary creation and sent it to Marti with the words, "Eat your heart out."

The guys follow me out to the patio hoping for something good to come their way. It was hard to enjoy my pizza with sad eyes locked on each and every bite. They were masters at the art of begging and with their sad looks Mr. Softy caved and shared the crust. My phone pinged again and it was another text from Marti, "I wish I was there. Looks good, but it's the company I really miss." I wished she was here too.

With the pizza gone I sat staring out into the backyard puzzled about Joy's reaction and our brief conversation. I couldn't help but think that if I lost a family member how shaken I would be. She voiced no sorrow. It was late and the patio lights came on so I went inside. I cleaned up the dishes, locked the door and went to bed to read. I was having a hard time concentrating on the story because my thoughts kept reverting back to my conversation with Joy. Maybe she was the person trying to sell the Trailer Queen. I listened to Annie's snoring and smiled happy she had become part of this family in such a short time. My phone pinged and it was Marti saying good night. We texted back and forth a few times with some small talk and then concluded with our "love yous."

I turned out the light and just laid there. There was a lot to process.

Chapter 8

Chuck had his hand on the door handle and we both had
our guns poised ready for what might be waiting for us
behind the door. I heard footsteps coming from behind
me. Our back up had finally decided to join us. I felt
some sort of relief. We all looked at each other and
nodded in unison signaling it was time to proceed. Chuck
opened the door slowly and a faint light came from within
illuminating and casting shadows on our faces. As the
door opened further there was a strange and eerie
silence. Just then something flew out and slammed into
my chest. I fell backward into the officers behind me and
we all crashed to the ground. The extreme weight of our
suspect pressed down on my chest and I struggled to
move out from underneath of him. Suddenly, someone
threw a bucket of water in my face. I opened my eyes and
that was when I saw those two familiar big brown eyes.

"Oz, what the hell are you doing?" Yikes! I glanced at the
clock, it was almost six a.m. and Oz was on my chest. I
hated it when he did that. Lucky for me Annie was still
asleep on the floor.

After getting Oz settled down on the bed I closed my eyes
and tried to go back to sleep. I realized sleep was not
going to happen. My mind was busy processing what I

would say to Joy if I could meet up with her this morning. In my current line of work as a private investigator I never interviewed or really had any communications with my suspects. Now that I was kind of looking into Ed's murder talking and questioning potential suspects was new to me. I wanted to make sure to ask the right questions and get the response I needed. I could see Oz was about to pounce again so I got up and started moving.

I needed to go to the place where I did my best thinking. It was time to pay a visit to my local Wally World. Our pantry was getting low and with Marti coming home for a couple of days I didn't want to spend my time away from her shopping.

For me the advantage of shopping at this time of the day was there were no screaming kids and no scooter people blocking the aisles. I could walk and think. It was amazing how much brain work I was able to get done while shopping. Shopping Walmart provided some great distractions and entertainment: you got to see some uniquely dressed people, which made you wonder how they survived in the real world. Marti figured that since I did most of the cooking then it made sense I should do most of the shopping.

While I walked the aisles I picked up what we were going to need in the way of food for the next week. Also, I was able to think about all the evidence I had gathered so far concerning Ed's murder. I had the where, the how and possibly the who although my suspect list was long. Hopefully, after I visited with Joy and Ed's co-workers, I would have the why. If time allowed it would be helpful to take another walk around Ed's house too as long as Rod would give me the key. The police had already searched and taken what they felt was important to their investigation but I wanted to satisfy my own curiosity. Before I knew it I was standing in a long line with a cart filled with groceries waiting to check out. I looked around the store and watched people as they scurried around trying to find something before they headed off to work. Why would someone take Ed's Cadillac? They had to know sooner or later the police would find it and trace it back to them. With a cart full of bagged up groceries I walked out of the store to see the sun rising over the mountains. The parking lot was filling up but thankfully I had beaten the morning rush.

As soon as I got home I was greeted with a "Did you get us something good to eat?" look. After putting the groceries away I made eggs, bacon and toast for breakfast. I put some bacon bits in the guys food and watched as they wolfed it down. I enjoyed my breakfast out on the patio and read up on my next case I had gotten from the state.

The report outlined a suspect's claim that he fell off a ladder at a construction job site and was unable to work due to his injury. The report read that he had pain when bending and lifting anything heavy. It went on to read that when he tried climbing a ladder he felt shooting pains throughout his back and legs. Unfortunately, the doctor's reports didn't show any conclusive back damage due to the fall. If anything did show it was a couple of pulled muscles which would heal over time. The state had been paying on this claim for almost a year. Since there was no record of this person having tried to get another job it was their opinion that further investigation was needed to justify the continuation of payment.

Most cases given to me by the state or by private insurance companies had something to do with back issues. They were hard to diagnose and easy for the claimants to fake. The report also read that none of his co-workers had seen the accident happen. They had heard him screaming and found him lying on the ground. He told them he had fallen off the ladder while carrying some wood up to the roof. After spending three months recuperating, which included some physical therapy visits, the doctors cleared him to go back to work. A week later he returned to the doctor claiming it was just too painful to continue working in construction. The state tried to find other lines of work for him but with each job there was another complaint about the pain he was in and shortly after he'd quit. The state succumbed to his complaint and continued to pay on his claim. I re-read the report and it was now time for me to put on my Sherlock Holmes hat and go to work.

I dialed Joy's number and after a couple of rings she answered, "Hello?"

"Morning Joy, this is Wes. We talked last night. Would this morning be a good time for me to stop by for a visit?"

She sounded perturbed that I had called but after a couple of moans and groans she relented and said, "Sure why not? I just got home from work and want to get to bed soon so how long before you can get here?"

"Give me your address and I'm on my way?"

I could tell by her tone she didn't want to meet with me but I wasn't going to let this opportunity pass me by. She gave me her address and I told her I would be there within the hour. I had a good idea of about where she lived and it would take about thirty minutes depending on the traffic. As I walk out the front door there were no sad eyes watching me leave. There must've been something out in the back yard keeping the guy's interest.

Traffic was light and I made good time. After our two brief conversations I already knew what kind of reception I was going to receive. By the tone of Joy's voice this morning, it would be cold and defensive. Joy lived in a low-income apartment complex on the south side of a neighboring town. After seeing where she lived, it was obvious there was no way she could keep Annie. I had to climb three flights of stairs to get to her door and I had to stop and catch my breath once I reached the top. Maybe this would be a good time to cut back on Betty's fritters. Nah, that wasn't going to happen anytime soon.

I knocked on the door a couple of times and when it opened I was greeted by an overwhelming cloud of cigarette smoke. There stood a petite, blue eyed blonde in her late twenties with a half smoked cigarette in her mouth and a cup of coffee in her other hand. She wore a stained diner's waitress uniform with her hair pulled back into a ponytail. Her face looked tired after working the graveyard shift and she blew a puff of smoke in my face. "You must be Wes. Come on in."

Inside the place reeked of cigarette smoke and stale beers like a neighborhood dive bar. There were ashtrays overflowing with used butts and empty beer bottles tossed around the floor.

"Yes, thanks for taking the time to meet with me."

"I just got off my shift at the truck stop, so let's talk now before I crash. It was a long night and I just want to get off my feet."

She lit up another cigarette and sat on the sofa while I found a safe place to sit at the counter. There was not much in the way of furnishings, a well-worn sofa and chair and an old television set. The walls had a couple of pictures like something you would find at a thrift store. We sat looking at each other with a cold silence in the room which kind of gave me the chills. I thought to myself "What the heck am I doing here? I should get up and leave and let the police do their work." I took a deep breath and swallowed hard. I was choking on the smoke. I heard what sounded like a cat meowing from another room. It was going to be up to me to break the silence. She hadn't said a word since we both sat down.

"How long have you been living here?"

"I moved into this dump about six months ago. I can barely afford this place it but was the cheapest I could find."

She took a long drag on her cigarette and blew the smoke toward me. I just about choked but tried not to show that it bothered me and continued to try to get her to open up.

"I am sorry about the passing of your brother. It must have been a terrible shock."

She looked down into her almost empty coffee cup and after a few moments of silence she then replied, "The state's making me responsible for burying my stupid brother since I am the only living relative." She took a sip of coffee and continued, "I'm going to have to pay for it. I don't have that fricking kind of money! I can barely afford to pay my bills as it is and they cut back my hours at the truck stop." Tears began running down her cheeks, her hands shook and ashes from her cigarette fell scattering on the floor. "My stupid brother is going to bankrupt me. That bastard!"

"I'm pretty sure Ed's estate will pay for the funeral."

"I don't have a clue what you're talking about. All I know is my stupid brother is going to leave me stuck with the bill, like he did before." Her tone was harsh as she regained her composure, "That bastard!" she said under her breath.

I heard some faint noises again coming from the bedroom and we both looked in that direction. Her face showed fear for the first time when she turned back and looked into my eyes.

"Why are you are here and what the hell do you want? I told that nosey police officer everything I knew when he stopped by yesterday at my work. He almost got me fired."

"Ed was a friend of mine and I wanted to offer my condolences and my services with anything I could do to help with planning the ..." More noises came from the bedroom which caused me to stop. I didn't think we were alone in the apartment.

The bedroom door suddenly opened and out ran a cat and the door quickly closed. The cat hopped onto Joy's lap and started purring. She turned her attention to the cat and the room filled with the sound of the cat purring. The cat seemed to calm Joy, the anger in her face had dissipated.

"I'm not supposed to have pets, but I found Tiger roaming the streets and he was in bad shape. I snuck him in the apartment since I don't have money for a pet deposit. I'm barely making my rent as it is," she repeated.

"Cat, what cat? I don't see a cat. Do you see a cat?" This brought a smile to Joy's face for the first time since I had arrived.

"Look, I understand you and Ed didn't get along but I am sorry for your loss. I do have one question though."

"So, what's your question?" Joy started tensing up again.

"Well, ever since Ed's death, I have been taking care of his dog Annie I mean Annabelle. My dog Oz and I have become very fond of her. I was wondering what your plans for her are?"

I knew she couldn't keep Annie. The management would find out and she would be evicted.

"If you want her, keep her. I don't want Ed's stupid dog. It would be just another thing Ed stuck me with. Besides, where would I get the money to feed the dumb dog? Then, there is the cleaning up after her which I really don't want to do. I would have to move because the apartment manager would find out for sure and I would have to put down a deposit. I can't afford to move and have to pay another deposit," she rambled.

I gave her a weak smile and thought to myself, "Looks like Annie has a new home and it is with us."

Joy abruptly stood up, "I think it's time for you to leave." I took the hint and headed for the door.

Just as I started to open the front door a tall, skinny man walked out of the bedroom. He was wearing only jeans and his chest and arms were covered with tattoos. Joy's eyes filled with fear as she looked at him and then with a quick motion she turned to me. "You better leave."

"Hey babe, is this guy bothering you?" His voice was raspy and his eyes were cold and dark. He had long scraggly hair which needed washing and a half smoked cigarette hanging out the side of his mouth. His body was lean, not an ounce of fat. My first impression was this was a person who you didn't want to mess with. He leaned up against the doorway and I saw a gun sticking out of his back pocket. I knew then it was in my best interest to get the hell out of Dodge and fast.

"Yep," I said to myself," It was time to leave." The door slammed behind me and as soon as I was in the hallway I could hear them screaming and yelling at each other. Unfortunately, I was unable to make out what they were yelling about. When I got to my truck I looked up at Joy's apartment and saw Mr. James Dean want-a-be staring at me with his hand on his back pocket. I got the message and left.

"Well, that was a fun time," I thought to myself. "When I get home I'm going to have to burn these clothes. I wondered if the love lost between Ed and Joy was two sided or if it was just Joy." I was beginning to feel it was just Joy. I didn't ever remember Ed saying he had a sister or much about his family or past at all. I rolled down all the windows since I reeked of cigarette smoke. The stench made it hard to breathe. I called Rod hoping I might be able to get some information about what he had found out about the Trailer Queen. Also I wanted to see if he would give me access to Ed's house. The call went straight to voicemail so I left him a message to call me back.

I parked in a strip mall a couple of blocks away from Joy's apartment. I wanted to gather my thoughts about what I had just experienced. Joy had a lot of animosity toward

Ed and it had certainly showed during our conversation. Joy had needed money and she reached out to her brother and he apparently refused to give her any. Ed's death could have been a robbery gone bad. Her tattooed muscle then could have taken matters in his hands and things had gone too far. Ed was shot and I was betting the gun in his back pocket was the gun used to kill him. That was one scary dude living with her. If I was to meet up with Joy again, I would definitely make sure it was not at her apartment. Joy and Mr. James Dean want-a-be had just moved to the top of my list of suspects.

I headed back home to change out of my smoke infested cloths but I made a side trip to a small bedroom community on the north side of town, a subdivision called "Station Village". That was where the suspect for my next state investigation lived. Driving down his street I could see by looking at the homes and yards that it was an older subdivision. The homes were single story ranches and the yards were good size with tall shade trees. Some of the yards could have used a good cleaning up, as well as some of the homes, but all in all it looked like a decent place to live. I found the address and drove by slowly. The house had seen better days and the grass desperately needed some water. I circled the block and stopped out front. I parked the truck and left the engine running while I looked around trying to find where a good place would be to set up my surveillance. I turned my attention to the suspect's house where there were kid's bikes on the grass and the curtains were drawn blocking my view. The driveway was littered with a broken down motorcycle and parts as if someone had been working on it. I sat there for a few minutes getting the lay of the land. It seemed no one payed any attention to me or the sound of my engine running.

My phone rang and it was Rod. I answered with, "Hey, are you keeping yourself busy?"

"What do you think Hot Shot?"

"Did you find out anything new on the Trailer Queen?"

"Not really. Some lady tried to sell the car, but then I have a feeling you already know that. When I talked to Mac, the owner, he said some guy had asked a lot of questions about the person who brought the car in to sell. I figured it was you."

"Hey, you asked me to find the car and so when I did I just asked a couple of questions."

Rod just chuckled and went on to explain what he found out but I was pretty sure he left out the good stuff. I listened while keeping an eye out for any movement at my suspect's house but there was nothing. From what Rod said Mac was not a lot of help. It was a Saturday when the lady brought the car in and he was there by himself. He had a lot full of customers and rushed through the paperwork processing the Cadillac. After she left he had helped a couple of perspective buyers and when he returned to his office all her paperwork was gone. Copies of the photo id and all the other information about the lady had disappeared. He thought she must have taken it with her by mistake but he figured she would be back for her money and he would get the copies back then.

"It sounds like she doesn't want a paper trail." I said.

"That's what it looks like to me. He wasn't very helpful with her description."

"If I were Mac, this would bring up a bunch of red flags. Do you think he runs a clean business?"

"We did a background check on him and he's pretty clean. He's been in the car business a long time but there have been a few complaints filed against him. Most of them were about the cars being lemons, nothing really solid."

Rod went on to say they were checking the car for fingerprints but he wasn't very optimistic.

"I talked to Joy this morning and she doesn't want any part of Ed's dog, Annie. Do you think I could get access to Ed's house to get Annie's things?"

"So is it the dog's things that you want or are you going to do a little snooping? I could tell by the way he answered me he was smiling on the other end of the phone. "We're done with the house so stop by the station and I'll have the key at the front desk for you."

"Thanks," and the call ended.

I noticed the neighbors next to my suspect's house were out working in their yard so I got out of my truck and walked over to them. Being the neighborly kind of person that I am I gave them my best smile and greeting but after we shook hands they took a step back to get away from the reeking smell of my smoke infested cloths. I told them I was a real estate agent and had someone interested in the house next door. They confirmed my suspicions that someone was living there and it sounded like it wouldn't hurt their feelings if they moved. They said the property was a rental and people were always moving in and out. They told me there were always a bunch of biker people hanging around all hours of the night. It made some of the neighbors feel uneasy being out in their front yards. I thanked them for their time and walked back to my truck taking one last look at the place but still there was no movement. I looked around for a good location to set up surveillance and spotted a convenience store at the end of the block. I pulled onto the stores lot and parked on the side. This would be the perfect location where I could see the front of the property and the driveway. I decided to start in the morning.

I thought this would be a good time to swing by the house and check on the guys. It was close to lunch time and I needed to get out of these smoke filled clothes. When I opened the front door I saw that Oz had taught Annie the finer points of our sofa. They each had their head on an arm rest.

Oz looked up as I closed the door and he casually got up and walked over to say "Hi" but once he got a whiff of my clothes he turned and walked away. As for Annie she had found her happy place and was not moving. I walked over to her and scratched behind her ears. "Well, lady it looks as if this will be your new home. Welcome to the family."

I changed and put the clothes into the washer adding extra soap hoping it would take out the smell. If not I was going to have to burn them. If I was going to put on clean cloths I had better shower and get the rest of the cigarette smell off my body. I showered, dressed in jeans and a polo shirt and made a couple of peanut butter sandwiches. I grabbed a bottle of water and was back out the front door. I was off to the police station to pick up the keys to Ed's house. Rod was not in but they were at the front desk like he said they would be. I drove up to Ed's house and saw the police tape had been taken down and it looked as if nothing had happened there. I wondered if the inside was still a mess.

Chapter 9

I got out of my truck and took a moment to look around the neighborhood. All I could hear was a dog barking down the street. The old, crabby looking lady from across the street from Ed's house was standing in her front window staring at me again. This was the second time I had seen her checking me out. The first time was when I had discovered Ed's body. I bet she was the neighborhood busy body. She looked to be in her later years and had a scowl on her face. This would scare away any person who came knocking on her door. I gave her a friendly wave of my hand as she continued to stare. I started toward Ed's front door and could still feel her beady little eyes watching my every move. She was starting to freak me out.

As the front door lock clicked open the hairs on the back of my neck stood on end. I pushed the door open and there was an eerie feeling as if being in a Stephen King novel. I was starting to creep myself out. The blood on the front hall floor was gone and the crime scene had been cleaned up, but the house still had a real sour smell to it. I opened all the windows and doors to let in the fresh air. I found Annie's toys and they surely had seen better days so in the trash they went. A stop by the pet store was in order to pick up some new toys for the guys.

If Annie was anything like Oz I was sure it wouldn't take long before they would have all the stuffing out of them.

Regaining my composure I started sleuthing and looking for clues. It was obvious the police had gone through the house with a fine tooth comb and gathered evidence important to their case. During my last visit the house had been trashed. Things now were back in their place as if Ed was still living there. My plan was simple, I would go through one room at a time, starting with the master bedroom and make my way through the house. I rummaged through the nightstands, the dresser and the closet. Despite my efforts I found nothing that could help my case. The second bedroom had only a bed and nightstand with a few ladies clothes in the closet. I stood looking at the clothes and wondered if Ed had a girlfriend. I knew they couldn't be Joy's. This created another path my investigation would have to explore. I walked into the master bath and on the counter was a toothbrush and paste. I opened the cabinet and there was the usual men's stuff along with another toothbrush and some ladies toiletries. I needed to find out who these belonged too.

Ed's office looked like this was where he spent most of his time. I sat behind his desk and admired all the pictures and trophies he had won with the Trailer Queen. It was strange though that there were no personal pictures of Ed's life outside of car shows. I went through the desk one drawer at a time and rifled through papers hoping for some kind of evidence. In the bottom drawer shoved in the back I found a picture of Ed and Linda, Ronnie's sister. There was also a second picture of Ed with his arms wrapped around a woman whom I had not met. Maybe the clothes and personal items belonged to her. She could be vital in helping me solve this case. I thought for a moment she could be the killer. The trick would be to find her. I turned the photo over but there was no writing on it. Darn! I also found a large photo book filled with pictures but unfortunately the pictures were all of the Trailer Queen. Not one picture showed Ed's personal life outside of the shows he had attended. I put the two pictures I had found in my pocket and I continued looking for a name, an address or anything else that would help with my investigation. I came up empty except for the two photos.

The patio screen door slid open and a female voice sang out, "Hello?"

It startled me and I walked back into the living room to see who it was. There stood Ronnie wearing tight shorts, a halter top and her hair tied back in a ponytail.

"Hey, I noticed the truck parked out front and the doors and windows open so I thought I would come by and see who was here," she said.

"Just me, I stopped by to get Annabelle's food and toys."

"Let me help you find them. They're usually all over the place. Ed spoiled that dog. That's funny, I don't see any now and they were here the other day."

"The toys had seen better days so in the trash they went. Any idea where Ed kept her food?"

"You'll find Annabelle's food in the garage in a cabinet by the side door," she said.

"Ronnie, how are you and your family coping after such a tragedy?"

"It's shaken our family. I don't know if I will ever get over seeing his body lying there. Poor Nick, he's been very distant these days. Every time I want to talk about Ed, he puts his hand up and walks away. I think he's really misses his friend. I noticed he's been drinking a lot more lately too. He has been struggling with Ed's death more than I would have thought. Linda is a basket case. She has been staying with us during this whole ordeal. She just sits in the recliner staring at the wall with a blank look on her face and rocks back and forth mumbling to herself. I can't get her to eat or talk to me. It's so frustrating. And poor Lyle, he keeps asking to go visit Uncle Ed. He's too young to understand."

"I bet it is hard on them but you didn't say how you're coping."

Ronnie just stood there looking around the room with tears forming in her eyes, "It's hard. I have nightmares from seeing poor Ed lying there in a puddle of blood. No one in my family will talk to me about it. I'm very stressed out and from time to time I breakdown and cry. I just want this nightmare to end and things to get back to the way they were before this mess happened." Tears streaked her cheeks.

I could tell this was the first time she had been able to speak to anyone about what had happened. As she walked into the kitchen she used the back of her hand to wipe away the tears. I followed her and used this time to continue to look for clues. I opened and closed cabinet doors and pulled out drawers and found nothing out of the ordinary. When I opened the fridge, the smell just about knocked me over. There were a lot of science projects growing inside, such as shriveled veggies and past expiration date meats. I quickly closed the door as the smell was starting to turn my stomach. I noticed it hadn't seem to bother Ronnie. She just sat at the table and watching me.

I stopped my search and joined her at the table. Her eyes were red and swollen. She blankly flipped through the mail and looked at one piece at time and then shuffled it to the back. She kept on repeating the process and after the fourth run-through it was time to get her to talk.

"You said your sister was taking this very hard, why is that?"

The question brought Ronnie back to reality," Yes, she is still shaken up. She's having a hard time, but we all are."

"I understand, I'm still struggling myself. Do you think Linda is having issues because she and Ed had been an item once?"

Ronnie's eyes opened wide and her mouth dropped. There was a look of shock as "how did you know?" crossed her face.

"You told me the other day when I came over to visit and found Ed's body," I replied.

She took a deep breath and looked around the kitchen. She then started in repeating her story from the other day either for my benefit or hers. I wasn't going to stop her. It was good to hear it again. "They dated for about a year, and things seemed to be going well, but then one night out of the blue, Ed told her he didn't think it was going to work out and he ended it. That night she cried in my arms. He broke her heart."

"Did Linda ever tell you why Ed ended their relationship?"

She paused to think then replied, "No, not really. Linda has always kept it close to her heart."

"So after the break-up they never really talked?"

"No, Linda didn't want anything to do with him after that."

"How long has it been since they stopped being a couple?"

"Some time last year, I think. It was around November but I can't remember exactly."

I was losing Ronnie's attention so I decided to change the subject.

"So, how long you've been living next door to Ed, if you don't mind me asking?"

"About four years I think. Our family was growing so we decided to look for a bigger home. I saw our place and fell in love with it. I thought it would be perfect to raise our family but I had to work hard to convince Nick it was our dream home. Have the police said anything about what happened? I noticed you seem to be buddies with the detective guy? What was his name?"

"No, Rod hasn't said anything to me about the investigation. I'm as much in the dark as you are. So how did you guys become friends with Ed?"

After a few moments of silence I repeated the question but suddenly she got up and walked out the back door without saying a single word.

I followed her and before she reached the side gate I yelled, "Ronnie, do you know who cleaned Ed's house?"

"Linda and I cleaned the place. The house was a real mess after the police finished investigating."

I stood there in the doorway with a puzzled look on my face. Strange they would take the time to clean the house. From what Ronnie just told me, Linda didn't want anything to do with Ed. So why did they go to all the effort? Why clean? Maybe it was a form of closure. I started for the garage when I stopped dead in my tracks and thought. "How did they get in?" The police would have locked up the house when they were finished with their investigation. Maybe Ronnie or Linda had a key."

I opened the door to the garage and the light came on and I found Annie's food right where Ronnie had said it would be. I was curious to find a basket full of children's toys there too. Ed didn't have any kids that I knew about. He never said anything about having kids. What was he doing with kid's toys? Had he once been married? Could the lady in the picture I found in his desk be his ex? If so then where were the kids? If she wasn't his ex then maybe she was a current girlfriend? Maybe she had a son or daughter? That would explain the extra toothbrush and ladies toiletries in the bathroom and women's clothes in the closet. So where were the kid's clothes? The more I found out about Ed's life, the more questions I had. I went around the house one more time looking for clues before shutting all the windows and locking the doors. I grabbed Annie's food on my way out.

As I started for my truck I saw Ronnie had left the side gate open so I walked over and closed it. I caught a glimpse of her peeking out from behind the curtain in her living room watching me. She tried not to be noticed but when I gave her a wave she quickly turned away. She wasn't the only one watching me. Ed's crabby looking neighbor from across the street was now joined by an elderly man. They both stood glaring at me out their front window.

I had collected plenty of information to add to my report from meeting with both Joy and Ronnie. With luck it would aid in solving Ed's murder. A quick stop at the pet shop and sixty dollar's worth of dog toys later, I was ready to call it a day. I spent the afternoon updating my notes but it took a lot longer than it should have. All the chasing and the squeaking of new toys made it difficult to concentrate. After sitting at a my desk for hours I was stiff and needed to get out and stretch my legs. I knew the guys would be disappointed if I didn't take them with me so I grabbed their leases and off we went. Our walks around the neighborhood were becoming more enjoyable as the three of us got used to walking together. Oz was always on guard and took the point and Annie walked by my side. Oz was such a ham that he would stop to socialize whenever there was someone to give him some attention. The guys got attention and I got caught up on the neighborhood gossip. We walked about two miles and by the time we arrived back home the guys were panting. Our walk around the neighborhood had given me an idea. I would take the guys for walk around Ed's neighborhood. I was sure someone would recognize Annie and they might give me some additional information to help with the case.

My phone was vibrating on the counter and I had missed a call from Bruce. I hit redial and after a few rings he said, "Hey Wes, our group decided to stay at the park after the car show on Saturday and have a short memorial service for Ed."

"That sounds good to me. We'll be there. I think I'll call Ed's sister, Joy, and see if she'd like to join us."

"Do you think she'll come? I'd like to meet her. Well, see you Saturday."

We hung up and I thought back to my first impression of Joy. It would be real interesting if she decided to show.

I'm taking Vegas odds that she won't, but if she did it would give me the opportunity to ask her a few more questions. Let's hope if she did decide to show up and she wouldn't bring her thuggish boyfriend. I dialed Joy's number and left her a voice mail.

I fed the guys and watched as they wolfed their food down. I wondered if they ever really tasted what they are eating. I started to prepare my dinner which consisted of a couple Cajun seasoned spice chicken breast along with a small spaghetti squash. I mixed in some olive oil, salt, pepper and feta cheese. I went out on the patio to enjoy the warm summer evening and waited for it to cook. I had a lot on my mind and it was hard to shut it down and relax. Finally the timer told me it was time to eat.

I found an old 70's Charles Bronson cop movie to watch while I ate. The guy's faces were inches from my plate hoping I wouldn't notice if they happen to sneak something off if it. With my plate empty they gave up and found a spot to lay down while I continued to watch the movie. The movie was about halfway through when I received a text from Marti wondering what I was doing. She must have had a vibe, like a sixth sense, because whenever I turned on a movie she would either call or send a text interrupting my concentration. We texted back and forth about the day's work and after about an hour we ended with our usual "love yous," and said good night. As usual I had missed the ending of the movie and didn't get to find out who the killer was. Oh well, I'd have to watch the movie another time. I made sure the doors were locked and by the time I walked into the bedroom I saw the guys had found their spots on the bed. I wasn't going to be comfortable but I was too tired to fight them. I worked my body around theirs in a kind of figure "S" shape and tried to get to sleep. Annie's snoring kept me awake but it was alright. My mind was re-processing my meetings with both Joy and Ronnie. There was a lot of information to sort out.

Chapter 10

The light of the sun was coming through the bedroom window when I rolled over I saw that the clock read seven a.m. My body was stiff and sore from having slept between the guys all night. This would be the last time Mr. Softy would let them sleep on the bed. Suddenly, the sound of the alarm clock going off shattered the peacefulness of the morning and I was besieged by licks and pouncing. The guys were letting me know it was time to get up. Between the alarm and all the pouncing I was wide awake so I got up and walked into the kitchen with them close behind. Once they were fed I made a large pot of oatmeal with lots of butter and brown sugar, one of my favorite breakfasts. Marti would be home sometime this afternoon and she would need to get a ride home from someone since I would be busy working.

I had two objectives today, the first being the insurance investigation I had started and the second was to stop by the bank where Ed used to work. For the state's investigation I had planned to use my traffic surveillance line on the store manager and hoped they would allow me to use their parking lot to set up my operations. It was the perfect location to view my suspect's entire front yard and driveway which allowed me to see all the comings and goings.

I put plenty of water out for the guys, jotted a note for Marti and headed out the door. Soon I was parked on the back side of the convenience store's lot and once in the store I located the store manager. She was short and somewhat stocky in her mid-thirties and wore a loose fitting store employee shirt with the name Sheila printed under the words store manager. I explained I was a traffic inspector for the city and that the city was looking at the possibility of making modifications to the traffic pattern on the residential street next to her store. I asked if it would be okay if I parked on the back side of their lot to watch and monitor the traffic patterns for a week or so. She was indifferent to the idea and had no problem with it so to show my appreciation I stocked up on water and snacks.

I set up my video camera on the dash and took a walk down to the end of the street and back. I stopped a couple times to get a close up view of my suspect's yard and house, once pretending to be tying my shoe. The curtains were still closed and there was no activity. When I returned to the truck I unpacked the rest of my camera gear and then sat and waited for something to happen. The first three hours were quiet and unfortunately for me nothing happened. This was the worst part of my job, just sitting and waiting. Since nothing was happening here and I was impatient to talk to Ed's coworkers I made an executive decision to leave and come back later.

The bank's parking lot was mostly empty and that gave me a chance to talk to the bank's employees without being interrupted by customers. I walked inside and saw there were four employees, two tellers behind the counter assisting customers, an older lady sitting at a front desk as well as another lady sitting at a desk in the back of the room, possibly the bank manager. As I approached I saw on the desk a plaque with the words, "Bank Manager" and introduced myself.

She stood and shook my hand and said, "Please have a seat. How may I be of assistance?" She was in her late forties, had short black hair, brown eyes and wore glasses. She was dressed professionally in a light grey business suit.

Reading her name tag I replied, "Good morning Michelle, my name is Wesley Johns and I was a good friend of Ed Wilson. He worked here as a loan officer."

Her demeanor changed from a smile to a sight frown, "Yes, what a tragedy. We are all going to miss him. He was a treasure to work with."

"Some of his car club friends are planning to have a small service at the park this Saturday and everyone here at the bank is invited. I was hoping some of you would be able share some stories you might have about Ed during the time he worked here."

She rocked back and forth in her chair, occasionally looking at the lobby making sure the customers were being taken care of. "I transferred here about six months ago. Ed had been at this branch for over two years. During that time he didn't share much about his personal life. He talked a lot about his car. He was so proud of it and of course Annie who was the love of his life." She pointed to her right and I turned to look. There were on his old desk two pictures, one of the Trailer Queen and the other of Annie and him. She continued her story, "Ed was well liked by all the employees and by our customers. There were rumors however that he would be leaving us soon and going to the corporate office in Portland. He was in line for a promotion since he had been such a good loan officer and had a high quality rating on loans. We all worked well with each other. We thought he might be leaving us soon, we just didn't expect..." She was getting choked up talking about Ed and tears were welling up in her eyes. She stopped and reached for a Kleenex. I allowed her to regain her composure before I asked a few questions.

"So Michelle, you're telling me Ed focused mostly on his work and did little socializing with the employees here at the bank."

"Oh, there was the day to day chitchat, but that's about it. Other than information about Annabella and his car I couldn't tell you much about his personal life. Sometimes a bunch of us would go out after we closed the bank and get a drink. I can't really tell you anymore than what I have said. Maybe some of the other employees might be of more help."

"Would it be okay if I took Ed's pictures for the service and possibly have a look around his desk to see if there's anything else I can use?"

"I think that'll be okay. I don't know what you'll find though. The bank has removed all important papers and the police have taken what they felt was important."

We stood and shook hands. I walked over to Ed's desk while Michelle walked over to talk to the lady at the front desk. They both turned and looked at me as I sat down at his desk, but looked away quickly when they saw I was watching them. They continued to talk for a few more minutes when Michelle made her way to the two tellers.

Sitting at Ed's desk felt kind of strange. I picked up the two picture frames and looked at the pictures, having remembered taken the one of Ed and the Trailer Queen. I set them on the corner of the desk to take with me and I methodically went through the desk drawers. Michelle was right. There was not any personal stuff left. I opened the last drawer and detected a small piece of paper stuck in the very back. It was a wallet size photo. After carefully working it loose I made sure not to tear it and was able to retrieve it. The photo took me by surprise. It was a portrait of Lyle, Ronnie's little boy. Why would Ed have a picture of Lyle? Pocketing the picture I kept looking for anything else that might help but there was nothing. I walked over to Michelle and the two tellers and thanked her for her time. As I started to walk out of the bank I turned to take in one last look when I saw a third teller who was now working by the drive up window. I waited for her to turn around and when she did, "Bingo!" She was "Miss Unknown" in the picture I found in Ed's home desk. The name tag on her shirt read "Donna." She must have been on break when I first walked into the bank.

"Well, this was a stroke of luck," I thought. I walked over to her and introduced myself. I told her why I was there and asked if I could speak to her about Ed. She was taken aback by my request, "I'm sorry but I can't talk right now," she said.

She was unaware that I had found the picture of her at Ed's house in the desk and I knew there was more to her story than just working at the bank with him. I took the photo of her and Ed out of my pocket and showed it to her. She looked closely at it and tears started forming. She wiped them away and handed the picture back to me. Just then a car pulled up to the window. Pointing to a place across the way she said, "My lunch is in thirty minutes. Meet me at the coffee shop over there." She then turned her attention to the customer after wiping her face dry.

I walked over to the coffee shop and ordered an ice tea. I found a table by the window while I waited for Donna. I watched as people came and went getting their midmorning coffee fix. I thought about the picture I found in Ed's bank desk of Lyle and wondered why he would have it. I realized thinking about Ed was like thinking about a stranger. He had never talked about family or his relationships with the ladies. I was convinced none of us really knew him.

My phone pinged with a text from Marti, "Will be home in about two hours. Are you going to pick me up?"

"Sorry you are going to have to find a ride. I'm working on a case but am excited to see you later," I texted.

She texted back, "K".

Donna walked into the shop placed her order at the counter and joined me. I formally introduce myself. She was a beautiful lady with long reddish hair and bright green eyes. She was tall above six foot, very slim and looked like she must work out. I bet she was in her mid-thirty's. Her picture with Ed didn't do her any justice, she was a knock out.

I started the conversation, "I found this picture of you in Ed's home desk and was wondering if you could tell me about it?"

She took the picture from me and after looking at it in silence, tears started to well up and finally trickled down her cheeks. She reached for a napkin and wiped them away. She sat there looking at the picture quietly sobbing, her hands shaking. I was now wiping tears from my eyes too and I could tell there was a lot more between them than just dating.

She looked up at me and said, "We were going to be married."

It was like someone threw a brick at my chest knocking all the air out of my lungs. "Married?" It's the only word I could muster as I sat there in shock.

"No one knew. We kept it a secret. You see bank employees at the same branch are not allowed to be involved. We started dating almost a year ago." I sat there with my mouth wide open. I couldn't believe what I was hearing.

Donna continued with her story, "We met at the bank's company party and at that time I was working at the branch at the corner of Indiana and Williams. Usually, Friday nights after work a bunch of us would go out and have a drink or two before going home. One night after an hour or so everyone else started to leave but Ed and I stayed since we were both single and not involved with anyone. Over time we became friends and would go to the movies, have a drink or even go out for dinner." She paused to take a sip of her now cold coffee and looked out the window. I could tell this was very hard on her. "Then one night we ended up in bed together. From that time on our relationship became more involved. About six months ago I was transferred to this branch and we kind of went underground to hide our affair. I couldn't afford to quit my job and so we had kept it a secret. I told Michelle about it after Ed's passing and she promised to keep it a secret. She told me she had suspected something had been going on between the two of us but never said anything."

Michelle was true to her word. She hadn't mentioned anything to me when I talked to her just a little bit ago. I sat there letting Donna take her time telling about their relationship.

She took another sip of cold coffee and continued, "When Ed was up for a promotion we started talking about eloping. I was going to move with him to Portland." She looked at me with her puffy red eyes and sat there in silence not really knowing what to say next.

"Why didn't Ed bring you around to the car shows or to some of our other social events?"

"We were afraid someone from the bank would see us and we'd get in trouble. Like I said, I couldn't afford to lose my job."

I was still trying to soak all this in when she stood up, "I have to get back to the bank, my break is almost over and by the way what's going to happen to Annabelle? I love that little girl."

"She's currently living with me and doing very well. Oz, my collie, has made her very welcome." That put a smile on Donna's face.

I wished we would have had more time to talk. I asked for her phone number since I still had a lot of questions for her. At first she was reluctant to give it to me but must have decided it was okay. She asked if she could keep the picture and I told her I'd be happy to make her a copy and that brought a smile to her face.

"I better hurry back. My lunch break is almost over."

As we walk backed to the bank I told her about the service we were having on Saturday and that she and the other bank employees were welcomed to join us. She just nodded and entered the bank through the back door. I walked around to where my truck was parked and I sat there trying to grasp what I had just heard. Ed had a girlfriend, serious enough that they were going to be married. "Crap!" I said out loud. I had forgotten to ask her if she had any children. If she did that would answer the question of the basket of toys I had found in the garage. I was betting the toiletries and clothes belonged to her, too.

I chuckled as I thought Ed must have been a secret agent in his past life. He sure could keep a secret. I had no clue of his love life. Just then there was a rap on the window and I jumped a mile. It was Rod.

"Hey, you scared the crap out of me!" I yelled at him.

"What brings you to the bank buddy?"

I told him about the service the club was planning and that I had invited Ed's co-workers. I also told Rod that I had asked them if they would like to share any life stories about him at the service.

He cocked his head to one side and gave me a smirk, "You're not trying to play detective on this case are you? You know that's my job."

"Whatever gives you that idea?" I tried to play it as cool as a cucumber but I knew he saw right through me. I continued, "So Mr. Hot Shot Detective, how's the investigation going anyway? Got any suspects yet?"

He gave me the police song and dance you see in all the movies, then turned and walked away. I thought about asking if he wanted the key to Ed's house back but thought better of it.

There was a lot to process after talking to Donna and the best way to process any new information was to get a sub from the deli. I found it was easier to think things out when my stomach wasn't grumbling.

When I got back to the convenience store's parking lot I continued my surveillance but still there was no activity to report. While munching on my roast beef with pickle I thought about my meeting with Ed's future wife "Donna" and tried to figure how she fit into all of this. I reached for a pad of paper and started making notes about our conversation. I also jotted down what the bank manager had said while everything was fresh in my mind. Occasionally I would look up to see if anything was happening down the street. I added Donna's name to my suspect list since I knew there was more to her than she had told me. I'd give her a call in the next couple of days and try to meet with her again. Also, the next time our car group got together I'd ask around and see if anyone knew about Ed and Donna's relationship. It was possible he had confided something to someone.

My suspect list was growing. There was Ronnie and her husband Nick, her sister Linda, Ed's sister Joy and her strange boyfriend and now Ed's fiancée Donna. Any one of these ladies could have been the one who had taken

Ed's caddy to Mac to sell. Although I had a suspect list there was nothing yet that really pointed a finger at anyone specific who might have been the murderer. As the old saying goes, "Something was rotten in Denmark."

Out of the corner of my eye I saw movement. A man exited the front door of my suspect's house and he matched the photo in the state's case file. I grabbed my camera and started taking pictures. He bent over and picked up the kid's bikes in the front yard and leaned them up against the house. Then he walked over to the motorcycle and started working on it. I watched and took pictures of him bending and lifting parts. There didn't seem to be an issue with his back since he was moving around pretty well. After a while he put his tools away and he went back into the house. It was late afternoon and I figured I had gotten all the pictures I was going to get for the day. I knew Marti would be home by now and I was anxious to see her. I had just put my camera away when the suspect came back outside and started walking toward me. "Crap!! Had he caught on that I was surveilling him?" I watched as he walked past me giving me a slight glance and then entered the convenience store. That was a close call.

I got out of my truck and followed him inside. He walked straight to the beer cooler picked up two twelve packs and grabbed a bag of chips on his way to the checkout counter. I went to the candy aisle by the front counter and watched from a distance as he walked up to the cashier. He must have been a regular by the way the kid behind the counter talked to him.

The clerk asked if he was going to the game on Sunday.

"Yea, you're not going to believe this but a buddy of mine won four tickets from a local radio station."

The clerk nodded in approval as he rang up the sale. They talked about how well the team was doing and I watched as he picked up a couple of bags of ice on his way out. I quickly paid for my candies, hurried back to my truck and took out my camera. I was able to get some great shots of him walking home, carrying the two twelve packs of beer, bag of chips and the large bags of ice. He definitely wasn't having any back issues today. These photos would be a good start into my investigation proving this guy was a fraud. It was getting close to five and most people would be getting off work soon. With all the beer he purchased I was betting he was going to have some company soon.

Marti sent me a text and picture of her chilling on the sofa with the guys, with their heads on her lap. Below the picture was just one word, "Home". It was cute.

I texted back, "Still working for a while longer but will make dinner when I get home." She replied with a thumbs-up. I couldn't wait until I had her in my arms.

The rush hour traffic was getting heavy as people were returning home after a day's work. I watched as they pulled into their driveways and got out looking exhausted. This made me want to call it a day but I kept watching my suspect's place hoping something would happen soon. Just then a couple of guys roared past me on their Harleys and parked in front of his house. He came out as soon as he heard them pull up carrying a large cooler. It looked to be heavy and probably full of beer and ice. I got some really good shots of him carrying it and figured my case was coming along nicely. All of them started working on his bike and I watched as he lifted the motor as the other two stabilized the bike frame. I could tell it was heavy but he wasn't having any issues with his back as he moved it. Once the engine was in place, they sat in camp chairs around the bike and started drinking beer. I felt like there was not much more going to happen and I was hot, hungry and wanted a long cool shower. It was time to go.

On my drive home I thought about the day and all the information I had gathered. Now however, it was time to take a sexy lady in my arms and show her how much I missed her and I wasn't thinking of Annie. I wondered if Marti would like to go to a baseball game.

Chapter 11

I unlocked the front door and was greeted by Oz. When I walked into the bedroom both Marti and Annie were sound asleep. I told Oz we'd better be quiet and let them sleep.

I was hot and tired after sitting in the truck all afternoon and I wasn't a person you'd want to get close too. A long cool shower helped me unwind and relax and I certainly smelled a lot better. I put on a t-shirt and sweats and went into the kitchen to prepare dinner. Oz followed my every step hoping something would fall his way and he would be there to clean it up. With Oz it was the two second rule and some times that was a stretch.

On the menu was grilled salmon, fresh corn on the cob, tossed salad, and a bottle of wine for Marti. As for dessert, we'd just have to wait to see what became of the evening. I made up a plate of cheese and crackers with some grapes and went out on the patio to enjoy the warm summer evening. Soon Annie joined Oz and me fearing he would get treats without her. With a click of a switch the gas grill came to life. I was not one to sit around and wait for the charcoals to heat up. I took a couple of bites of cheese and waited for Marti to wake up and join the three of us. I was pleased that the day of investigating had been so productive. From inside of the house I heard a rustling sound and when I turned, there stood Marti, still half asleep with her hair standing up like a chicken head.

"I see you found a sleeping buddy. I'm jealous." I said.

"Annie has been glued to me ever since I got home. Wherever I go, she goes. It's like we're joined at the hip. So what's on the menu tonight my sexy chef? I'm starving?"

"For you my special lady, the chef will prepare a culinary feast for the eyes and for the soul," I said handing her a glass of her favorite wine.

"I meant for dinner. That something special will have to wait until later this evening. It will be my treat," she replied with a devilish smile.

I left Marti to fend off the guys who were begging for a hand out. I returned with the salmon and corn and saw Marti had caved in to the guys begging and had given them some cheese. She was such a softy and she was my softy. As our dinner cooked we talked about the events during our days apart. I chose to leave out the fact that I had been looking into Ed's murder. I felt this wasn't the time or place to share this information since it might upset her. Marti talked about a passenger who had gotten the hiccups half way through the flight and couldn't stop. As she told the story about this passenger's unfortunate situation she giggled like a school girl. Everyone on the plane gave the man suggestions on how to stop them but unfortunately none worked. When the plane landed and he stepped off they suddenly stopped. As they would say in baseball, I came out of left field with, "How would you like to go to a baseball game Sunday afternoon?"

She gave me a funny look and replied, "Since when do you like baseball? We've never gone to a baseball game, ever. Why do you want to go to a baseball game? How about we see a movie instead?"

"Well, it's part of the investigation on my insurance case. My suspect has been taking the state to the cleaners with his workman's comp claim and I overheard he's going to a baseball game. I thought you might like to join me."

She startled me when she burst out singing, "Take me out to the ball game..."

We laughed and talked while we ate our dinners. Every now and then we would accidently dropped something for the guys. After we finished Marti got up and went into the bedroom with Annie following close behind. I looked down at Oz and said, "I don't know how it happens buddy, but I set the table, prepped the food, cooked the food, served the food, and in the end get stuck with the dishes.

Something is wrong with this picture." He just sat there looking up at me with a look as if to say, "I will happy to clean the dishes for you. Just put them down here on the floor."

I had just finished wiping down the counter when the ladies appeared in the kitchen. Marti had changed into a floral short summer dress with matching sandals and she was waving the keys to the truck, "Hey studs, us ladies would like to treat their men to some ice cream!"

"Well, you don't have to ask us twice," I replied throwing my dish towel in the sink.

As we all headed to the truck, Marti and I chanted, "Ice cream, you scream, who wants ice cream?" It was a beautiful summer evening with temperatures in the high eighties. We cruised with the windows down and the radio playing oldies. Our favorite ice cream shop had an outside patio where four-legged family members were allowed to participate. By the time we arrived the place was hopping, but on a warm June evening what would you expect?

"Okay, you guys get a table and I'll place our order," Marti said.

I watched as Marti walked to order our treats looking sexy in her short sun dress and her hair was flowing with each step. I said to myself, "Hmm, maybe there will be two desserts tonight."

Both Oz and Annie were hits with all the kids who took turns petting them. Marti soon joined us with two cones and two cups of delicious frozen treats. For me and the guys it was vanilla and Marti had chocolate. The guys gulped theirs down before I was able to taste my first bite. I wondered if they got brain freeze like humans. We talked about our plans to attend the car show on Saturday and the baseball game on Sunday. We decided to take the rest of the week one day at a time. It was great to have her home for this length of time and we would have to make the most of this precious time.

The sun had set and the street lights were coming on as we drove home. The guys were asleep in the backseat and Marti's continuous yawning made it obvious she'd soon be doing the same. As soon as we got home Marti and Annie went straight to the bedroom and I locked up the house while Oz watched my every move. Annie found her spot on the floor and Oz laid by her with their butts touching. I joined Marti who was already under the sheets and almost sleep. We kissed and said our "love yous" and it was lights out.

I was up early and drove the Bird to a do it yourself car wash. It didn't take me long to wash it since I was the only one there. By the time I parked it back in the garage it was mostly dry but I wiped down any remaining wet spots. The house was still quiet so I fed the guys and started the coffee. I knew Marti would be up soon so I threw some frozen biscuits in the oven. I sat out on the patio and enjoyed the morning stillness and read the paper. I heard footsteps and when I turned there stood Marti with her first cup of coffee. Coffee was the secret to getting her up. I had tried other methods but coffee worked the best. Marti grabbed the local section of the paper and I read the sports. I heard the oven buzzer go off and soon returned with hot biscuits and jam plus the pot of coffee. Marti's favorite saying was, "Until I've had my first sip of coffee in the morning, don't even think about asking me anything important!" Marti was such a coffee junkie that I bet she had at least four or five cups a day.

We watched the guys busily chase the squirrels as we ate our breakfast. They were never fast enough to catch one and I was pretty sure they wouldn't know what to do if they did. Marti told me that she and Annie were meeting some of her friends. They were going hiking along the river and afterwards have lunch. This meant it was just Oz and me today.

I was in the shower planning my surveillance for the day when Marti walked into the bathroom and told me Mike had just called and he wanted me to call him back. She then climbed into the shower and joined me. "Hey sexy do you have room for one more?"

We let the hot water splash off our bodies as we kissed and held each other. Marti looked into my eyes and I could see she was happy to be home. The feeling was mutual.

I got dressed and I returned Mike's call. He wanted to let us know his plans for the brief memorial after the car show on Saturday. After our short conversation I made sure both Oz and I had plenty of water and some snacks for our day. I kissed Marti goodbye and out the door we went. Our first stop would be the car lot where I'd try to get some additional information out of Mac and take another look at that Pontiac. I really did want the car but I wasn't sure what Marti would think of the idea.

Mac was sitting at his office desk watching the front window waiting for potential victims to appear so he could pounce. I told myself to be nice as I walked over to the Pontiac. He soon joined me with a big smile.

"So did you talk to the little lady last night about this incredible ride?"

I lied, "I did bring up the topic but she's pretty lukewarm about the idea if you know what I mean. Hey, I see that couple picked up the Cadillac." Even though I knew full well the police had impounded the car.

"Nope, the police have it. It seems it was stolen and is part of a murder investigation of some kind."

"Wow!" I just stood there waiting for him to share the details, but he didn't say any more about it.

"I talked to the owner of the Pontiac last night, and he's motivated to sell. Make him an offer."

He opened the car door again and gave me a gentle nudge inside. I sat looking out the windshield staring at Oz in the truck and I knew I should leave now before doing something stupid.

"Mac, I'll bring the wife by in the next couple of days and if she thinks it's a good deal then we'll talk," I told him as I climbed out of the front seat and closed the door behind me.

Oz started barking like he needed a break. Mac nodded in agreement and we shook hands. I was disappointed that I hadn't gotten any additional information, not much of an investigator if you asked me. We stopped at the dog park and as soon as I opened the door Oz leaped out of the truck. He was so excited when he saw some playmates. We liked coming to the park because it allowed me time to think and gave Oz time to work off some energy. He busied himself with his new friends and I found a shady spot and started to put what information I had together. In my mind I listed the six suspects who might have had a reason to murder Ed. The list didn't include the people from our little car group, yet. At tomorrow's show I would ask around and see if I needed to add anyone else to my list. Besides, it could also have been a complete stranger. Anyone could have broken into his house he interrupted them and they shot him. Maybe it was someone he knew and he just let them in. For now though it was probably best to concentrate on my list: Joy and her boyfriend, Ronnie, Nick, Linda, Donna, and possibly someone from our club. As I watched Oz having a good time with his new friends, I thought about how little I really knew about my friend, Ed.

It would be nice to just sit here for the rest of the day and relax but work called. A couple of whistles and Oz reluctantly met me at the gate. This park offered a little of everything for the community; a place for dogs to play, a playground for the kids, a picnic area, a soccer field and even a couple of baseball diamonds. Maybe later this week Marti and I could bring the guys back to play while we have a picnic.

Just as we got into the truck my phone rang. I was shocked to hear Joy's voice and curious how she got my number. In my line of work I only gave it to those who were in my inner circle. My out-going calls were blocked and didn't allow call backs.

"Wes? This is Joy. I hope you don't mind but Detective Miller gave me your cell number. I hoped you might have a few minutes to talk to me."

"No, that is fine. What's on your mind?"

"I don't know what to do about Ed's funeral. The guy from the funeral place keeps calling me and wants to know what they should do with Ed's body. I keep telling him to call someone else but he keeps saying I'm his only family. The other day when you came by you did offer to help. I just don't know what to do."

I wondered what had changed her mind. At first she didn't want anything to do with the funeral and now she was asking for help. Her voice had softened since the last time we talked. "Sure, I'll be glad to help. Let's get together later this afternoon. Where would you like to meet?"

The line was quiet and for a moment I thought we had gotten disconnected, then she said, "If it's alright with you I would like to meet at Ed's house."

I agreed and we decided to meet there around three. I was really surprised when she asked for his address. Maybe she was the murderer and was trying to make it sound as if she had never been to his house when she actually had. Was she trying to throw me off? I hoped her boyfriend wouldn't show up with her or things could get weird. A chill went through my body when I realized there was the possibility that she hadn't found whatever she had been looking for the other day and she wanted a second chance to try and find it today. I wondered if I should call Rod and have him meet us there just to be safe. I looked over at Oz and decided that we could handle it. If her boyfriend did show up Oz would take care of the situation. If it looked as if things were taking a turn for the worse I'd go to plan B which was run out of the house like a screaming fool.

It was lunchtime and both of our stomach alarms were now going off. I looked at Oz and said, "I guess it's just you and me buddy. What sounds good?" He turned his head toward me and back to look out the window. "Okay, burgers it is."

We pulled up to the drive through and placed our order and by the time we reached the window Oz was on my lap with his head in the drive-up window. At first the lady pulled her hand back but then started to laugh. When she was face to nose with Oz, she patted him on the head as I tried pushing him back to his side of the truck. It wasn't easy once he smelled the food. I put our lunch in the back seat where I hoped it would be safe until we got to our stakeout. Oz kept looking back at it and once attempted to climb over the seat but I caught him just in time and wrestled him back to the front.

Finally we arrived at the convenience store's lot. My right arm was sore from trying to restrain Oz from getting into our lunch. I opened the bag of food and placed his burger and some fries, with no ketchup in front of him. I took a handful of the fries and looked down the street to see what was happening at my suspect's house. Suddenly Oz was in my face with one of those "Hey are you going to finish those fries and how about that burger you haven't even touched?" look.

I was just about to take my first bite when my suspect came walking toward me. I watched as he entered the store.

Oh, crap I thought, "Here we go again! Oz, you be a good boy and don't touch my food. I will be right back." I knew that was a dumb thing to ask but I needed to follow my suspect inside the store. While he was in back getting more beer I grabbed a lint roller. After riding around with Oz all morning I was covered in dog hair and needed to get some of it off me before I met with Joy this afternoon. I had at least a dozen of these things at home but one more wouldn't hurt. I should have bought stock in the company since I'm one of their best customers.

The clerk behind the counter asked my suspect, "How's the bike coming along? You've been working on for a long time."

"I have the engine just about put back together and I hope to get it done within the next couple of weeks. I want to join my buddies and ride to Sturgis if I get it done in time. This will be our sixth year going together."

"So are you going to take the family?"

"Just my honey. The ex will take the kids."

I followed him out the store and by the time I returned to the truck there were food wrappers all over the place and no food. Oz sat there with a "sorry, I couldn't help myself and I didn't want it to get cold" look.

I cleaned up the mess and gave Oz my famous dirty look which didn't have any effect on him. I watched as my suspect started working on his bike. I was still hungry thanks to Oz pigging out on my lunch of which my stomach was constantly reminding me. My camera was clicking away as I took picture after picture of my suspect bending over and lifting heavy parts. It was interesting that he planned to ride to Sturgis with his buddies. That trip must be at least a thousand miles each way. It would be a tough ride for a person with a good back let alone a person with the type of back injury he claimed to have. The smell inside the truck of the missing food kept setting off my stomach alarm which made it hard for me to concentrate. I glanced at my watch and realized I would need to leave soon to meet with Joy at Ed's house. I watched for another fifteen minutes but since nothing much was happening I decided to leave and get something to eat. I drove through the drive up for a second time today and you should've seen the funny look on the lady's face. She was the same person who had helped me the first time through. I explained to her someone had pigged out on all of our first lunch and pointed to Oz. She just smiled.

This time I wolfed down my burger before Mr. Mega-mouth had a chance to snatch it from my hand. His "sad eyed look" didn't work on me this time and he turned his attention to the world outside of his window. We arrived at Ed's about twenty minutes before Joy was due to arrive. This gave me an opportunity to look around for some additional clues.

Chapter 12

When Oz and I pulled up to Ed's I realized his yard could
do with some work. I would get ahold of Vern and have
him come over and cut the grass. Oz jumped out of the
truck and I saw Ed's neighborhood watch lady on duty
looking out of her front window again. The keen eyed
lady had now been joined by the elderly man again and
they both were staring at me. I gave them a friendly wave
but only the man returned my gesture. I opened the front
door and I thought about all the times I'd been over here
these past few days. I was having a hard time
comprehending everything that had happened. Oz made
a beeline to the back yard since someone had left the side
gate open again and he started barking. I looked out the
patio door to see what he was barking at and there was
Ronnie looking over the fence at him. I still had time to
look around the place before Joy arrived even though I
wasn't sure if any clues were still to be found. In the past,
every time I tried to do some investigative work I had
been interrupted by Ronnie. I hoped this time she stayed
on her own side of the fence.

Across from the sofa in the living room, mounted on the
wall was one of the biggest televisions I had ever seen.
Next to it were two cabinets each about 6 feet tall. I
opened the first cabinet and it was full of electronics, a

DVD player, a sound system and other electronic components which I had no clue about. Before closing the door I chuckled at the fact that Ed still had a VCR. In the next cabinet were his movies and music collection. There must have been over 400 DVDs not to mention hundreds of CDs. Ed was obviously serious about his entertainment, having thousands of dollars in equipment alone. I closed the cabinet and looked around the room. There were a few pictures on the walls mostly of mountain scenes, the kind you purchased from a poster shop. The room was very sterile, nothing personal, no family pictures, no pictures of Annie or any pictures that Ed might have taken himself.

The dining room had the usual table and chairs and nothing else except for the mail neatly sorted by size sitting on the table. I started to leave and then stopped and turned around to look at the stack of mail again. It had grown since I had been here the last time. Someone had been in the house since my last visit. I flipped through the stack of mail and saw that nothing had been opened and it was organized by type, bills first, junk next and magazines on the bottom. As far as I could tell there was nothing out of the ordinary so I put everything back the way I found it. I sat there and stared at it which got me thinking about who had access to Ed's house and why were they bringing in the mail? If it had been me, I would have just tossed it on the table and not taken the time to sort it.

Just then the front door slowly opened and Oz bolted through the doggie door, barking as if there was no tomorrow. He had cornered Joy in the front hall but once he saw me he let down his guard and started sniffing her.

Poor Joy, she was scared to death. She stood there shaking and could barely get a word out, "So this is Annabelle?"

"No, this is Oz. He's my dog. Oz back off." He gave her a couple more sniffs and walked back to my side. "He's my personal bodyguard".

She let out a nervous laugh and said, "He does a great job. Sorry for being late but I got lost getting here. I don't get over to this side of town very often. The GPS on my phone kind of messed up."

She started for the living room and I looked out the front door to see if her boyfriend had come with her. I was ready for him today, I packed Oz. Luckily for him he didn't come with her. If he had tried to lay one finger on me, Oz would have turned him into ground chuck. I followed Joy into the living room.

"So you've never been here before?" I asked.

"No. I'm going to look around if that's okay with you."

She slowly walked around running her fingers along the furniture, opening each cabinet and exploring its contents. She moved into the dining room and I watched as she picked up the stack of mail and slowly looked at each envelope. When she noticed me watching she quickly put the stack back on the table and continued to explore the rest of the house. Her eyes and her expression showed sadness. She was living the loss of her brother. Oz stayed close and followed her from room to room.

As I watched her I could tell she hadn't a clue about Ed's life and what he was all about. I realized I was finding out the same thing these past couple of days. She finally returned to the living room and sat in the chair next to the sofa. There was a period of silence as we sat and looked at each other.

I posed the first question in an effort to try and get her to open up, "Why did you want to meet me here?"

She looked around the room avoiding eye contact. Tears began coming and sobs escaped her lips. Oz, mister sensitive, walked over and put his head in her lap. She stroked him for a couple of minutes.

"Is Annabelle here? I'd like to see her."

My heart jumped when she said that, "No, she's at home with my wife." I hoped she wasn't having second thoughts about me keeping Annie.

"You see, I never really kept in touch with my brother after our parents died. Our lack of communication was entirely my fault," she paused. "He is or was six years older than me. Growing up we had some good times but when our parents died things changed between us. I was just out of high school and the shock of their passing was hard for me and I put up this wall between us. Ed tried to reach out and help but I just shut him down. I was so angry that my parents had left me. They had set aside money for my college education but I blew it. Ed was living in Nevada at the time working for some bank and he offered to let me stay at his place while I went to college but I was too full of anger to accept his offer. I was a stupid, know-it-all kid. I thought I could take care of myself so I hung out with friends who I thought liked me. It turned out they liked my money and when the money was gone, so were they."

"Where did you and Ed grow up? Was it here?" I asked.

"No, we grew up in Florida." With that she got up and walked into the kitchen. I could hear her getting a glass of water and when she returned the tears had been wiped from her face.

Joy started back in with her story, "I traveled around aimlessly and blew the money I had. I realized I didn't have any left for college or even for a place to live. I found an old friend from high school who let me crash at her place for a while and I went to work as a waitress. I called Ed a couple of times, but selfishly all I really wanted from him was money. I never asked much about him personally or about how he was doing. Every year he would text me on my birthday, on Christmas and on New Year's. I was so mad at him and at the world I just blew him off. Looking back now I realize I was really just mad at my parents for abandoning me. Then one day I got a text from him and he said he was moving here and asked me if I needed a place to stay. My pride and anger got in the way and I blew him off again."

"Do you know the reason why Ed moved here?" I asked.

"No, I just thought it was for work, he never said. I didn't really care anyway."

"So how did you end up living in the valley? It sounds like you had been living on the other side of the county?"

"I had been but then last year I met this guy and thought he was going to be the love of my life. He was a long-haul truck driver so I quit my job and traveled with him for about six months. It was great in the beginning and we had some really good times but living together in the back of his truck twenty-four seven was not good for our relationship. It took a turn for the worse. We started getting on each other's nerves. One night we stopped at truck stop outside of town, on our way to Seattle with a load of camping coolers. We started our usual arguing over something stupid so I stormed off to the ladies room and when I came out he was gone. Truck and all! My few belongings had been dumped right there in the middle of the parking lot. I couldn't believe it! He just left me! I sat down right there and lost it in the middle of the parking lot. I cried for what had seemed like hours. People who saw me must have thought I was nuts."

Oz suddenly moved toward the patio door and I turned to see Ronnie standing there. I walked over and unlocked the door and she walked in uninvited.

"I saw someone was here and just wanted to come by and see who it was," she said.

I introduced her to Joy, "Ronnie, this is Ed's sister, Joy."

Joy acknowledged her with a small smile but I could tell she was upset having Ronnie interrupt our conversation. I asked Ronnie to join me on the patio and as we walked out together she turned and looked at the stack of mail on the dining room table. It was not in the neat pile it was when I first walked into the house this afternoon and I could tell this bothered her. What was her interest in the mail? Outside I asked her to please leave explaining this was not the best time for her to visit. She gave me one of those "Who are you to tell me what to do" looks. She started to open her mouth to object but thought the better of it and stormed off.

I looked down at Oz, "I wonder what her problem is?"

When I returned to the living room I could see the puzzled look on Joy's face.

"She was your brother's next door neighbor."

"Oh, I must be boring you. I'd better go."

I assured her all was good and after a few quiet minutes she continued on with her story. "When I was crying in the middle of parking lot one of the waitresses came out to catch a quick smoke and saw me sitting there. She invited me to come inside the restaurant and gave me some coffee and a shoulder to cry on. I explained my dilemma and she took pity on me. She gave me a place to crash for a couple of weeks and got me my job at the truck stop. I was too ashamed to tell Ed I was living in a neighboring town. There were times when I wanted to call him but was afraid after all the stupid things I had said and done he wouldn't want any part of me. Boy, I really messed up my life. I just couldn't handle the thought of his possible rejection. I felt like I had no family and was really all alone."

She looked up at the ceiling and broke down crying. Not knowing what to do I just sat there and watched as Mister Sensitive did his magic and put his head in her lap again. He looked up at her with his sad eyes and she looked down and smiled. "He sure is a great dog. I wish I could have met Annabelle."

"I tell you what, give me a call sometime and we will make plans to meet and I will bring Annie", I replied.

"Annie?"

I didn't reply, just waited for her to get it together. Looking into the dining room I glanced again at the stack of mail both Ronnie and Joy had been so focused on. Was there more to the story concerning the mail? I had flipped through it and didn't see anything of importance but had made a mental note to ask Rod whether he knew anything about it.

Joy stood up and nervously walked around the house one more time. Finally she came out of the office with tears flowing and an old teddy bear in her arms. "Do you think it would be okay if I took this with me? He was mine when I was growing up. I can't believe Ed kept it all these years."

I didn't see any reason why it would be a problem and she hugged the bear tightly to her chest as she walked toward the front door. I quickly made sure the patio door was locked and Oz and I both walked out with her.

She turned and thanked me for listening and letting her walk around Ed's place. "I'm not sure I can get time off tomorrow for Ed's ceremony because the weekends are pretty crazy but I will try to make it."

In the truck with Oz I thought about what Joy had told me about her brother. I also wondered why Ronnie came over. What was going on with that stack of mail? I saw Ronnie watching me out her front window and felt there was something strange about her. I needed to find out what it was. I gave her a slight wave and she immediately turned away. As I turned the truck around in the street, Ronnie was not the only one watching. The lady across from Ed's house was still standing at her front window with her arms crossed. She had a scowl on her face but I waved at her anyway as we drove by and she reluctantly waved back. When we got home I saw Marti's car parked in the garage. There was barking coming from behind the front door and this perked up Oz. He jumped out the truck window and started barking and running to the door.

Marti opened the front door and the guys started chasing each other around the yard like they hadn't seen each other for years. I was welcomed home with a wonderful hug and a warm and inviting kiss. We all walked inside and a very familiar smell made my mouth water. I looked into her eyes and they said, yes, "I'm making meatloaf with mashed potatoes." I responded with a kiss.

"You go take a shower and clean up. I'll feed the dogs and get dinner on the table."

I quickly went into my office and made a few notes from my meeting with Joy. I thought that later I'd make time to review them and add any additional information. I was in and out of the shower in record time. Now it was meatloaf time, Marti's special meatloaf. I could hardly wait. Marti didn't cook often, but when she did it was always something special. The guys finished their dinners as Marti set two place settings on the counter. It looked like we were eating in the kitchen tonight. I walked over and gave her a big hug and a kiss on the back of her neck. "It's been a while since you have made your famous meatloaf. Did I miss a special occasion or something?"

"It's always special when I get to cook for my man and don't you forget it."

I sat at the counter and refilled Marti's glass of wine while she served dinner. The meatloaf had hot melty cheese coming out from the center. "What a surprise," I thought. "This looks great and you put cheese in the center."

She smiled and said, "This time I decided to stuff the inside with cheese instead of mixing it throughout. Hope you like it."

I leaned over and kissed her and then I took my first bite. It was fantastic as always and my taste buds went into flavor overload. "This is the best you've ever made, my compliments to the chef," I mumble with my mouth full.

She smiled and replied, "If you like this then wait until you see what I have planned for dessert."

As we ate we talked about our day and Marti told me how much fun it was hanging out with her friends and how they all loved Annie. I noticed the guys were under our feet waiting for something to drop with their sad eyes looking up at us as if to say "Please sir, could you spare some table scraps?" Oops, I dropped a couple pieces of bread, but there was no way they were getting any of this meatloaf. I made sure to save some for tomorrow's lunch. I loved cold meatloaf sandwiches loaded with lettuce, tomato and mayo. Although the food was delicious, the best part about the night's dinner was not eating alone. Okay, I should rephrase that. The best part was eating with someone who didn't have four legs. Since Marti cooked the dinner I had kitchen duty. Boy did she use a lot of pots and pans. She sat at the counter and sipped her wine while I cleaned up. I brought up that I had met with Ed's sister Joy and how hard she was taking her brother's death and how nonexistent their relationship was. I gave Marti the impression I was trying to get some more information about her brother for his upcoming service. I left out the key part which was I was investigating Ed's murder. With the last dish rinsed and put in the dishwasher I turned to see tears in her eyes and I walked around the counter and gave her a hug. I didn't realize how deeply Ed's death had affected her.

She took the guys for a walk so I could have some time updating my notes pertaining to the state's case and my conversations with Mac, Joy, and Ronnie. As I recalled the events at Ed's house today, first and foremost I focused on the mail. Why had it been moved from the kitchen to the dining room and why had it been sorted by size as if someone was looking for something? None of the envelopes had been opened but someone had been bringing the mail into the house and sorting it. My second question was about Ronnie's attitude today. Why did she act like I had no right telling her to leave, and what about her fixation on the mail? Just then I remembered Joy was also focused on the mail. This whole thing puzzled me. Joy seemed truly shaken this afternoon about the loss of her brother and I wondered if she actually hadn't ever been to Ed's. Had she really gotten lost? She walked around the house looking and touching things as if she'd never been there, but was it an act? I had the feeling her loss was genuine but then again she could have been playing me. She could have wanted access to the house to look for something, something she didn't find the other day when she killed Ed. I might have made the mistake of not following her and maybe she found what she was looking for and I didn't notice. I hoped she would come to the car show memorial this weekend. Spending a little more time with her could possibly help solve Ed's murder. Hopefully, if she did decide to show up then I hoped she would come alone.

The guys came bounding into the office all excited to tell me about their walk. A quick look at the clock showed I'd been working for two hours and I was ready to call it a night.

Marti joined the three of us and wrapped her arms around me and whispered: "Are you ready for some dessert?"

I closed my notebook and replied, "Do you have to ask?"

"You lock up the house, and I'll meet you in the bedroom."

It didn't take long to complete the nightly check around the house. I made sure the house and garage doors were locked. We didn't need one of those fancy alarm systems because we had what I called "Secured by Oz." I walked pass the guys who were busy enjoying the dog bones Marti had given them and saw a sticky note on the bedroom door. "Close the door behind you and don't let the dogs in". "Oh boy, we're going to have some private time," I thought to myself.

I was greeted with the sound of soft music, the scent of strawberries, and candles casting a warm shadowy glow throughout the room. Marti was under the covers and had a plate of chocolate covered strawberries on the bed.

"Hey stud, how about you get out of those clothes and join me?"

She didn't have to ask me twice. I did my superman impression and in a flash I was under the covers with her. I closed my eyes and moved in for a kiss but instead I was greeted with a strawberry against my lips. Who was I to refuse such an offering? It was soon my turn to return the favor and I gently pressed a strawberry against her lips. I moved in for a kiss and the chocolate melted as my lips touched hers. We shared a couple more strawberries before I pulled her body into mine and whispered, "You sexy lady! You are so romantic."

We kissed while I caressed her body and soon our fires ignited. The evening was filled with love, desire, and passion. We moved as one until we could no longer move.

I held her in my arms and whispered, "I love you."

"You're my sexy man."

The moment was perfect. We laid there with our bodies locked together and let the music slowly rock us to sleep. Unfortunately, our perfect moment was interrupted with scratching and whining at the bedroom door. The guys had finished their bones and wanted in. When I started to open the door and I was pushed aside as they rushed in and hopped onto the bed. Marti dove for cover under the sheets. After licks and hugs all around I was able to push a reluctant Annie off the bed. Oz got the message after a slight prodding and jumped off. I climbed under the sheets and I embraced my love. We said our Love yous and fell asleep in each other's arms.

Chapter 13

It was going to be beautiful day for a car show I was up early giving the Bird a quick going over with a feather duster making sure it looked presentable. I stood back and admired my work. I loved how cool the chrome bumpers shined and reflected the sun which was something you didn't see on the new cars these days.

I walked back into the house and Marti was already taking a shower. Usually I had to wake her. She loved sleeping in when she was home because it was a luxury she didn't get on the road. The guys were prancing around with excitement. When Oz heard the rumble of the Bird's engine he knew we were going to a car show. This being Annie's first show I wondered how she'd act. The temperature was going to be in the 90's so it was shorts, my favorite t-Bird camp shirt that my honey had gotten me and a baseball cap. Marti came out of the shower and we kissed.

"Are we stopping by Betty's this morning?" she asked.

"Of course. Do your really have to ask?"

While Marti got dressed I retrieved my camera and fed the guys. It was not long before we were out the door.

"The Bird looks great. You did a very nice job cleaning it," Marti commented. I had to coax Oz to the back seat since he was used to riding shotgun with me.

Oz had a smile on his face because he knew we were stopping at Betty's and boy howdy he loved her donuts. With all four windows down we cruised in style. At the donut shop, Marti stayed in the car with the guys while I got our treats. Being Mr. Nice Guy I also picked up an additional dozen donuts for the gang. On the way to the car show Marti guarded them with her life because both Oz and Annie made numerous attempts to get at them. We sang along to fifties songs on the radio but as we drove into the park we both became silent realizing that Ed would no longer be joining us.

There must have been at least a hundred cars already parked when we arrived and many more were in line behind us. Knowing most of them to be classic car junkies as I would call them, they must had been here since the crack of dawn. Ed also had been an early bird. It was strange not having him save us parking spots. I swore he must have been the first car parked at every show.

I saw Jeff standing next to his Buick signaling to us to where our car group was parked. I pulled in next to Dave's 57 Chevy and we all piled out of the car like a circus act. At first I thought everyone was excited to see us because they came rushing over for hugs and hellos but then I realized Marti had placed the box of donuts on the hood of the Bird.

Doug bent down to pet Annie, "Who's this little girl?"

Marti kneeled down next to Annie and Doug, "This is Annie. She is our new family member. She belonged to Ed."

Marti started to tear up so Doug pulled her close to him and said, "We all miss him."

"Hey, hey, hey get your hands off my lady! You have your own to hug," I said jokingly.

Doug stood up and pointed his finger at me and said, "And you keep your paws off her or I will smack you." Doug was always saying he was going to curse you or smack you to someone or another.

I left to register the Bird while Marti set out our chairs and blankets for both Oz and Annie. Cars kept arriving and filled the park with old fashion Detroit steel. There had to have been at least two hundred and fifty cars. This was going to be a big show. The band started playing and the air filled with country music. This meant the show had officially begun. Soon the onlookers started to arrive and check out the Detroit steel on display. Annie was lying next to Marti on her blanket and Oz was at his usual post out front of the Bird. Oz was getting his share of attention and loved every minute of it. He had a thing for the ladies and they reciprocated. From time to time Annie would join him but mostly she spent her time close to Marti.

After sitting for a couple of hours socializing with our little group it was time to stretch our legs so we took the guys for a walk and checked out the other rides. We had seen most of them at previous car shows throughout the years but every now and then there would be a new classic or two we hadn't seen. Marti and I would occasionally stop and visit with the owners. A few commented how sad they were to hear about Ed since they knew he was part of our group. Ed knew almost everyone who brought a car to a show. He would say things like, "There's Bart who owns the white Dodge Dart or there's Roger and his Mustang." He was good at getting to know each of them and their cars.

We walked around admiring the cars when something got Oz's attention. It was a familiar smell that was at each and every show we attend. He started to pull on his leash as he dragged me across the park. After taking a deep breath I knew that smell, the smell of burgers cooking. It was all I could do to restrain him since his attention was focused on Bill's famous burgers. When it came to food Oz had a one track mind. We tried to continue looking around at the rest of the cars but it was no use. My right arm now was two feet longer than my left so it was time to get a burger. I looked over to Marti who was also having a hard time not being dragged by Annie and smiled.

"Okay guys, you win. Who wants a burger?" I asked.

Oz excitedly wagged his tail and Annie joined in not sure what it meant, but if Oz was happy she was happy.

"If I wag my tail like them do I get a burger too?" Marti whispered in my ear and then kissed it.

"You bet! I'll get you two," I said with a big grin.

She gave me a smile and started walking in front of me moving those sexy hips from side to side.

"Okay, I'll make it three and throw in a couple bags of chips."

We both laughed and walked arm and arm to burger heaven. The line was not long and Bill saw my signal on how many burgers to put on the grill as we walked toward his stand.   By the time we reached the window our burgers were ready. Marti gave me a puzzled look, "How did he know what we wanted?" I just smiled as we walked back to our group to enjoy our lunch. I gave the guys each a burger which they devoured in less than sixty seconds. Marti and I tried to enjoy ours but as always Oz and now Annie were in our faces with those big, sad eyes begging for more. However, their plan wasn't working on us this time. Jeff returned from getting his burger and they immediately turned their attention to him hoping he'd be the soft touch. Jeff smiled and pulled out a couple extra burgers, one for each of them.

"After attending all these shows with Oz I've learned to have one for him or he would overpower me for mine," Jeff said. We all laughed.

Once the burgers were gone Annie crashed on her blanket and Oz went back to his post in front of the Bird. Our little group sat around talking mostly about Ed and remembering some of the funny stories he used to tell us. It was good to laugh. From time to time there was a moment of silence as we all thought about how much we were going to miss him. I listened to what was being said and I realized Ed talked a lot about cars but little else about his life. Jane mentioned that it was Ed who had helped her and Dave purchase their Chevy with a loan from his bank.

The more we talked the more I realized we were all in the same boat. Ed never shared his personal life with any of us. When I brought up the subject that Ed had a girlfriend and they were going to be married, you should have seen the look on everyone's faces. After the initial shock had worn off I was bombarded with a barrage of questions from every direction. They all wanted to know who she was, how I found out and if I had any other juicy information to share. The biggest question was why Ed hadn't brought her to any of the shows.

Just then Oz jumped up and started barking. It wasn't his "I am here" bark but his "alarm" bark. I quickly stood and watched him looking around to see what had gotten his attention. His eyes were focused on a man who was running toward the street and away from the cars. It looked as if he had some sort of a bag in his right hand. As he ran past us he looked back to see if Oz was going to chase after him. Oz started to pursue the man but I called his name and he stopped and came to me with his tail wagging.

Bruce pated Oz behind his ears and said, "Hey big fella, what was that all about?"

"Did anyone get a good look at the guy?" I asked and they all shook their heads no in unison.

We stood around trying to figure why that stranger had gotten Oz so upset. The day was getting on and it was time for the trophy ceremony so we all headed to the stage for the presentations and to see who the lucky winners would be. The master of the ceremonies said a few words about the loss of a fellow car enthusiast and a moment of silence followed for Ed.

This time our group came up empty on the trophies. In my opinion trophies were just something else to dust and for us the car shows gave Marti and me time to get together with the group. After the presentations on our way back to our cars I saw Bruce talking to an unfamiliar face. We walked over and joined in on the conversation.

"Hey guys, this is Pastor Tom. I asked him to stop by and say a few words for Ed. I told him Ed lived for these shows and with all of us here I felt there would be no better place to say good bye."

Pastor Tom smiled as we all nodded in agreement. I looked around and was surprised that only a few cars were leaving. Almost everyone who participated in the show were staying to honor Ed. Somehow the word had gotten out about our little memorial. The sponsors walked over to our group and offered us the stage and sound system.

We all walked back to the stage in a quiet and somber manner. I reached for Marti's hand and noticed tears flowing down her cheeks. . Marti looked up and squeezed my hand. I looked around and the same was happening with all the ladies. They had tears running down their cheeks. I saw Bruce and Doug were also tearing up but they couldn't beat the champ, I was the master. My eyes were red and my shirt was wet from wiping the tears away.

Out of the corner of my eye I spotted Joy standing on the edge of the park. Apparently she was able to make it after all. I waved her over to join us and quietly introduced her to Marti. They started crying and hugging each other and Doris put her arms around them. Soon we all followed suit, hugging and crying over the loss of a friend.

We looked at each other not saying a word when the sound of a man's voice broke the silence.

Bruce started off saying a few words, "It's a sad day when we have to say goodbye to one of our own. I am honored to have known Ed Wilson and will greatly miss him. So many of you have stayed to wish him farewell and for that I am deeply touched. This is such a great tribute to our friend." Bruce could no longer hold back the tears and broke down sobbing on the stage. Sue ran over and hugged him. There was not a dry eye in the park. Both Oz and Annie were sitting by Joy's feet and Joy kept patting them on head for comfort. From time to time Joy would look down at Annie and give her a slight smile.

Pastor Tom took a moment to comfort Bruce before giving his eulogy. It was touching and uplifting, especially coming from a man who never had the privilege of meeting Ed. Using the car show as a background helped us to say goodbye. All you could hear were sobs when he finished. I looked at Joy, her eyes were red, tears stained her cheeks and she hugged the guys. People came up to us and offered their condolences, many teary eyed. Ed had touched a lot of people but probably not more than anyone within the classic car community. Marti and I comforted each other. This was by far the hardest thing we had ever been through together.

The band which I had thought had packed up and gone home started playing "Amazing Grace" and the water works continued to flow unabated. Yes, Mister Softy was at it again. You know those coffee commercials at Christmas time, the warm and fuzzy ones? I tear up each time I see them and I don't even drink coffee. The band finished playing and everyone just milled about not sure what to do next. I introduced Joy to our little group and there were more condolences and hugs.

People started to return to their cars when the PA system broke the somber silence.

The man who sponsored this show announced that in each of coming years this show would now be known as the "The Ed Wilson Memorial Classic Show and Shine".

A loud cheer went up in approval. He also informed everyone there would be a celebration of Ed's life at Donavan's Pizza and everyone was invited. The band announced they would also be there and another cheer arose from the crowd. I could see off to my right four motorcycle officers at the entrance of the park. One of them was Detective Rod Miller.

I said to the group, "It looks like we're going to have a police escort."

Cars started lining up behind our group with Bruce and Sue in their Ford leading the way. I stood there amazed at the scene which unfolded before my eyes. It was a beautiful sight. There must have been at least a hundred cars in line. I watched as Jeff offered Joy a ride in his Buick and the band played "Hotrod Caddie," I wondered how they knew Ed owned a Cadillac, but then I saw the smile on Doug's face. As Bruce and Sue drove out of the park leading the caravan, sirens wailed and the procession followed.

Rod drove up to my window and gave me a wink and roared past. Traffic on the street parked and watched our long classic car procession pass in front of them. They honked their horns in recognition of Detroit Steel and I started to tear up again. Marti reached over and squeezed my hand. I looked over and tears also filled her eyes.

"This is so cool," I said choking on my words.

Marti nodded and was unable to find words to reply. Being part of a long freight train of classic cars "days gone by" of American Steel choked me up. Car horns continued to honk and people cheered as we drove by. "Ed, I hope you are watching this! It's for you, buddy."

We filled the parking lot in front of Donavan's Pizza. It was a good thing it was located at the end of a strip mall and most of the businesses had closed for the day.

I couldn't believe how many cars showed up. The great thing about the classic car community was the bond we had for old cars and for the people. Ed must have touched a lot of lives. Rod walked over and told me he counted at least ninety cars and I just stood there with my mouth wide open. There was no way Donavan's Pizza would be able to hold that many people inside so we set up our chairs in the parking lot. As we were getting things organized Joy walked over to me and gave me a big unexpected hug.

"So what's that for?" I asked.

"For opening my eyes. I was so stupid to have not been a part of my brother's life. Thank you for showing me how great of a person he was."

We both stood there looking at each other and I could see she was genuinely touched.

Bruce joined us and said, "I thought it would be just our little group. Can you believe this?" We all stood there in amazed disbelief as the parking lot continued to fill with cars.

Doug and Doris joined us and Doris said, "Good news, Donavan has called in re-enforcements because of the turnout. In honor of Ed he is selling all pizzas at half price."

Bruce laughed, "I just reserved the meeting room in the back but there's no way we can fit everyone in there now."

"There's one catch," Doug said with a funny looking smile on his face. "Donavan wants to join our car group with his classic Lincoln."

We all started to laugh and I thought how sometimes strange things happen. Here we were saying goodbye to one friend and hello to another.

All the ladies in our group whisked Joy away. Marsha looked back and said, "It's gal time. Will you gentlemen please order the pizzas and drinks?"

I turned around to check on Oz and Annie since they weren't by my side. I was amazed as they were already begging for bites from those who had already gotten their pizzas. They were moving from group to group giving everyone their sad-eyed looks and apparently being very successful at getting free nibbles. Annie was catching on to Oz's tricks. He was a bad influence on her. I looked at Joy and hoped she hadn't decided to keep Annie.

The band started playing classic rock and roll as Bruce, Doug, Jeff and I all headed inside to place our orders and get the drinks. It was sheer madness as customers stood in the long line and waited to place their order. I overheard people talking about Ed and discovered they knew he had been murdered. I tried to work my way closer to hear what they were saying but Mike suddenly pulled me aside, "I thought it would be a great idea if our group bought the band pizza and drinks but....."

I had to ask him to repeat what he had just said because it was hard to hear with all the noise. Besides, I was trying to listen to random comments about the murder. He just laughed and repeated, "When I placed my order I thought it would be a great idea to buy the band pizza and drinks but Donavon told me the band already had plenty. Almost everyone who had been ordering their own pizza had the same idea and also ordered for the band. In fact people were paying full price for their pizzas even though they knew they were half price. They were asking the difference to be set aside for a charity in Ed's honor."

I stood there trying to all take this in. I would have never imagined how this was turning out. What a blessing to be a part of something so amazing after something so evil had happened. This made me want to push even harder to find who murdered my friend.

We sat in our circle eating and talking about this afternoon's memorial and how many people had turned out for a final tribute. Oz and Annie realized we had food and turned their begging act on us. I would have thought by now they'd be stuffed, but from past experience I knew Oz was a bottomless pit. Word had gotten around that Joy was Ed's sister and I watched as people walked up to her and offered their condolences. Joy's emotions were on overload as so many shared with her their experiences about Ed.

I heard a familiar voice, "Do you mind if I join you?"

There stood Rod with his hands full of pizza. He smiled and said, "Holy crap, everywhere I turn someone is either handing me a drink or a slice of pizza!" Doug got another chair from the trunk of his car and I introduced Rod as a friend, not as the officer who was heading up Ed's investigation. Everyone took turns thanking him for the escort he and his fellow officers provided for the cars today. The rest of the night was filled with laughter and tears as we took turns telling car stories about our friend. I could see Rod was on the job. He sat and listened, absorbing as much information as he could without writing it down.

Oz and Annie had had enough pizza and they crashed next to my chair. I never thought I'd see the day Oz stopped begging for food. I had watched them work the crowd as if they were professional panhandlers and they had been very successful.

The temperature started to drop as the sun was setting and people started to pack up to leave. Marti sat slumped in her seat yawning and showing the strains of the day. I started putting our chairs away and noticed Joy and Rod has separated themselves from our group. They were off in a remote spot of the parking lot away from the cars and people. Their conversation looked to be friendly and I wished I could be a fly buzzing about to hear what was being said. Rod glanced over and noticed we were packing up so he returned to our group to say goodbye, leaving Joy standing there alone.

I walked over to Joy, "Hey, are you okay? It's been a rough afternoon for you."

She looked up at me, her body had nothing left, "Yea, I'm pooped. It has been a very long day."

I could see she was emotionally drained. "I noticed you spent quite a bit of time with Rod," I said hoping she would open up.

"Yea, you know he asked me a lot of questions," she replied with a half-smile.

I could tell she was done talking for the night. Jeff walked over to us, "Hey little lady, what do you say we get you home," he said trying to do his best John Wayne impersonation to impress her.

She nodded in acceptance then gave me a hug and whispered, "Thank you" in my ear.

She walked over and thanked everyone in our group and gave them each a hug. The ladies, including Marti, exchanged phone numbers with her. Oz got up stretched then walked over to Joy. She bent down and gave him a big hug. Annie decided she didn't want to be left out so she joined the two of them. Marti and I watched and I said, "Do you think Joy will let us keep Annie?"

The ladies in our group gave her a group hug and the tears flowed freely again. Joy whispered something to Marti who smiled and hugged her again.

Jeff reached for Joy's hand and as they walked to his car he didn't let go. They both waved goodbye as they pulled out of the lot.

There were just a few of us left in the parking lot. The band had packed up and it was pretty quiet. What was left of our little car group walked inside to thank Donavan and all his employees for their hard work.

He offered up his place for our monthly social gatherings with a, "I know the owner and I can get you a good deal," wink and we all laughed.

It was decided we would meet here for all our future gatherings. He promised he would have his Lincoln parked out front at our next get together so we could ooooh and aaaaah over it. After a short discussion we decided the monies people donated this evening would go to the "Fallen Peace Officer Fund" in Ed's name. He would have liked that. We huddled together one more time and said a goodbye prayer for our friend.

The engines fired up and we waved goodbye as we started for home. It felt like the Bird was riding a little lower with all the pizza we had eaten.

"May I suggest Chinese tomorrow night?" Marti just smiled and patted me on the hand.

We were about to pull out of the parking lot when Donavan came to our car and said, "Here's a pizza and two small hamburgers. The burgers are for your dogs. You guys might get hungry later and need a late night snack."

Oz and Annie were almost in our laps once they smelled the food. Donavan laughed as Marti tried to fend them off. They would have to wait until we got home to enjoy their treats. By the time we arrived and cleaned out the

Bird, it was time to relax on the sofa and veg out in front of the TV. I put the pizza in the fridge and gave Oz and Annie their burgers. Marti flipped through the channels but there didn't seem to be anything on to hold her attention. She finally she settled on a channel. When I sat down and she put her head in my lap and closed her eyes.

"It was a good day. I'm glad things worked out the way they did. I think Ed would be very happy with his tribute," Marti said.

"I agree. It gave us some closure and Joy got to see how much her brother was loved and respected," I replied.

Marti was falling asleep so we retired to the bedroom where the guys were already on their beds most likely dreaming about all the pizza. They had stuffed themselves tonight. My mind couldn't stop processing all I had learned.

Marti kissed me goodnight and I started to say "I love you" when she smiled and said, "Joy's happy Annie is going to be part of our family. She asked if she could come and visit her from time to time."

I smiled and was excited about the good news.

It wasn't long before Marti and Annie created a snoring symphony. It was hard for me to fall asleep as usual. My mind was racing, the car show, Joy, the amazing memorial, the night at Donavan's, and Oz's strange behavior with his hackles up at the car show. This had been the second time he had focused on that man who had run from the park. Whatever this guy was doing he put Oz on alert. You never wanted to get on Oz's bad side. It's not a good thing.

As I laid there staring in the darkness I remembered not seeing Donna or any of the bank employees at the memorial this afternoon. That was kind of strange since she told me they were going to be married. 'Donna, what are you hiding," I thought. She and I were going to have another conversation. The Sandman finally came knocking and I joined in the symphony.

Chapter 14

There must have been a celestial incident where the sun, moon and earth were all in alignment because when I opened my eyes it was well past eight thirty in the morning, and I hadn't been pounced on. I couldn't remember how long it had been since I had slept in this late. When I rolled over Marti was missing from her side of the bed and something wasn't quite right. The house was very quiet, actually too quiet for my liking, so I got up to investigate. That's what I do. The first clue was the bedroom door was closed and the guys were missing. When I opened the bedroom door I spied both Marti and Annie sound asleep on the sofa. Oz was out in the back yard sniffing around. I wondered why Marti had chosen to come out to the living room to sleep. Not wanting to wake her I figured this would be a good time to update my notes with the information I had gathered from yesterday's encounters.

My suspect list started to shrink as I removed everyone from our car group. I hadn't found one bit of evidence or one reason why any of them would have wanted Ed dead. For the time being I removed Joy from public enemy number one but kept her boyfriend high on my list. There was just something about the guy I just didn't trust. In a couple of days I'd reach out to Joy and ask her some questions about him but today I had to work on my other case. After an hour of adding to and reviewing my notes I realized I wasn't any closer to solving this case than I was yesterday. I wrote myself a sticky note as a reminder to call Vern and ask him do some yard work over at Ed's house the following day. That would give me an opportunity to look around the place one more time. I bet Ronnie would be stopping by while I was there. She hadn't missed coming by on one of my visits yet. There was something very strange about her and she definitely was having issues with Ed's death but what were those issues.

It was time to get back to reality and go to work. I checked to make sure my camera was fully charged for the afternoon's baseball game and I felt a warm wet nose pushed against my elbow. I turned to see two sad faces looking at me giving me the look of "How much longer before breakfast? We're starving."

"Okay, what do you say to some pancakes?" I asked as we all walked into the kitchen.

I put on a fresh pot of coffee for my lady, threw some bacon strips in the oven and mixed up the pancake batter. I had just put the griddle on the stove when a pair of warm and inviting arms wrapped around my body.

"Marsha, Marti's asleep in the other room," I joked.

My comment was followed by a slap on the back of my head and the words "Ha, Ha, Ha, how funny you are. Make mine with blueberries please," she requested while pouring her first cup of coffee.

"Yes, ma'am, your wish is my command," and with that I put the first pancakes on the griddle. "So, what was with the sleeping on the sofa?"

"I couldn't sleep last night. All I could think about was poor Joy now that Ed is gone. She doesn't have any family. It's very sad."

I could see tears forming in her eyes so I walked over and gave her a hug. We stood there for a few minutes hugging while the first pancakes cooked. I always gave the guys the first pancakes after they had cooled and they wolfed them down within seconds. I served Marti her breakfast on the patio which was a plate full of blueberry pancakes and side of bacon. I then went back inside for the most important item.

"Hey, don't forget the syrup," she mumbled as she chewed on a strip of bacon.

Okay, so there were two most important items. I returned balancing my plate of food, the syrup and of course the freshly brewed pot of coffee. I was followed by prancing feet with hopes my juggling act would fail and food would fall their way. I was not going to let that happen since I didn't share my blueberry pancakes with anyone.

"You know if you ever want to try a new occupation you could become a short-order cook at the diner down the street or maybe even a waiter somewhere," Marti said as she shoved another bite in her mouth.

I couldn't give her a snappy comeback since I had a mouthful of pancakes, so I just smiled. We sat there munching away on our breakfast not saying much and the guys had given up begging and were sound asleep in the sun.

"Beside the game, is there anything you would like to do this afternoon?" I posed the question to her.

"No, I'm looking for some down time after yesterday. I really need to relax," she replied as she finished the last bite.

We spent the morning cleaning the house, mostly vacuuming up the floating hair monsters both Oz and Annie had left behind. Even though I was working this afternoon, it was always fun to spend time with Marti. With the house clean for another week, okay maybe a day, it was time to leave for the game. Marti walked out of the bedroom wearing a pair of short jean shorts showing off her long sexy legs, a white tank top and a baseball cap with her ponytail sticking out the back.

"Wow, my lady! You're looking pretty fine this afternoon," I said giving her a wolf whistle.

"Well, it's not every day I get to go to a baseball game with my stud and get to watch him work at the same time."

"You will be mystified and amazed by my many talents," I assured her.

I gave her a kiss and took her hand as we walked out the door. The guys sat there with their "Can't we go too?" looks. We were just about to the truck when I realized I had forgotten my camera so I went back inside to find both Oz and Annie had already staked out their spots on the sofa. "So the sad act was just a scam," I said to them as I closed the front door with camera in hand.

During the drive to the ballpark Marti sang, "Take me out the ballgame…" and I joined in. We pulled into the parking lot and surprisingly there weren't many cars. Maybe we were early.

"In all the years we've been married this is the first time you've ever taken me on a case," Marti remarked as we got out of the truck and she wrapped her arm around mine. "This is kind of exciting."

"Stick with me Sweetheart. You're going to see a pro in action."

We pretty much had our choice of seats which was good since I'd overheard my suspect telling the clerk at the convenience store they would be right behind third base. I handed the kid at the gate our tickets and he stopped me with a, "Hey, no cameras allowed."

I wonder if he also checked cell phone since they had cameras built in them. I showed him my press pass and he nodded in approval and allowed us to enter camera and all.

"Where in the hell did you get a press pass?" Marti asked with a puzzled look on her face.

"I have connections. I did a workman's comp case for the paper and they won their case. They liked my pictures so much they made me a photographer just in case they needed me for a story or something."

"Well, then how about increasing your tax deductions and buying me a hot dog and a cold beer?" she asked directing me toward the food court.

Boy, you should've seen the look the lady at the concession stand gave me when I had asked for a receipt. I bet she thought I was nuts. Marti and I both laughed and headed to our seats. Our baseball team was what I would call a pre-pre-farm team to the majors. If a player had some skills then they could move up to the next level and even possibly to the big show. I had watched all the

Major League movies many times and knew how the system worked. Many of the players out on the field today hoped someday to play in the majors and other players were living their fantasy of being a local sports hero. Let's face it, I was not what you would call baseball fan by any means. I only watched it on television when I wanted to take a nap. It was the best sleep aid ever.

The small crowd of fans stood and cheered as the teams took to the field. My suspect and friends hadn't shown yet. I would be very upset if I had to sit through this entire game and didn't get one bit of evidence to use in my case. Marti said between hotdog bites, "So, what's the plan, Stan?"

After I took a bite of my own hotdog I replied, "Besides being out on a date with one sexy lady, we are here to monitor my suspect for any activity that shows he shouldn't be receiving disability checks."

"Okay, so point him out for me so I know who we're watching."

"So far he's a no show," I told her. The fact he hadn't shown up was really getting on my nerves but I then I spotted him. As we stood for the opening ceremonies he and his buddies were making their way to their seats. Their hands were full of beer and hot dogs and as luck would have it our seats were five rows above theirs and no one was sitting between us. They all wore community baseball team jerseys and their spirits were high. I snapped a couple of pictures but nothing of value.

"Will any of those pictures help your case against this guy?" Marti asked.

"Probably not. I take a lot of pictures and then go through them all and choose which ones I can use and which ones I can't. It's best to take too many than not enough. You just never know what's going to happen or when you might get the perfect shot that will bust the case wide open."

Just then the stadium came alive as those famous words came across the P.A. system, "Play ball!"

The first three innings were very long and boring. There were a lot of strikes or balls but not much cracking of the bats. Marti though was getting into the game and occasionally stood and cheered. I watched as my suspect and friends returned again with more beer and hotdogs. I clicked off a few more shots but felt this was turning into a bust. Marti enjoyed the game, but as for me I could take it but mostly leave it.

Finally it was the seventh inning stretch and I was ready to give my butt a break from sitting on the hard metal bench. Our team was ahead by two and Marti headed off to the ladies room asking, "Boss, can I have some money and yes I will ask for a receipt?"

As she walked down the steps passing my suspect and his friends I watched as they eyed her every step and made comments about her to each other. Lucky for them I wasn't the jealous type. I said to myself "Eat your hearts out suckers, she is mine. If you even think about touching her, I will have my enforcer, Oz, address the issue."

My suspect and one of his buddies got up and walked down the steps probably going for more beer and hotdogs. I counted that between them they had made five beer and hotdog runs in the first seven innings of the game. That was good because the more they drank the more stupid they would act and I could take more photos.

Marti returned with a bag of peanuts in her hand and sported a great big smile. She bent over and gave me a warm and inviting kiss. I thought I heard a bunch of male egos deflate in the crowd.

As she sat down, I commented, "I guess I am going to have to stock the house full of peanuts for the future if they make you this excited."

My suspect and his buddy returned, this time he carried a small metal tub filled with ice and at least a dozen beers. I quickly grabbed my camera and snapped shot after shot.

"Hey sexy!" Marti whispered in my ear.

This got my blood flowing, "Yesssss."

"Would it help if I told you that your suspect will be playing baseball tomorrow night? I even know the where and the when."

Now I was really excited "How did you come across such valuable information?"

"I was in line behind them at the concession stand and I overheard them talking about their game tomorrow night. They play every Monday and Thursday nights at the Dwayne Evans Sports Complex. Do you know where that is?"

I looked into her amazing brown eyes and replied, "That's where Oz and I were the other day. They have a dog park there."

"Great we can take the dogs and make it a family evening of spying," she said with a twinkle in her eyes.

"We?" I asked.

"You brought me in on this case as your hot and sexy assistant and I'm going to make sure you don't mess it up. Here have some peanuts and watch the game."

"I have no objections," I replied and grabbed a handful of nuts.

I was able to snap a few more photos of my suspect before the game was over and I watched them head for the exit. We followed close behind just in case there were more photo opportunities but unfortunately there were not. I thought I had a few pics I could use for my case, but no smoking gun yet. Hopefully, he'd be playing in the game tomorrow night and I'd be able to get some great video of him showing off for his buddies. I would like to be able to close this case and concentrate on Ed's murder.

It was fun spending the afternoon with the love of my life, but would I spend it again at another baseball game? No way in hell! I remembered then that was exactly what I would be doing tomorrow night.

After all the pizza at Donavan's the night before I made a lazy chef's decision and we picked up some Chinese takeout. When it came to Chinese food Marti and I had somewhat different tastes. I liked the spicy food, Marti not so much. I ordered the general's chicken with an egg roll and Marti ordered chicken chow mein with noodles instead of the rice. We agreed on pork and seeds and pot stickers as appetizers. We always seemed to order more than we could eat, but the best thing about Chinese food was the leftovers the next day.

We returned home to a jubilant reception of wagging tails and prancing feet. We ate our dinner on the sofa and watched a movie. We shared some of the pork with the guys. When the movie was over I turned off the television and handed Marti her fortune cookie.

I read her mine, "You have found your true soul mate." She melted at the sentiment and gave me a kiss.

Her fortune read, "Make sure to take advantage of all the opportunities which come your way."

Marti cleaned up after our dinner while I called Vern to see if he could mow Ed's lawn the next day. Marti picked up my fortune, "Hey buster, that's not what your fortune said. It says here "Your balance will be in the seventh sun with the moon on the horizon. What the hell does that mean? I think I like yours better," she added with a smile.

Oz and I did our nightly patrol making sure the house was secure. By the time we reached the bedroom Marti was in bed reading her book and Annie was snoring on her bed. I kissed Marti good night and we said our "Love yous". Before I knew it I was out like a light.

Chapter 15

The sun peeked through the window to let me know it was a new day. I had struggled to get to sleep last night and now I was struggling to wake up. I rolled over with plans to get a little more shut eye but the crows out in the backyard had different plans for me this morning. When the guys joined in with their two cents I knew the reality of more sleep wasn't going to happen. The only way to stop the backyard conversation was to get up. The guys finally stopped barking once they heard me tap on the patio door but the crows continued on with their squawking. With all this noise I was amazed how Marti was able to sleep through it.

Oz and Annie came crashing through the doggie door excited to see that I was up. We went for an early morning walk to burn off some of their excess energy plus this gave me time to plan my day. As we made our way around the neighborhood I watched with interest as it emptied out. I was glad not be one of those poor souls tied down to an 8 to 5 job. In short time we had covered about seven blocks and when we returned home the guys went straight for the water dish slopping water all over the floor. Thank goodness the crows had stopped their squawking.

Since Marti was still asleep I figured this would be a good time to get some work done. Reviewing the photos from yesterday's baseball game I discovered some good ones for my case but I still needed more conclusive evidence. I went through the mail which was something I hadn't done for a couple of days. This got me to thinking about Ed's mail. Who had been bringing it in the house and why go through the trouble to sort it unless they were looking for something specific? Yesterday I had made arrangements with Vern to take him over to Ed's so while he was there I'd thoroughly inspect Ed's mail again to see if anything jumped out. I tossed my junk mail into the round file and decided to look at bills and new cases later. My workload from the state and insurance companies were starting to pile up and I needed to make time to concentrate on their cases since they paid the bills. At this rate I wasn't going to have much more time to spend on Ed's murder.

The guys came rushing into the office all excited. They had been outside playing but now they had food on their minds. How could I resist those eyes? While I was getting their breakfast ready I suddenly thought about the Trailer Queen and I wondered if the lady had ever claimed her money. Surely she'd noticed the caddy was no longer on the lot. I made a mental note to stop by the auto lot and try to pry some more information out of Mac. This would also give me a chance to check out the Pontiac one more time. Maybe I should take Marti with me. Naw, once we finished looking at the car she'd want to go shopping and I had too much to do today.

Marti walked into the kitchen and gave me a big hug, "Hey, where's the coffee?" She walked over to the machine and pressed the start button.

"I didn't want to have that glorious aroma wake you from your beauty sleep." It was good having her home, but unfortunately in a few days she would be back in the air working.

"What are your plans for today?" I asked.

She gave me that look and held up one hand, "I just got up, let me have my coffee and then we will talk."

She headed out to the patio with her java fix while I fed the guys. I whipped up a batch of my special oatmeal loaded with dried cranberries, honey from Alaska, pecans and a touch of cinnamon. I would be the only one eating it, since oatmeal wasn't on Marti's culinary list. She saw my bowl of oatmeal and got up and walked into the kitchen and returned with a bowl of last night's Chinese food. She loved to eat her Chinese food cold the next day. I was a cold pizza guy myself.

I watched as she took a couple of bites and her eyes started watering. There was a small choke from the spices, "its good" she tried to get out before taking a quick sip of coffee.

She had mixed some of my spicy chicken in with her chow mein. I laughed and took another spoonful of oatmeal. We talked about our plans for the day and I told her I was taking Vern over to Ed's to cut his grass. I asked if she would like to come along, but she declined, "I just want to have a lazy morning around the house."

We talked a little bit more about what she might like to do over the next couple of days while she was in town. I checked the time on my phone and thought I'd better get moving since Vern would be here soon. As I bent over and kissed her Chinese fire coated lips, I took her hand and pulled her out of her chair, "Come with me my sexy lady."

There was no hesitation on her part. We snuggled in the shower until the hot water ran out and while I got dressed she climbed under the sheets and waved good bye. Both Oz and Annie hopped on the bed and joined her.

Just as I finished loading the lawn mower into the back of the truck Vern came riding on his bike. Talk about perfect timing. He asked if he could put his bike in the back too. He told me he was going to buddy's house once he finished mowing Ed's yard.

On the drive over to Ed's we stopped at the local convenience store and picked up one giant soda for Vern and a couple of bottles of water for me. He told me that in August he was going to try out for football and asked if it would be okay to cut the grass on Sundays. I had no objection and I wasn't going to argue with his plans since I didn't want to cut the grass or pick up after the guys. When we drove up in front of Ed's house it was obvious why I had brought Vern. The yard definitely needed some of his loving care. Vern started mowing the front yard and I headed to the house to do some more investigating. As I opened the front door I turned around to see the lady from across the street staring at me again with a scowl look on her face. I thought to myself she needed to get a life. I walked into the house and left the front door open to air out the musky smell.

I had a feeling with Vern cutting the grass and my truck out front that it wouldn't be long before Ronnie showed up. I concentrated on the mail and noticed the stack had grown since the last time I was here. Taking my time I read the outside of each and every piece of it looking for anything that might be a red flag. About eighty percent was junk mail and the rest just bills. I had a feeling that someone was looking for something particular and I hoped I wasn't too late and they had already found it.

I made a call to Rod to see if he had any more information about the murder and to see if he or the police were bringing in the mail.

It took just one ring and the voice on the other end answered, "Hello, Detective Miller here."

"Gee buddy you sound so official," I said.

"You know me. I'm here to protect and to serve. What's on your mind?"

"Just wanted to thank you again for the police escort the other night, it was appreciated."

"Not a problem, it was my pleasure. It allowed me to walk around afterward and eavesdrop on some bits and pieces of conversation."

"I figured that's what you were up to. Did you get any hot leads or juicy information you'd care to share with your buddy here?"

There was a long pause and I could tell he was debating whether or not he wanted to share, "No, not really," he replied.

"Could you tell me if the department has been able to lift any prints from the caddy?"

Again a long pause, "I will tell you that the guy at the car dealership was not too happy that we came and picked up the car. You should have seen the look on his face, it was a priceless."

We both had a good laugh, "Hey, I am over here at Ed's place."

"What the hell are you doing there?"

"I brought my neighbor's kid over to cut the grass and clean up the yard. I was just wondering if you guys had been here lately."

"No, why do you ask?"

I didn't want to give away any of my findings yet and have him shut me out of the investigation. I replied, "No reason, I just wanted to see if it would be okay to clean up the house is all."

By his tone I knew he suspected I was up to something, "Let me check with the lab and see if they've finished processing the crime scene. If they have then clean to your heart's content, Cowboy."

"Great, call me Mr. Clean," and we ended our conversation. I looked around and the place was spotless. It wouldn't do any good for the lab team to return. I knew the police and I had a key but who else did. Since the police nor I were the ones bringing in the mail then who was and how were they getting in? Also, why take the time to sort and stack the mail so neatly? If it had been me I would have just dumped it on the table. I had the feeling the mail was the key in solving Ed's murder.

I heard Vern in the back yard and he was making quick time of cutting the grass.

A man's voice came from the front of the house, "Hello."

I turned to see who it was and there stood a man in his seventies with silver hair at the temples, "Hi, can I help you?" I asked.

He looked around for a moment and then answered, "My name is Eric and I live across the street. My wife and I have noticed you have been coming around a lot. We were wondering if you were with the police department."

"Oh, so you are with the neighborhood watch lady from across the street?"

"Yes, you could say that," he said with a knowing smile. "Lois is my wife and has this thing about putting her nose into everyone else's business. Please don't tell her I said that," he said with a quiver in his voice.

The look on his face and the tone in his voice indicated his wife had sent him to get the scoop. I invited him inside and looked to see his wife watching us out their front window. I smiled and waved to her and she hesitatingly waved back. We walked into the living room and I waited for him to start talking but after a few minutes of silence I started the conversation.

"No, I'm not with the police. I'm just a friend of Ed's. Had you known him long?" I asked.

He paused and thought about what to say, "I didn't know him very well. We would say 'Hi' when we saw each other. Occasionally I would visit with him when he was out washing his car but that was the extent of it."

I thought for a moment. I'm sure this guy's wife knew all the comings and goings at Ed's house. I looked out the living room window and she was still standing there. Her hands were on her hips and she had that familiar scowl on her face while keeping an eye on us.

"With you being Ed's neighbor, was he one to have a lot of parties or friends over?"

"Not really, I think he dated a couple of ladies from time to time. He seemed to spend a lot of time with his next door neighbors. They were over here a lot, especially the dark haired lady. Overall I would say he was a very quiet neighbor and got along well with everyone on the block."

I could tell he was starting to get nervous about being here for this long. I looked out the front window again and his wife still hadn't moved from her post.

"Eric, I have a silly question to ask you. Do you know who keeps bringing in Ed's mail?"

He looked puzzled, shook his head no and got up to leave. We started to say our goodbyes when he suddenly turned around and said with a big smile on his face, "You should be asking my wife about the mail. She's the neighborhood busybody but please don't tell her I said that either."

I knew who wore the pants in his house and assured him his secret was safe with me. I watched as he made his way home. His wife hadn't moved and was still looking out their front window. I watched as Eric almost got to their front door when suddenly it opened and his wife quickly ushered him inside. She was probably going to grill him like an old time police investigator for all he had just learned. That poor guy, I kind of felt sorry for him.

Still no Ronnie and Vern was just about finished cutting the grass in the backyard so I decided to take another room by room search starting with the garage. As I opened the door from the kitchen the light in the garage immediately went on. Ed kept the garage spotless. It was so clean you could have eaten off the floor. Mine was a pig sty compared to his. Not a tool out of place or a speck of dust anywhere. The floor had been coated with epoxy and not a drop of fluid had leaked on it from the Trailer Queen. Everything had it's proper place and as far as I could tell there was nothing out of place. On one wall a glass cabinet ran the length of the garage and was filled with trophies he had won at previous car shows. There must have been dozens of them. Another wall was covered with pictures of his car. On the back wall of the garage were shelves filled with cleaning supplies for the Trailer Queen and a section of antique oil cans. Next to these shelves was a workbench. Ed's other car was a late model Ford about five years old. It was parked in the spot next to where the Trailer Queen would have been. I didn't see anything that looked out of place or might have helped me solve Ed's murder.

Vern popped his head in the garage door and scared the crap out of me, "All done."

We loaded up the lawnmower in the back of my truck, I paid him for his services, and watched as he pedaled down the street. Back inside I moved into Ed's office hoping to find something to help with my case. I had just finished going through the last desk drawer when there was the usual knock at the patio door. As if I didn't know who it was. I walked into the living room and there stood Ronnie smiling.

"I noticed that boy cutting the grass and wanted to stop by and say hi. It was nice of you to take care of the yard. I tried to get Nick to do it but he kept blowing me off about it."

"No problem, just helping out a buddy. So what's going on?"

She looked around the room, "I wonder who our new neighbors will be when this mess is all cleaned up? Did you get any more information about who killed Ed from your buddy the police officer?"

"Nope, I'm just as much in the dark about it as you are." She walked into the dining room and I closely followed behind. "But I'm sure they're getting close to finding out what happened and who the killer is."

She looked at the messy stack of envelopes on the table and started to clean it up but when she noticed me watching she stopped. She then backed away from the table and walked back into the living room.

"You know, I am going to miss Ed," she blurted out and turned to face me, tears streaking down her cheeks. "Even Lyle keeps asking to visit Uncle Ed. And whenever Linda comes to visit she just stares at this house. We all miss him. Even Nick, he is so depressed he hardly talks to me anymore. He spends most of his time either at the store or hangs out with some guy he knows. This has become a nightmare for me and my family. What a frick'n mess!"

I really hadn't had a real chance to talk to Linda or Nick but maybe I should.

Ronnie sat on the sofa and I sat in the chair next to it. "Ronnie, could you tell me about Ed and Linda. He never said a word to any of his friends about dating her."

She sat there looking at the wall and after a couple of minutes of silence she replied, "Why do you want to know?"

"I also am having a hard saying goodbye."

She nodded in agreement, "Linda and Ed had some good times and it seemed like they were a happy couple for almost a year but then things took a turn for the worse and Ed started distancing himself from her."

"So do you know the reason why," I questioned.

Ronnie looked around the room and then continued on with her story, "I think Ed was seeing another woman on the side. Yes, I'm pretty sure that was it. One day he just told Linda it was over and it broke her heart. She still hasn't gotten over the breakup."

Ronnie started to get restless and suddenly stood up, "I must be getting home. Lyle is going to wake up from his nap soon." I had more questions but she jetted out the backdoor before I could ask them. There was more going on with Ed and Linda's relationship but Ronnie wasn't going to tell me.

After another twenty minutes going through the office I realized there was nothing there that was going to help. I did a quick look around the rest of the house and came up empty. I locked the front door and started for my truck when I noticed the lady from across the street was back at her front window giving me the evil eye. What's with this lady? Oh, what the heck, I decided to walk over and pay her a visit. Maybe she'd shed some light on what had been happening around here. Before I could even ring the doorbell Eric opened the door with a big smile and invited me into their home. I introduced myself and he introduced me to his wife, Lois. She gave me the once over with her eyes, the scowl still on her face. She offered me a seat in the living room and I had the feeling I was in for the third degree.

Lois was petite and looked to be her seventies. Like Eric she had silver hair and wore her glasses around her neck on a chain. I bet they were mostly for reading because I noticed she hadn't been wearing them while she was watching me out the front window.

"Eric tells me you are the neighborhood watch." I glanced over at him and got a dirty look. "I'm hoping you'll be able to tell me what you know about Ed, your neighbor across the street."

She gave Eric a "you are in big trouble buster" look and said, "You think I'm some nosey, busy body, don't you? Don't answer that?"

Eric joined the conversation "Yes, you're always looking out the window spying on the neighbors."

"Well, I never," she said in a huff and then a little smile crept across her face.

I smiled back and let the tension eased a bit, "I'm just looking for any information that might help me understand why someone would want to kill him."

Lois smiled, "Okay, let me get us some refreshments and we'll talk." She quickly hopped out of her chair and almost ran to the kitchen with excitement. Soon she returned with tea and sugar cookies. For a few minutes we sat there looking at each other sipping on tea and munching on cookies.

"These are great cookies. Mine always turn out hard as rocks," I said while reaching for another one.

"My secret is I use half butter and half Crisco, but let's cut the crap. You're not here to learn how to bake. I can tell you about all the comings and goings at his house and it would make a hooker blush. I have a front row seat to see it all. I could write a New York Times best seller with what I have seen going on in this neighborhood. For example did you know: the people who live behind us have a hot tub and they have sex every time they're out there?"

This got me squirming in my seat thinking about Marti and me out in our hot tub. I hoped we didn't have a neighborhood watch like Lois around our place.

Eric started to say something but when she gave him a "you better not," look, he quickly shut his mouth and munched quietly on his cookie.

"Your friend Ed, he seemed to be real buddy, buddy with the next door neighbors. Someone was always over at his house but he was hardly ever at theirs. It was usually either one of the two ladies or the little boy visiting him. I remarked to Eric once that since those ladies were always visiting they should move in with him. One of them spent a lot of one on one time with him if you know what I mean." She stopped to catch her breath then she continued, "Also from time to time there would be lots of classic cars out in front of his house. You know the other night when all the police were around the house there was a classic one there too. If I'm not mistaken it was yours, wasn't it?"

"Yes, it was mine, and yes, sometimes we would come over after a car show and have a barbeque," I said with a smile. I reached for another cookie. I couldn't stop eating them because they were so much better than mine. At this rate I was going to have to walk an extra twenty miles to burn off the calories.

"Now where was I? Oh yea, I think it was the neighbor's sister or friend, the blonde one, that came and went all hours of the day and night and got down and dirty with him. She's a real piece of work. I caught her spying on Ed at various times. She would look in the kitchen and living room windows when he was home and there were times when she would do it when he wasn't home. You know, come to think of it, there was this one time when Ed must have been at work or something and I saw her inside his house. That's strange don't you think?"

I nodded in agreement since I couldn't speak with my mouth full of cookie. Lois took a sip of her tea and started in again. "I think Ed was having a relationship with her."

"Why do you say that?" I asked already knowing the answer but wanting to get her side of the story.

"Well, they were always driving off somewhere together and she would come and go inside of his house whenever she wanted," Lois stopped talking in midsentence and just looked at me. "Oh what the hell, we are all adults here," she said and continued talking. "Almost every night I would notice they weren't watching the TV but it was lighting up the whole room and you could see all the action. I thought the neighbors from behind us were bad with their hot tub, but you would have thought your friend and his lover were making dirty movies the way they were carrying on. It was out there in the open for anyone walking by to see."

Eric made the mistake of opening his mouth, "Even nosey busy bodies from across the street!"

I could see he regretted what he had just said.

Lois gave him a dirty look and replied, "I didn't see you turn away when I pointed out what they were doing, Mister."

It took a couple of minutes for things to settle down and that's when Lois continued on with her story, "But then something must have happened because it all stopped. That blonde stopped her comings and goings and things started to get a little weird. A different woman started hanging out with Ed and she was very cute. She was over there a lot. That's when the blonde lady next door increased her spying on Ed. There was this one time when Ed and this new lady friend were getting it on in the living room and the blonde was spying on them. I watched as the blonde picked up a rock and almost threw it at Ed's front window but instead she threw the rock at this new ladies car parked out in front of his house. She then went running to the house next door crying."

Lois pause and that's when Eric opened up, "Tell him about the time the police were over there a couple of months ago and lighting up the whole neighborhood with their flashing lights in the middle of the night."

Lois gave him a dirty look, and then smiled at me. "Yes, it was late and you could hear shouting coming from Ed's house, someone must have called the police. We watched from our window as the police had to separate two women who were arguing and fighting. It looked like they wanted to kill each other! The new lady friend who had been coming around lately and the other, well, I couldn't tell who the other one was, but I assumed it was the blonde. They were yelling and screaming at each other until the police put one in the backseat of a patrol car. All the neighbors were out in their front yards watching the excitement."

Taking a sip of my tea, "Did the police take the ladies away?"

"Only the one in the back of the police car but I wasn't able to see who she was. The other one went back inside Ed's house. She left soon after the police did and when the excitement was over."

I looked at my watch and it was getting late. "I appreciate all the information but sorry I have to run. I'm investigating another case and I need to be somewhere in an hour."

Lois showed a look of disappointment that I was leaving and I could tell by the look on her face she was thinking hard trying to remember anything else. She was obviously in seventh heaven having an audience to tell her story to. I stood up and headed for the front door when I remembered about the mail. "Would you have any idea who keeps bringing in Ed's mail?"

They both shook their heads no but agreed they would be happy to watch and let me know. I gave her my card and she looked at it and then me, "Are you really an investigator?" she asked.

"Sort of, I work fraud cases for the state. I'm not like those private eyes you see on television. I don't go around getting in fights and carrying a gun. I mostly sit in my truck and do what you do, spy." I winked at her.

I thanked them for the tea, cookies and all the neighborhood gossip, as I walked toward my truck I saw Ronnie watching me from her front window. Boy, I guess everyone does spy on everybody else in this neighborhood.

On my drive to the car lot, I had a ton to process. Why had the police come to break up a disturbance involving two ladies? I had a feeling Donna was involved so it was time to pay her another visit. As I pulled onto the classic car lot I saw the closed for business sign on the office door. Strange they were closed at this time of the day. I would have to come back another day.

I decided to stop by home and see what had been happening. When I opened the front door, the guys greeted me with such enthusiasm, the kind of "You are home! We have been so lonely" kind of greeting. After a couple of scribbles behind their ears, they ran off happy as could be. I walked into the kitchen and found a note from Marti, "Out shopping, if you want to meet for lunch, text me." I thought about it, but needed to update my notes with all I had learned from Eric and Lois while it was fresh in my mind.

I started to text Marti that I wasn't going to make it for lunch when my phone rang. It was Bruce, "Hey have I got some news for you," he said. Before I could say anything he started telling me that someone had been stealing valuables from the cars at the car shows.

"Really, how did you find out?" I asked.

"I just got a call from one of the guys in another club. He told me that whoever was doing it walked around looking at the cars and when no one was watching he helped himself to whatever he could find. Not everyone puts their valuables in the trunk during the shows you know."

"That's just not right. I hope the police catch this jerk and...." Just then Bruce cut me off.

"Got to go, I'll have to tell the guys in our club to not leave anything valuable in their cars during the shows."

Before I knew it he had hung up. Standing there I looked at Oz and thought back to the times when he had focused on a man running from the show and wondered if it was that guy doing all the stealing. Next show I would pay better attention to Oz's actions.

I finished texting Marti, "Sorry can't make it. Please bring me a treat."

I made a peanut butter and jelly sandwich and went into my office to update my notes. The things Ronnie, Lois, and Eric had told me today were very confusing. Why hadn't Ronnie said anything about the fight at Ed's house? I bet it was Linda who the police had hauled away that night. I was concentrating so intently that I didn't hear Marti come in. I just about jumped out of my chair when she touched my shoulder.

She laughed and said, "It must be some heavy stuff you're working on?"

I nodded as she put a slice of carrot cake in front of me. First, it was Lois's sugar cookies. I think I ate about six of them, and now a slice of carrot cake. If I wasn't careful I was going to lose my six pack; but who was I kidding, I lost it years ago. I took the first bite and smiled, "Thanks, this is great."

She reached down, dipped her finger into the icing and turned away smacking her lips, "You're welcome."

An hour later my notes were updated and I had a lot of information but it didn't seem to get me any closer to finding out who had killed my buddy. Ed had two girlfriends, Donna from the bank and Linda, Ronnie's sister. Either one of them could have been the murderer. Donna could have been upset over Linda being Ed's ex and coming over whenever she was there or Linda could have been upset that Ed had dumped her and was dating Donna. Either way I was going to have to talk to both of them and try to pry out more information.

I also I found out there was a lady who had been taken away by the police the night of the fight. Lois wasn't sure who it was since it was dark and she didn't get a good look at her. Who knew Ed was such a ladies' man? The other thing that puzzled me was who'd been bringing in Ed's mail and sorting it? I was just about finished jotting down my ideas when I thought back to Ronnie saying Nick had become distant. I'd need to speak to him too. I had moved Joy to the bottom of my list because of her emotional reactions yesterday at her brother's memorial. She appeared to be truly shaken by his death. However, that could have been a con job and she and her James Dean boyfriend could both somehow be involved. I still had it in the back of my mind about Donna not showing up for the services the other day. There was something strange about that and I needed answers to why she didn't show.

It was getting late in the afternoon and I needed to get things ready for the baseball game. I wasn't very excited about sitting through another game since I had had my fill of baseball yesterday. My stomach rumbled and the guys were at my feet thinking the same thing. I filled their dishes and they happily wagged their tails as they ate. I seasoned the pork chops I had taken out the previous day and put them in a hot skillet. I peeled some potatoes, started them boiling in chicken stock and then grab some frozen veggies from the freezer and nuked them in the microwave.

Marti joined me in the kitchen with a kiss and hug, "So chef, are we still going to the baseball game tonight?"

"Only if you're up to it," I said.

"As long as I am with you, I'm a happy camper," she kissed me and asked what she could do to help.

"You can set the table on the patio while I finish preparing dinner," I replied. We ate outside as the guys watched our every bite and hoped that something would drop their way.

Chapter 16

I finished loading the truck with my camera gear and chairs when Marti and the guys climbed into the truck. We drove to the park, Marti sang to the tunes on the radio. The guys were checking out the sights, sounds and smells of the city with their heads out the back windows.

The park was crowded on this warm summer evening and the baseball diamonds were filled with community league play. At the dog-park there were lots dogs and their owners and the playground was filled with kids laughing and screaming. I found a parking spot close to the diamonds so I wouldn't have far to carry all the gear. With a quick kiss on the cheek Marti headed with the guys to the dog-park to play. I set up camp along the third baseline which gave me a great vantage point to surveil the dugout my suspect's team was using.

I was really disappointed when his team took to the field and he just sat there in the dugout. I had hoped he'd be out playing in the first few innings relieving me of my suffering of sitting through another game. If truth be told I would rather be with Marti and the guys at the dog park. The first couple of innings had been very uneventful, long and boring like yesterday's game. "Oh God, not this crap again," I thought to myself. Why don't they shorten the game, you know maybe two outs instead of three and two strikes instead of three. I was having a hard time trying to stay awake and focusing at the task at hand. I watched as my suspect just sat in the dugout and I was beginning to really dislike him. I prayed he'd take to the field soon and end my misery. I had yet to take one good shot of him doing anything which would help me close my case. I got up, stretched and walked around my chair a couple of times but it didn't help much.

From time to time I looked over at the dog park and watched Marti and the guys. They were all having a lot more fun than me. I was jealous. The guys were busy running and chasing their new found friends and Marti sat talking with a couple of ladies as they all watched their dogs play. The next two innings were no different from the first ones; long, slow and boring. "I must be in hell," I thought to myself. I had almost fallen asleep and was startled when someone hit the ball with a loud crack of the bat and people started to cheer. As the sun set the lights came on and gave me a little boost of energy but not much. I was ready to call it a night and go back to watching my suspect work on his bike tomorrow. As far as I was concerned so far this night had been a bust.

"Yes! Finally, the seventh inning stretch," I said as I stood up with the rest of the fans. I watched as some of the players carried a keg of beer out to the mound. Soon players from both team along with their families and friends walked out on to the mound to drink and socialize.

"It looks to me that not many are sampling the brew." Marti said as she and the guys join me on the sideline. "Hey buddy, is this seat taken or are you saving it for some hot lady?"

"Why yes, I'm saving it for a hottie. You know me, I always like some arm candy." The guys looked exhausted from running around chasing their friends and they immediately crashed next to my chair.

"So how is the investigating going? Have you broken the case wide open yet?"

I gave her a funny look like "duh" and she handed me the leashes and wandered toward the party on the mound. I watched as she stood in line talking to a couple of ladies and soon returned with a cup full of what looked like a very dark beer.

"So how does it taste?"

"It's not for everyone, hardly anyone is drinking it." After taking a couple of sips I could tell this wasn't one of her favorites either. "Nope this is not my taste," and with that she poured the rest on the grass. Oz got up and walked over to where she had poured out the beer. He took one sniff and went back and laid down next to Annie. It obviously wasn't one of his favorites either.

We watched the party on the mound and I noticed my suspect was the only person really drinking and enjoying the beer. The game finally continued and we settled in to watch the remaining innings. If this went into extra innings I might have to do something drastic like go for a jog to keep myself awake. Yea, right, like that would ever happen.

The last two innings were just like the first seven, long and boring, and I was totally excited to see the game end. My suspect's team lost by two runs and unfortunately, I didn't even get one good photo I could use for my case. I packed up my camera gear, chairs and started for the truck. I really hoped I never would have another case where going to a baseball game was involved.

Marti and the guys started walking toward the truck with me when one of the ladies and her poodle from the dog park came over and started talking to her. I watched as they typed each other's contact information into their phones while the guys sniffed and pranced around their feet. I continued to the truck thankfully not having been invited to join in on the conversation. I sat and waited for Marti and the guys and was entertained by watching the bottle neck of traffic as everyone else tried to leave the park all at once. Soon Marti and the guys headed my way.

She had a smile on her face from ear to ear and I gave her a puzzled look as I helped load the guys in the back seat.

The traffic had thinned and we were on our way home when I looked over at Marti who was still smiling. "You must have met a new friend?" I said.

"It's better than that. I'll tell you all about it when we get home," she replied.

Marti was acting like a two-year-old who couldn't wait for Christmas morning and it was hard for her to sit still. I wondered what was so special about her new friend that made her this excited. She busied herself by texting and within a few seconds my phone started to vibrate in my pocket. Sporting a big smile she said, "It's for you, Mr. Ace Investigator."

I pulled into our driveway and we all piled out. Marti quickly wrapped her arm around mine and smiled, "Hey aren't you going to check your phone. It could be important."

"I will check it once we get in the house," I replied.

She gave me her pouty look, a look I was unable to resist. I reached into my pocket and pulled out my phone. "Hey, I got a message from a sexy lady and I wonder what it says?" I opened the incoming text. It was a video she had taken at the ball park. All I could say after watching it was

"OMG, OMG!" This is amazing!" I let out a loud scream "YOU ARE SO BUSTED!" I just stood there frozen in time watching it a second time.

Marti jumped up and down all excited as I watched and rewatched the video. I gave her a big hug, "You did good! You did really good. I have a smart and a sexy assistant," I said.

Apparently while I was waiting at the truck and Marti was talking to her new friend she noticed my suspect picking up the keg and lifting it onto his shoulder. He walked toward the other parking lot which must have been at least 75 feet away from the baseball diamond. She was able to capture the whole scene on video. This made tonight's boring adventure worth the struggle. I had my smoking gun! I watched the video two more times before I noticed I was the only one standing out in our front yard. Marti and the guys had already gone inside. "What the hell," I thought and continued to stand and watch the video a couple more times.

In the house the guys were busy chomping on doggie treats and Marti's clothes were strewn all over the living room floor. The patio door was open and the cover was off the hot tub. "Hey, sailor don't just stand there. Aren't you going to join me?" she asked.

"You don't have to ask twice," and with that I hopped into the hot tub clothes and all. Good thing I had put my phone, keys and wallet in the bowl by the front door when I first walked in. We both laughed. Marti slowly started taking my clothes off and I thought back to what neighborhood watch, Lois, had said this afternoon about watching her neighbors and their hot tub activity. I looked around the yard and hoped our neighbors weren't spying on us through the fence.

After our play time in the hot tub, it wasn't long before I was in bed trying to read. Oz was snuggled in his bed and Marti and Annie were in the living room watching some reality T.V. show. I was having a hard time focusing on my book since my mind was busy processing the evidence we gathered tonight at the baseball game. In the morning I would complete my paperwork and close out the state's case. There was a growing stack of fraud cases on my desk I needed to get busy working on but I wanted to concentrate on Ed. There were a lot of unanswered questions I needed answered and I had the feeling in the back of my mind the key was Ed's love life. The love life I didn't know he had. Before I knew it the Sandman visited and I fell asleep.

The room was getting light as the sun broke over the mountains. As I started to wake up I felt a warm body pressing against my back, "it was good having Marti home" I thought. I reached behind me and instead of soft warm skin I felt nothing but fur. I turned over and there was Oz. He rolled his head my way as if to say, "You were expecting someone else?"

I sat up and focused my eyes; yep it was Oz, not Marti. The sound of the television coming from the living room sparked my curiosity. I walked in and I found both Marti and Annie sound asleep on the couch. Hmm, she never made it to bed last night. I turned off the television and went to take a shower. Marti joined me in the bedroom as I was getting dressed.

"I guess I fell asleep on the sofa again," she said as she crawled into bed next to Oz. Annie wasn't going to let him have all the fun and jumped up on the bed to claim her spot. "Please close the door and the curtains on your way out," Marti said while stifling a yawn.

Being the good husband that I was, I did as I was told. Oz decided three was a crowd and joined me in the kitchen. I grabbed a yogurt for me and a doggie treat for him and we both headed into my office. I added last night's video to my report along with my revised notes. After reading my report I decided to make one more surveillance attempt. I really wanted to nail this guy after he made me suffer through two baseball games. The hall clock chimed ten when Oz and I left with Marti and Annie both sawing logs. I left a note on the kitchen counter to let her know my plans.

When we arrived at the convenience store's parking lot I saw there was no activity at my suspect's house. Oz knew the routine and crashed in the back seat as I lowered all the windows hoping there would be some kind of a breeze. The temperatures were on the rise and it was going to be another hot day in the city. Two hours later and still nothing, I was beginning to think after last night's video I had enough evidence to close out this case. The yogurt hadn't lasted long and my stomach let me know it was time to eat, maybe we should stop at Betty's. I started the engine and was about to back out when two teenagers walked out of my suspect's front door struggling with the keg from the previous night. I turned off the engine and turned on the video camera mounted on the dash. I got out of the truck and started taking pictures. The boys dropped the keg four times, apparently it was still pretty full. That confirmed Marti's comment that no one was really drinking from it last night.

Someone from inside the house yelled "Be careful with that! I have a deposit on that keg." My suspect then walked out and said something I couldn't hear. He then lifted the keg up on his shoulder just like he did in the video from the night before. He loaded it into the backseat of the car parked on the street. There were no issues with this man's back. He was lazy and didn't want to work so he was scamming the system.

I was just about to get back in my truck when my suspect stared right at me. He stood there for a second glaring at me and then my camera and started running toward me. I quickly took a couple more pictures but before I knew it he was in my face.

"Hey," he yelled. "What the hell do you think you're doing?" I had never been caught while observing a suspect so this kind of confrontation was new to me. "Okay asshole, why have you been following me? I noticed you have been hanging around these past couple days watching me and last night I saw you at the baseball game. Did my ex-wife send you to spy on me? Well, tell her I'm not paying her one goddamn penny of child support. She can take me back to court if she wants!"

I was so caught off guard I couldn't answer. I just stood there like a fence post. It would be no problem for this guy to pound me into the ground with one hit of his big fist.

"Okay, out with it. Why have you been spying on me?" he shouted in my face and splattered his spit all over me.

"I work for the state." I was surprised how strong I made that statement sound.

He just stood there glaring and huffing and puffing trying to catch his breath. He looked down at my camera and I knew what he was thinking. If he took it then I wouldn't have any evidence on him. Luckily he hadn't seen the small video camera on the dash which had been filming ever since the two teenagers tried to carry the keg out to the car. I just hoped it didn't run out of disc space or battery power anytime soon. I couldn't remember if I had put in a new disc or battery this morning.

We stood there with our eyes locked on each other and I was thinking this was not going to turn out positive for me. I may have looked like Superman on the outside, but on the inside I was shaking more than a California earthquake. This guy was big and well-built. After watching him carry the keg of beer as if it was a bag of potato chips, I knew he would have no problem pounding me into hamburger. Just as he started to reach for my camera I noticed movement of behind him.

"I wouldn't do that if I were you," I said as my confidence began to grow.

His quick and not so clever reply, "Who's going to stop me, you?" and he let out a light chuckle.

He started to ball up his fists and was about to take his first swing when I answered with a smile, "Oz!"

He gave me a puzzled look and then said, "Oh, I see Mister Smarty-pants so you think the Wizard of Oz is going to save you? Who do you think you are Dorothy? You look more like the Cowardly Lion to me."

He laughed at the funny he had just made until I said, "Turn around."

As he turned a low, gravely growl slowed his pivot. He looked confused at first but soon noticed that Oz was right behind him. Oz must have jumped out the back window when my suspect started getting in my face. The guy froze as Oz, with his Elvis curled-lip snarl, dared him to move. For a brief moment their eyes were locked upon each other. I knew this guy wasn't going to win. Oz wasn't going to let anything happen to his meal ticket.

"I see you've met Oz." I suggested it would be in his best interest to slowly back away and go home. He nodded his head nervously in agreement and turned toward home. Oz followed him for a distance making sure he wasn't going to do anything crazy. My suspect turned and looked at me and then Oz. After a few choice words he followed them up by giving me the finger. I watched as he huffed and puffed all the way home. He knew his free ride on the state's payroll was coming to an end. Oz must have sensed he wasn't coming back so he walked over to me and gave me a smile.

I bent down and gave him a hug, "Thanks, big guy. You saved my bacon."

As we got back in the truck I took a deep breath and allowed my body to relax. Almost having the crap beat out of me had made me tense and nervous. A Marti size smile came across my face and I thought how my suspect had just about crapped in his pants when he saw Oz. I couldn't wait to get home and check out the video. I hoped it had captured my entire encounter with this guy. Just then my phone rang and it scared the hell out of me.

"Hey, how is it going?" It was good to hear Marti's soothing voice.

"Great," I said weakly. "We're just finishing up and heading home."

"I'll make some tuna sandwiches and wait for you. By the way, Annie was upset she didn't get to go with you guys on your stakeout this morning but we had some good snuggle time."

I ended my call with Marti and turned to Oz, "Let's call this case closed."

When we got home we were greeted at the front door by Annie. The guys sniffed each other and then out they went to play in the backyard. I bet Oz was telling Annie about his great adventure and how he saved my butt. A hard lump grew in my throat because I knew sooner or later I would I have to tell Marti about almost getting my butt-kicked.

Marti had lunch ready and we sat out on the patio and watched the guys take turns chasing each other around the backyard. Between bites I told my story and saw the look of concern on her face.

"Oh Wes, weren't you scared?" she asked.

"Naw, you know me, Mister Fearless." I gave her a weak chuckle and reached for her sandwich since I had already polished off mine. I double checked to make sure I hadn't also eaten my napkin. The encounter had not only made me nervous but very hungry.

After lunch we went into my office and I loaded the video onto my computer. It started with the teenagers bringing out the keg and I was relieved the camera captured the whole incident. Marti sat there frozen in her seat as she watched.

I decided to lighten the mood, "Did you see the look in my suspect's eyes when he turned and saw Oz?" She just shook her head.

We watched the video a couple more times. Marti gave me a big hug and then walked over and gave Oz a bigger one. "Hey big guy, tonight you get a big, fat, juicy steak," she said to him.

"Hey, what about me?" I asked.

Marti looked at me, "Mr. Fearless my ass. I saw you shaking in your boots." She walked away laughing.

While Marti was out shopping I spent my time finishing up case notes and getting them ready to submit. I sure hoped they wouldn't laugh too hard when they saw my encounter with this guy. I knew Marti was home from the store when the house suddenly filled with barking and clicking on the hardwood floors. She held true to her word, "Hey, who wants a steak?"

I went running to the front hallway and joined the guys by jumping up and down excited for steak. Marti stood there with a funny look her on face and watched us dance around her. After a few moments she broke out laughing and said, "You could at least help me carry these groceries into the kitchen."

I was assigned the job of cooking the steaks since I was the grill master. I prepped them with salt and pepper and fired up the grill while Marti made a tossed salad and put some tots in the oven. As we waited for the grill to get up to temp, she poured herself a glass of wine and a club soda for me. The guys were busy eating their dinner in the kitchen. I sat at the patio table and thought about how I had only tonight and tomorrow before Marti had to be back to work. It had been great having her home for this many days in a row.

I got busy grilling the steaks and Marti watched. It would have made the perfect cover for Life Magazine an Americana Setting with me standing there at the grill on a warm summer evening, the guys lying on the grass at my feet and a beautiful woman watching as she sipped her wine. The scene was perfect.

Out of the blue Marti interrupted my dream moment with, "Honey, have you ever thought about getting a gun? I was thinking about it while out shopping today. What if something bad had happened to you today? You know it might be a good idea to have some kind of protection, something for emergencies."

She knew I was not a gun person. The last thing I wanted was to carry around a gun of any kind. I would most likely shoot myself in the foot or someplace even worst, like in my butt. I flipped the steaks over and looked down at Oz and smiled. "Why would I need a gun when I pack Oz? The worst that could happen with Oz is that he would eat my lunch. It's much safer than me shooting myself."

She gave me a weak smile and went inside to get the rest of our dinner.

We ate in pretty much silence as neither one of us talked much. Afterwards we all went for a walk stopping from time to time to visit with our neighbors. By the time we got back home we had caught up on all the neighborhood gossip.

We settled in for a movie which happened to a Charles Bronson classic "Mr. Majestyk". While we snuggled and ate popcorn I knew this was what married life was meant to be. Not long after the movie I started to yawn up a storm and Marti was already asleep. I turned off the television and I gave her a little nudge. Tonight she should sleep in our bed and not on the sofa. When we walked into the bedroom I saw she had also purchased two new dog beds while she was out shopping. Annie had staked out hers and Oz settled onto the other one.

"Their old ones were worn out and I felt they needed new ones. Besides, I don't want them sleeping on the bed with us all the time," she said as she climbed under the sheets.

I joined her and gave her a kiss good night. We said our "Love yous" and soon were both asleep.

Chapter 17

I rolled over and looked at the clock. It was 4 o'clock in the morning but I was wide awake. I was up even before the crows had started their morning ritual of squawking and crowing. I closed my eyes and tried to get back to sleep but my mind was already in processing mode. I decided to get up and look at my next case for the state. There was still that stack of case files I had yet to complete. My stack was growing like Ed's mail. I settled on reviewing the one on top. A lady claimed that last winter when she fell in a grocery store's parking lot she had hurt her hip. Now, because of the injury she was unable to do her job which required a lot of standing and walking. She had been employed by the store for three years and worked as a checker but on the day of her accident she was asked to help bring in the empty shopping carts. It had been raining and she slipped on some oil residue. She was suing the store for negligence, citing a failure to properly clear and maintain the lot. She was currently living off the state on a workman's comp settlement but the state requested my expertise investigating whether she was or was not scamming the system. The state had added a note asking for a rush because it was due to go to court in a couple of months.

Whenever I had a rush case my rates doubled and that was something I liked.

I recalled an old Perry Mason show I had seen and remembered they always started the show with the "Case of the....." After all these years working for the insurance companies and state I just called the people I was investigating "suspects." I made an executive business decision that it was time to start giving the suspects a name appropriate for the case I was working on. No more just using the name suspect. I decided after reviewing this new case I would call it "The case of The Cart Lady." That had a pretty good ring to it. I would call her the Cart Lady.

I was having a hard time concentrating on this new case since my mind kept going back to Ed. I decided to shelve the Cart Lady case to concentrate on my friend's murder. I figured it would be in my best interest not to tell Marti of my plan especially after yesterday's run in. I didn't want her to flip out and suggest again I carry a gun.

I heard Oz and Annie both go crashing out through the doggie door as the crows started their usual morning squawk fest. Between the crows and the guys, soon the whole neighborhood would be awake. I tapped on the patio door several times and they came rushing inside. They both gave me the look of "Hey, we tried to tell them to be quiet. Do we get a treat for doing our job?" I couldn't believe Marti was able to sleep with all the racket. I gave them their morning treat and they followed me back into my office. My first stop would be the auto dealership to see Mac. I still had some questions that I needed answered. I wanted to show him my two pictures and hoped he could identify who had brought in the caddy to sell. Stop number two, Ed's house. I had devised a plan on how to catch the person who had been bringing in his mail. I also hoped Linda would be visiting Ronnie so I could talk to her. The challenge would be getting Linda alone long enough to talk. Ronnie was always interrupting me and protecting Linda from something and I wanted find out what it was.

I heard the rumblings of empty stomachs including mine. We walked into the kitchen where my first priority was to start the coffee and feed the guys. I decided to make Marti's favorite breakfast, a Dutch Baby with some bacon. Just then an apocalyptic zombie came stumbling in and headed straight for the coffee maker. Oops, my bad, it was only Marti. After couple of sips of the dark brew she started to shed her zombie demeanor and become more human.

"What the hell was all the barking about?" she asked sipping her coffee.

"Well, the birds were having a party out back and the guys were upset they weren't invited." I refilled her cup and received the smile I fell in love with. She started cleaning and prepping strawberries, we worked well as a team.

"I have a couple of projects this morning, but I'm all yours this afternoon," I remarked while taking the bacon out of the oven and replacing it with the Dutch Baby.

"That works for me. I need to get a couple of things ready for work. How about after work we go for a picnic up at the lake?" she asked as she poured honey over the strawberries.

"Let's plan on leaving around two. I'll stop by the deli and grab us some sandwiches and it'll just be the two of us."

She nodded in agreement. We ate out on the patio and she filled me in on her schedule for the next couple of days. I was happy when she told me she'd be home Monday for a three day layover.

By the time I stepped out of the shower she had already left to run her errands. It was not long after I was also out the door leaving Oz and Annie to guard the home front. Soon I pulled into the car dealership and I noticed the Pontiac was still there. It looked at me like a lost puppy begging to be taken home.

Mac was busy washing a 1960 royal blue Buick Riviera with lots of chrome. He turned off the water and walked over to me and started the conversation, "So are you ready to drive the Pontiac home today?"

I told him no but that I was seriously thinking about it. He was pushing hard to sell me that car. I figured sales must be down this month.

"Mac, please take a look at these two pictures and tell me if one of them brought the Caddy in to sell." I asked.

"Why are you showing me these? What's it to you anyway who brought the car in?" He questioned with a puzzled look.

I handed him my business card, "Look, whoever brought the Caddy in to sell had something to do with the death of a friend of mine. I'm just trying to get some answers."

He stared at my business card and then turned his attention to the pictures for a few minutes and then looked up at me, "You've been working a case this whole time. I bet it was you who tipped off the police. Here I thought you were interested in buying the Pontiac. Get the hell off my lot!" He threw my card and the pictures on the ground turned and walked into his office and slammed the door behind him.

Mac had looked at the pictures but didn't say which lady it was. I had a feeling by his reaction he knew who it was but he wasn't going to tell me. I picked up my card and the pictures. I gave the Pontiac one last look and walked to my truck. Maybe I would come back once he'd cooled off or maybe not. I started to drive off when I saw Mac in my rearview mirror talking on the phone to someone. He was quite animated in his conversation so I must have said something to get him nervous, I just smiled. Mac was still high on my suspect list.

As I drove to the state office I kept thinking that Mac knew who had brought the Trailer Queen in to be sold. Maybe the lady and Mac were both in on it and my investigation was getting a little too close to home. Maybe it was his partner in crime that he was talking to on the phone. It was a quick visit at the state office, just a drop and run and I was glad they didn't have any new cases for me since I had a big stack still sitting on my desk.

When I pulled up in front of Ed's house, I turned to look for Lois. She wasn't at her window post this morning. I guess she couldn't be on watch twenty-four seven. I looked over at Ronnie's house and no one appeared to be watching me from there either. That was a good thing I thought. I wasn't surprised when I checked the mail box and it was empty. However when I opened the front door the mail wasn't stacked neatly on the table but it had been scattered all over the floor. What the hell? Very interesting! Whoever had been looking for something was getting frustrated and obviously they hadn't found what they wanted. I picked up the scattered mail and threw it back on the table.

I started for the office when there was the usual rap on the patio door, as if I didn't know who that would be. "Ronnie, what a surprise. How are you today?" I ask as I opened the door for her. "So what brings you by on this beautiful morning?"

She walked in before I could even get the door completely opened. She stopped, looked at the mail on the table then walked into the living room. "Oh, I just wanted stop by and say hi. You've been coming over here a lot and I wondered if you had any more information about Ed. I'm hoping to find out what happened because I want this nightmare to end. I just got off the phone with detective Miller who asked me a lot of questions."

"I have no idea what happened here. I'm just looking after a friend's house," I replied while taking a seat in the living room. I hoped she would take the bait and join me. She didn't and instead she walked into the kitchen. "Ronnie, I was wondering why your sister doesn't stop by?"

I could tell by her body language she was struggling to answer. "Well, she's trying to get over Ed and what happened to him. It's been very hard on her you know. She was so much in love with him. She's been staying with us these past couple of days and just sits and stares at the walls."

I continued to talk to her trying to get her to open up, "I would really like to talk with her."

I'm no poker player, but those words must have sent chills down her back because she turned toward me with a terrified look on her face.

She immediately turned away and started to walk out, "Linda doesn't want to talk to you or anyone else. The police have already upset her enough. Leave her the hell alone! Just butt the hell out of our lives. This has been a goddamn mess from the start. Just leave me and my family alone. You're just like the police. You think we all had something to do with Ed's murder. Go to hell!" She stormed off slamming the side gate on her way. I bet the whole neighborhood heard some choice four letter words as she marched home. I had hit a nerve.

I wonder what she meant by, "This has been a goddamn mess from the start?" She knew more than she was telling me. Maybe it was Mac and she who had conspired to kill Ed and steal the Trailer Queen, but why?

Before meeting with Marty there was just enough time to run to the hardware store and get a couple of things I needed to help execute my plan. I locked the patio door and as I walked into the kitchen I noticed a slight breeze coming from the doggie door in the pantry. I found the inside panel to the doggie door in the garage. For good measure I put a strip of tape across the bottom, you know like they do in the movies. This way I would know if any two legged animals had tried to get in.

It was a quick trip to the hardware store and when I returned there stood Lois back on duty at her front window. I waved and she waved back. I replaced all the locks with new ones just in case someone I didn't know about had a key. With the first part of my plan completed, it was time for part two. I walked over to Eric and Lois's house making sure I wasn't being watched by anyone from Ronnie's. I explained what I had in mind and they both excitedly agreed to help.

I left them to execute my plan and smiled as I walked to my truck. Things were starting to come together. It didn't appear anyone had been watching me from Ronnie's house and I knew my short conversation with her had shaken her. I still needed to find a way to get past her and speak with Linda.

I needed treats for our picnic so a quick stop at the store where Nick worked would kill two birds with one shot. I could try to get some information out of him before Ronnie got to him. The last time I saw him was when I discovered Ed's body. At that time he was very distant, his eyes cold, dark and his body tense. He had been more focused on what the police had been doing inside the house than on our conversation. During that time he never once comforted his wife, but did wrap his arms around her sister, Linda. That was a little strange, but it could have been because she had just lost her lover. Maybe this time he'd be more talkative. I parked in front of the small local market. It was one of the last independent stores of its kind in the city and it had a hard time competing against the big chains. Fortunately though, downtown was slowly being renovated and new apartments and condos were being built. Hopefully it would help this store make a comeback. There weren't a lot of people shopping at this time of day and there was only one checker up front and she looked bored.

I grabbed a basket and headed straight for the produce section. It was small but had everything I was looking for: a couple of apples, pears and grapes. Next, I grabbed some crackers and a couple types of cheese. I loved my cheese. I navigated the aisles looking for Nick but with no luck. I hoped he hadn't taken the day off since Ronnie mentioned he'd been putting in long hours. I added a few more snacks to my basket and as I rounded a corner there was Nick. He was helping a lady reach for something off the top shelf.

I walked over to him, "Hi, Nick. How's it going today?" He turned toward me with a smile. I could see he was trying to place where we had previously met. Before I could re-introduce myself he must have realized who I was since his attitude instantly changed to distant and defensive. His eyes became as harsh as the first day we had met. They had that same glassed over look.

Ronnie must have called and filled him in on our little visit this morning. I'd try to use my charm to get him to open up, "Nick, how's your wine selection here?"

He softened and seemed to be a little more upbeat, "We have one of the best wine selections in the valley. Let me show you."

As we walked towards the department, he told me how he was instrumental in selecting the variety of wines they offered for sale. I was amazed to see they had a room which was bigger than my garage dedicated to nothing but wine and beer.

"So, what are you looking for?" he asked.

"Going on a picnic with my lady this afternoon. She likes light and fruity wines. You know something sweet, kind of like me." I hoped some humor would continue to lighten his mood but it didn't.

Nick demonstrated his knowledge of wines by throwing out lots of technical jargon which went a mile over my head. I wasn't a wine drinker, just give me a good bottle of club soda and I'm a happy camper. He showed me a couple of different varieties. I recognized Marti's favorite by the label I had seen at home. I put it and another one he suggested in the basket. I hoped this would ease his mood. Now stocked up on wine I moved our conversation to a more personal level by asking him about his family. "So how are you guys holding up after the murder next door? I talked to Ronnie and she still seems very tense."

He immediately changed back into a defensive mode. "Ronnie called and said you'd been coming around asking a lot of questions about our family. What's it to you anyway? It's none of your business so butt out! Ronnie told you to leave us alone and I'm telling you the same thing. Now get out of here before I do something you'll regret."

This family was guilty of something and I needed to find out what it was. Nick stood there no more than a few feet from me staring into my eyes. I could feel his breath on my face and the glare. It looked as if he was about to take a swing but I kept asking questions and he kept being evasive and nonresponsive. He tried walking away but I matched him step for step until he turned and said, "Get the hell out of this store and leave me and my family the hell alone!"

I continued firing off questions one at a time in an attempt of to get an answer, "Nick, do you know who took Ed's Caddy? Who is bringing in the mail? Do you have a key to Ed's house?" He kept on trying to walk away from me. I still kept up my barrage of questions with, "Nick, how is Linda doing?"

That got a reaction and he turned and gave me a "deer in the headlights" look just like the one I had gotten from Ronnie earlier this morning. "Get the hell away from me before I call the cops."

Just then the store's intercom came alive, "Nick, you are wanted up front please."

Before I could say another word he ran up to the front of the store putting as much distance between us as possible. Things were starting to move along in my investigation. I was getting on people's nerves which told me they were hiding something. I felt I was on the right track in solving Ed's murder.

While I waited in line to checkout I looked around for Nick but he was nowhere in sight. Just then a familiar face walked into the store carrying an old red gym bag. I watched as he went to the front office as if he had been there before. A few knocks on the office door and it opened. This was an interesting turn of events. I had no idea Nick and this person had anything in common. When the door opened they turned toward me giving me the old evil eye. I hadn't noticed the checker had finishing ringing up my total and she was talking to me. I stood there frozen as the two men continued to stare and point in my direction. It gave me chills.

I paid for my groceries and started for the front door when the second guy pointed his finger at me like a gun and pulled the trigger. They both laughed and walked into the office and closed the door. Maybe Marti was right. Maybe I should start packing some heat, either that or Oz. It looked like Oz and I would be spending a lot more time together. I didn't waste any time leaving the parking lot and I drove across the street to the lot of an old office complex. I needed time to process and this gave me a good location to keep an eye on the front of the store and think. I parked behind a couple of cars so I couldn't be seen.

Twice in two days I'd had an unfriendly encounter of "Wes gets the crap beaten out of him" kind. Maybe it was time to let the pros handle this case and I would go back to working my fraud cases. I sat there and stared out the windshield while I tried to figure out how those two knew each other. Were they both involved in Ed's murder? Wow, this was an unexpected twist in the case. Maybe I should call Rod and let him know what I had witnessed. Nah, it would probably be a good idea to keep this to myself for now. I especially didn't want Marti to know because she would worry. Good thing she was going to be out of town for the next couple of days.

I was just about to leave when Nick and Rex left the store. Yep, somehow Nick knew Joy's boyfriend. What a small world. They were each carrying a bag, James Dean had his red gym bag and Nick a smaller gray one. Against my better judgement I decided to follow them. I was able to keep my distance since I was familiar with Nick's truck and it stood above most cars.   After ten minutes of driving through town I watched as his truck pulled in the drive up lane at Ed's old bank. This was getting more interesting by the minute. I parked in the coffee shop's lot across the street where Donna and I had talked. I reached for my binoculars as Nick finally reached the teller window. Holy crap, there was Donna, Ed's girlfriend. My mouth was wide open as I watched the three of them talking and laughing as if they were good friends. Soon an irate customer behind Nick started honking their horn to get him to move on. Rex gave the person the finger as they drove off in the opposite direction from the way they had come.

I couldn't believe what I had just seen. I was totally confused and things just weren't adding up. I tried to put two and two together and all I got was three. Donna, Nick and Mr. James Dean all knew each other. Maybe the three of them conspired to murder Ed. Maybe it was

Donna who kept bringing in Ed's mail since she may have had a key to his house. She could have been the lady trying to sell the Caddy.

I reflected on the three of them and my meeting earlier this morning with Mac. When I asked him who had brought in the Trailer Queen to sell, he froze up and acted strangely. Maybe two and two does add up to four, Nick, Donna, Mr. James Dean and Mac. For now it looked like Donna and I were going to have to have another heart to heart.

I started the truck to continue following them when my phone rang. It scared the hell out of me again, "Hey, when are you coming home?" Marti asked.

"On my way to the deli and will be there shortly."

I wanted to continue following Nick and Mr. James Dean but plans changed since I had promised to spend my afternoon with Marti. I called the deli and placed my order. My conversation with Donna would have to wait. I continued to replay over and over my interactions today with the four suspects hoping something would connect. Also there was the strange way Ronnie acted when I asked about Linda. They were all hiding something, but what? Are they all in this murder together? It was almost like the Orient Express where everyone was in on it. Maybe Rod should just arrest them all. Seeing Rex this morning made me wonder if Joy had also been playing me all along. It was time to pay her another visit too. Wow! This was turning into one of those daytime police dramas, "Who shot Mr. Ed?" What a mess!

Chapter 18

As soon as I walked through the front door of the deli they had my two sandwiches, a roast beef and cheddar on sourdough bread and a Ruben with pickles ready for me. Oz and Annie were excited to see me when I got home but I imagined the smell of the sandwiches had something to do with that. Marti finished packing the cooler while I quickly changed into picnicking attire. With the truck packed we were ready to go. I turned to say goodbye to the guys and four sad eyes gave me the "You aren't going to leave us here are you? We like picnics too," look.

I patted each one of them behind the ears and said, "Sorry guys, it's going to be just the two of us this time."

Marti was looking hot and sexy as usual. She wore a tank top along with one of her summer skirts with her long black hair pulled back in a ponytail through her baseball cap. She also had on her big Hollywood rimmed sunglasses. As we pulled out of the drive there were two sad looking faces staring at us from the side gate. Oz was obviously teaching Annie the art of the guilt trip. I had to admit there had been many times in the past that his guilt trip look had worked on me. Oz knew I was Mister Softie. No matter how much they begged I wasn't going to cave in today, but it was starting to work on Marti, "Honey, maybe we should bring Oz and Annie along with us?"

"Hey, it was your idea that it be just the two of us this afternoon."

She sighed, "You're right."

We drove up to the lake and Marti filled me in on her flight schedule for the next few days. I listened halfheartedly since I was still processing everything I had learned this morning. I was startled when a loud voice echoed throughout the cab of the truck, "Earth to Wes! Hello is any one home? Are you listening to me?"

"Sorry, I was thinking about a new case I'm starting tomorrow for the state. I scoped out the location this morning. I am going to call it the "Case of the Cart Lady," I said with a cheesy grin. I lied, which I didn't like doing especially to Marti but there was no need for her to worry while she was off working. Knowing her she'd tell me to stop investigating and let the police do their job. "Soooo, what time are you leaving in the morning?"

The great thing about where we lived was the short drive up to the lake. At this time of day the traffic was light since everyone was still working. There weren't many boats out on the water either but by this weekend the place would be packed. We drove past the boat ramp and a few of the picnic sites and soon arrived at our special spot. We were in luck and had the place all to ourselves. One of the reasons we loved this location was the view of the lake, shade from the tall pine trees and the privacy. Marti spread out the blankets as I walked up from behind her and pulled her in close wrapping my arms around her warm body, "I'm going to miss you these next couple of days."

She turned and looked into my eyes, "I'll miss you too." We stood there locked in each other's arms until she said, "Enough of this mushy stuff. I'm starving so let's break out the food."

We soon had a picnic bounty spread before us, our deli sandwiches, cheese, crackers, and a variety of fruits. Marti must have stopped at a bakery while she was out shopping because there was an Italian cream cake for later. I opened one of the bottles of wine and started to pour some into a glass but Marti grabbed the bottle out of my hand with a, "Who needs a glass?" look and took a big swig.

"While in Rome, do as the Romans do" was my motto and I did the same with my bottle of club soda. No formality here. We spent the afternoon eating, laughing and watching the boats out on the lake and basking in a warm summer breeze.

"Honey, how do you think Annie will react tomorrow when I leave? She's claimed me as hers. Whenever I'm home she follows me where ever I go," Marti said after taking another bite of her sandwich.

I just shrugged my shoulders, "I have no idea but the good thing is she has also bonded to Oz."

We made plans to take a trip in the fall. Marti could get tickets to fly almost anywhere for free. It was a perk for working for the airlines. We'd ask Vern to watch the guys since it was something he had done in the past. With our bellies full we laid back and watched the clouds pass over, pointing out unique shapes. Except for the background noise from the boats it was very peaceful.

I turned to face the love of my life and removed her sunglasses, "You know I have bonded to you and I will greatly miss you too," I said with a smile.

She wrapped her arms around me and pulled me in close. "It is always hard for me to leave, but I love what I do, and I have an amazing man who supports me."

"You're damn right you do." I kissed her gently on the lips.

With each kiss the fires within us started to ignite. As I started to run my hands along her leg, she pushed me onto my back. I gave her a puzzled look until she climbed on top of me. Looking into my eyes she bent down to kiss me. To my surprise she pulled off her top exposing her sexy breasts and when she bent down again to kiss me she whispered, "I have nothing on under my skirt."

We spent the afternoon making love and didn't care if anyone noticed. The sun moved toward the horizon and Marti hinted it was time to leave. She had a few things to finish up before her flight left in the morning.

I loaded up the truck and as I opened the door for her I gave her a kiss, "You are one sexy lady and you are mine."

She smiled and as she hugged me and whispered back, "I'm yours."

The drive time home was taking much longer since we had to navigate rush hour traffic. People were in a hurry to get in some lake time before it was too late in the day. When we got home I unloaded the truck as Marti started packing for work. I put away the food, fed the guys and went into my office. This was a good time to update my notes from my conversations with Mac, Ronnie and Nick as well as what I had witnessed in the store. Marti was busy cleaning her uniform and the guys were shadowing her every step. She was getting frustrated and I heard her repeatedly asking them to move out of her way as she walked around the house trying to get ready. Her knight in shining armor came to the rescue when I grabbed the guy's leashes and jingled them. This brought them running and Marti gave me a "thank you" look.

A walk would do us good and the guys wouldn't be under Marti's feet. Besides, I needed some time to think and burn off some of the calories from lunch. It'll help to make room for seconds on the Italian cream cake.

The guys dictated our path while I thought about Ronnie and how she had blown up when I started asking about her sister Linda. Something must be going on between the two of them. What could be Ronnie's motive for killing Ed? Maybe she was jealous of Ed and Linda's relationship or maybe she was jealous of the other lady, Donna, in Ed's life. They were supposed to being getting married or at least that was what Donna had told me. Maybe Ronnie might have easedropped in on Ed and Donna's conversation about getting married while they were out in Ed's backyard. Maybe Linda had also heard them. Per Ronnie, Linda hadn't been able to get past the break up with Ed and with him dating Donna. Maybe she couldn't stand it any longer and murdered him in a jealous rage.

My attention turned to Nick and what I had observed this morning. I wondered if Nick, Donna and Rex were in it together and committed the murder. Nick obviously knew Joy's boyfriend, Mr. James Dean want-a-be and he also knew Donna. Between the three of them had they had planned, murdered and had stolen the Trailer Queen? That left me with Joy and Mac and the role they played in this mess. Mac was very defensive when I showed him the two pictures this morning, actually down right pissy. Had Joy been playing the empathy card trying to throw me off her trail? Tomorrow I would pay another visit to Ed's girlfriend, Donna, and get some straight answers. I really wanted to know if she was telling the truth about them getting married and why didn't she show up at the service? Plus another chat with Joy wouldn't hurt either.

Before I knew it the guys had walked us home and I had to stop and think about where we had actually been. Marti was on the sofa with a big bowl of popcorn. I wanted to sit next to her but it was too late. Oz had claimed the spot on her right and Annie was on her left, both of their heads in her lap begging for a kernel or two. Once the three of them had finished off the popcorn the guys closed their eyes and laid their heads back on her lap. Marti gently stroked them behind their ears and they were in heaven. I settled in my recliner with a big slice of cake. Both Marti and I were classic movie buffs and we watched an old black and white drama starring James Cagney. It wasn't one of his best but still okay. It was around nine o'clock when the movie ended I got up and turned off the television. Pulling her away from the guys, who were content to stay where they were, we headed to bed.

I asked her, "What time do I need to get you to the airport?"

She replied, "I don't need a ride. They're sending a shuttle to pick me up. It's supposed to be here around four in the morning."

We snuggled into each other's arms. Our time together was coming to an end. We said, our "Love yous" and kissed and it wasn't long before we were asleep.

Holy crap! You would have thought it was World War III and the apocalyptic zombies were coming to get us. Marti's alarm shattered the quiet of the house which set the guys off and they started prancing, dancing and barking. The sun hadn't shown any signs of coming up yet and I nudged Marti numerous times to get her up. We went through this every time she needed to get up to go to work. I sometimes wondered what she did on the mornings when she was away from home. When she was home she would set her alarm to some weird rock music and shit it was loud! Regardless how loud it was though I was still the one who had to get her up. She could sleep through anything. Finally, after a couple more nudges she got up and danced around the room as she got dressed. It was some of the best entertainment a man could get. She rushed this way then that way, hopping on one foot and then the other. For fifteen to twenty minutes it was nothing but sheer pandemonium. Both Oz and I had experienced this madness before and knew when Marti was on a mission it was best to get out of the line of fire. Oz's instincts were to hop up on the bed and get out of the path of hurricane Marti, while Annie followed her every step. Over time Annie would also learn that during this madness the bed offered the only safe sanctuary. I offered to make coffee but she declined and said she'd get some at the terminal. Her phone pinged letting her know her ride was out front. We all walked her to the front door to say our goodbyes. She bent down and kissed Oz and then Annie trying not to get dog hair on her uniform. We held our hug for a while, kissed, said our "Love yous" and she walked out the door. Six very sad eyes watched her leave. Once inside the shuttle she waved and was gone.

It was too early for me to stay up so I headed back to bed. Unfortunately, the guys had the same idea and by the time I reached it they had claimed their spot on the pillows. I was able to find a small patch they hadn't covered up and I was almost asleep when my phone pinged, "I miss you already," Marti had texted with a sad face.

"Me too," I returned the sentiment and quickly fell back to sleep. The next thing I knew it was almost ten. The guys were still sprawled out on the bed and I decided this sleeping arrangement was not going to become a habit.

Chapter 19

I fed the guys before hopping into the shower. My first stop would be the bank to speak with Donna. I had a long list of questions I needed answers too. I want to find out more about the fight at Ed's house, how she knew Nick and Mr. James Dean and why she wasn't at the service. Next I want to track down Joy and ask her some questions. Finally, I needed to talk to Linda. I didn't know her last name so unfortunately I couldn't look up her address. Some investigator I was. Maybe she would be visiting at Ronnie and Nick's. It seemed she has been spending a lot of time there lately. I hoped I could talk to her alone and not have Ronnie listening in on our conversation. It would be better if Ronnie wasn't even home. Great, I planned to spend my day with three ladies, none of whom I really wanted to be around and I was sure they didn't want to be around me either. The one I'd rather be around was currently flying off to somewhere. On my way out the door I gave the guys a goodbye ear scribble and I heard my stomach let me know I should have eaten breakfast. That would have to wait because I wanted to catch Donna on her break.

I had just parked in the bank's lot when my phone rang, "Hey Wes, it's Mike. I just wanted to remind you that the group is meeting tonight."

"Oh crap, I had forgotten all about it. Are we meeting at the usual location and time?"

"No, we're meeting at Donavan's Pizza. Remember Donavan wanted to join our group?"

"Oh yea, yea I remember. He wanted to show off his Lincoln. So, what time?"

"Six o'clock and bring your car. He wants us to park them all out front and he will save us spots."

"Sounds good, I gotta run. Catch you tonight." Darn, I had forgotten about the meeting. I was glad Mike had called to remind me.

I saw Donna walk into the sandwich shop next to the bank so I quickly followed. The smell of fresh bread reminded me I was hungry so I got in line behind her. She looked back and saw me standing there and gave me a puzzled look and a weak wave.   By her facial expression I could tell I was the last person she wanted to talk to today. I got my sandwich and pickles and joined her at her table.

"What do you want this time?" Yep, she was not happy to see me.

I thought I would try to break the ice knowing she didn't want to talk. "I was talking to my buddy Nick, who said he knew you and wanted me to pass along his greetings."

She gave me a blank look, "I'm sorry but I don't know a Nick."

That was not the reaction I was hoping for, "Nick, he's Ed's neighbor."

Still same blank look, "No, no. I really don't know a Nick. You say he was Ed's neighbor? I don't think I ever met him."

Either she was playing it real cool or didn't know him, so I tried a different approach. "You know, Nick. He works as the manager at the Wilson Street Market downtown." That got a reaction.

"Ah, Nick. Yea I do know him. He comes to the bank to make the daily deposits. I didn't know he was Ed's neighbor though. How strange is that?"

I wondered if she was feeding me a line of BS. "So you only know him from the bank? He said he had seen you hanging out at Ed's."

She sat there for a while thinking before she replied, "No. I really never met him except at the bank. I only met one person when I was at Ed's and that didn't turn out so well."

I still wasn't getting the reaction I was hoping for. Her tone and body language was telling me she didn't have any connection with Nick. I waited until she had taken a couple of bites of her sandwich before I started asking her more questions. "You said when you met Ed's neighbor it didn't go well. What happened?"

She gave me a "how did you find out about that" look and after a couple more bites of her sandwich she shrugged and started telling her side of the story. "Yes, I was over at Ed's one night. We barbecued a couple of steaks and ate out on the patio." She took a sip from her soda and wrapped up the rest of her sandwich. "We had some extra circular activity and I went into the kitchen to pop some popcorn for the movie. The doorbell rang and when Ed opened the door this woman barged in screaming and yelling. He tried to talk to her and calm her down but she kept swearing and cussing. He couldn't get a word in edgewise."

"Could you hear what she was saying?" I asked.

"Yes, she was shouting so loud the whole neighborhood could hear. She was all over him about how he was sleeping with a tramp. Well, when she said the word 'Tramp' I'd had enough and walked into the hallway. She took one look at me and started calling me every kind of vile word in the book. Then she slapped Ed in the face. That's when I stepped in and punched her in the face and she went crashing to the floor. I told that bitch no one touches or talks me or my man that way. She looked at me with sheer hatred, jumped to her feet and started hitting, kicking and spitting on me. I wasn't going to take anymore of her crap so I hit her back. Poor Ed! He tried to stop us, but she hit him a couple of times too. Once was really hard and he went down." Donna stopped and took a sip of soda.

"So who won the fight?" I asked.

A smile crossed her face, "I did. In college I was in gymnastics and I lifted weights. Someone must have called the police because when they arrived, she had a black eye, a swollen lip and was bleeding from her nose."

We both laughed. Looking at Donna I would have never figured she had that kind of spirit.

"So who was your sparring partner that night?" I asked.

She looked down at her watch. I knew she was going to have to be back to work soon. "Ed said that she was his neighbor. I said she was one crazy bitch. Before that night I think I had met her once when we first started dating. I even caught her looking in the front window at us once while we watched a movie. I asked Ed about her and he just shrugged it off. So, I didn't let it bother me. You know, come to think of it, I even caught her a couple of other times looking out her front window at me as I left Ed's."

"Anyway, she kept trying to attack me and the police officers had a hard time restraining her. In her blind rage she even hit one of them who had been trying to get her to calm down. They finally had had enough and arrested her. They took her away in a police car." Donna stood up, "I'm sorry, but I have to get back to work now."

I grabbed my sandwich and followed her out the door. While we walked back to the bank I showed her the two pictures I had with me and she pointed at one of them, "That's the crazy bitch that attacked us! Do you think she's the one who killed Ed?"

"I'm not sure. I don't think the police have made any arrests at this point."

"Did you know Ed had to get a restraining order against her?"

"A restraining order?" I repeated with a surprised tone in my voice.

"She was nuts. She would stand out in front of his house every time I would visit. He got the order so she would leave us alone. Now that I think about it, I bet she was the one who threw the rock at my car."

We reached the employee's entrance of the bank, "Donna how come you didn't show up at the services we had at the park for Ed the other day?"

She stopped dead in her tracks and stared at me, tears running down her checks. She then took a deep breath, "I don't really know why I didn't show up. I guess that I'd be embarrassed that no one really knew who I was and why I showed up. I didn't want people thinking I was some kind of tramp sleeping around with their friend." She wiped away the tears and ran inside the bank. I stood there as the door slammed in my face.

I sat in my truck and ate the rest of my sandwich. It was not as good as the deli made, but it would due in a pinch since I was starving. I had this feeling she was telling the truth about only knowing Nick whenever he came through the drive up at the bank to make the store's deposits. She was also genuine when telling me why she chose not to show up at the services, if it was me I might have felt the same way. I then pictured the chaos that must have taken place the night of the fight and I felt sorry for Donna and Ed. I looked at the picture one more time and after listening to Donna's side of the story I knew it would be a good time to stop by Ronnie's.

I parked in front of Ed's house and I looked across the street and there stood Lois peering out her window. She smiled, winked at me and I just waved back. There was no sign of Ronnie's car or Nick's truck parked in the driveway. As I walked to their house I could hear Lyle out playing in the back yard. There was a white Ford Escort parked out front of Ronnie's house which I had seen there many times. I figured it belonged to Linda. Maybe I was in luck.

I rang the doorbell and after a couple of minutes, Linda opened the door. "Hi, can we talk?" I asked.

She took a moment to respond, "Ronnie and Nick warned me about you and if you were to come by not to talk to you. So get the hell off our property!" She slammed the door in my face. Well, that didn't go as I planned. She was hostile and downright rude if you asked me. This was the second time today I had a door slammed in my face. I stood there wondering whether or not I should push my luck and knock on the door again or walk away. I could hear her talking to someone on the other side of the door so I chose to walk away.

Doing the walk of shame back to my truck I glanced up to see Lois flashing me a smirky smile. I just waved and sat in my truck. Before I knew it, Ronnie came screaming past me in her car and she slammed on her brakes as she pulled into their driveway. I could see she was on the phone and I could guess who was on the other end. As she got out her car she glared in my direction and ran to the house. The door opened and Linda popped her head out and then gave me 'the finger' as she let her in. Maybe I should go back home and re-read *How to Win Friends and Influence People* because it sure hadn't worked on this family.

I arrived home to a hero's welcome. At least the guys were happy to see me. I bent down and gave them each ear scribbles. "Do you guys want a doggie treat?" and with that they danced with excitement. They got their treats and I grabbed a water bottle and went to my office to do some further research.

I updated my findings from my conversation with Donna and noted she and Nick were just business associates. I didn't get any negative vibes from her when I had mentioned his name but for now she was still on my list. I started searching on the web to see what I could find about the night of the fight. Since there had been an arrest it would be public record but I had made the big mistake of not asking the date it happened. Finally, after an hour I found the information I was looking for. The police had booked her for assault and disturbing the peace. Her police photo didn't do her any justice but then they never do. It was the police who had filed the complaint, not Ed or Donna. Nick had posted her bond and no court date had yet been set. Digging a little further, I discovered she had a past history of assaults. This was her third time arrested and I read each arrest in detail. They happened over a ten year span and each arrest was because of a fight with another woman. After reading each case I had a better understanding why she fought with Donna. I had experienced her temper just the other day.

Okay, so it was Ronnie who had gone nuts and not Linda. But why? As far as I knew she and Ed had never dated or had they? It was my understanding it was Linda who had dated Ed. Right? So did Ronnie try to sell the Caddy? So what set her off the deep end the other day at Ed's? Did she have a secret crush or even and an affair with Ed? Up until now I hadn't given Ronnie much thought other than the she was the nosey neighbor, but now maybe it was time to move her up on my suspect list. I bet she was the one who brought in Ed's mail, but why? There were so many unanswered questions and a web of suspects which were all tied together in one way or another. For now, "Ronnie you have become number one the list."

I just finished updating my notes when my phone dinged and it was a text from Marti, "In Atlanta tonight. Call me later."

I replied with a smiley face, "You got it."

I looked at my watch and it was almost four. Unfortunately, I hadn't caught up with Joy to ask her some questions but she would have to wait. I needed to get moving but first I had to feed the guys. The car group would be at Donavan's Pizza and I wanted to beat the traffic.

The drive was long and hot with no air conditioning in the Bird. I was sweating and how I hated to drive in rush hour traffic. It was moving slower than a snail just inching along. I was afraid the Bird would overheat and I'd be stuck in this mess but I luckily I arrived at the pizza parlor without any issues. There were nine classic cars already parked out front. I recognized six of them and one I assumed was Donavan's Lincoln. I had seen the other two at various car shows but I didn't have a clue who owned them.

When I entered the pizza parlor I was directed to the back room. When I stepped through the doorway everyone yelled, "Wes!" I felt like Norm at Cheers.

I made my way around the room saying hello to everyone and Marsha made the introductions of our new members. An older couple owned the green 1972 Plymouth Fury and a white hair gentleman owned the yellow 1960 Ford Falcon. They were at the show last week and the gathering here. They asked to join our little group and I always thought the more the merrier.

I took a seat next to Bob and his wife who owned the 1960 Chevy Pickup. They had been in this group ever since it was formed and Marti and I had been to their house a couple of times for dinner and movie.

Donavan walked in the meeting room with two large pizzas, followed by one of his employees with two more, "Okay guys! Let's eat."

The pizzas were great as usual and we had a good time getting to know our new members. They were going to fit in just fine. They didn't belong to any other car clubs and wanted to be included in one to make new friends. After we stuffed ourselves Jeff started the meeting. "Okay folks, if you don't mind, let's have a moment of silence for Ed." We all stood and bowed our heads remembering our friend.

Jeff had made himself our leader and quite frankly we didn't mind. "This coming Saturday we have a show at small park off Gekeler. We have attended this show before and had a great time. I thought we could all meet at the market on Broadway about eight o'clock and cruise over as a group. Who's interested in attending?" We all raised our hand and it was a plan. The rest of the evening was spent talking about future car shows and checking out each other's rides. It was a pretty cool collection of cars and we were all proud to show them off.

Donavan showed off his Lincoln like he was a proud papa showing off his baby. Dave walked over to me and asked if I had heard any more about Ed's murder.

"No, I haven't," I replied. I wasn't going to let on that I was doing my own investigating. "I'm sure the police are investigating any lead they have turned up."

"Do you think the police have found Ed's secret camera," Dave said with a smirk.

My mouth dropped wide open and my eyes bulged out of my head like in those Saturday morning cartoons. "What are you talking about?" I choked.

"Ed invited me over to his house a couple of months ago and he told me he was having some kind of woman problem. He said she was a real nut case. Well, you know Ed and his love for the Trailer Queen. He was afraid this woman was going to do some damage to it so he installed a hidden camera in the garage to keep an eye on things."

"What? How do you know about all this?" I asked.

"When I was over there one day he showed me the setup. It was pretty sweet. Every time either the door from the house or the door from the garage would open the garage lights would come on automatically activating the filming."

"I'm pretty sure the police will have found it by now," I said standing there still in shock.

Dave shook his head and laughed, "I bet they haven't. You see it was state of the art. He had a camera placed in an oil can on the shelf facing the queen and it filmed the entire garage. You could see everything."

"If the police had thoroughly searched the garage, which I'm sure they did they would have found the setup," I replied.

"You don't know Ed. He was big into the latest electronics and the camera lens was the size of the head of a ten penny nail. You had to look really hard at the can to see it. It was also wire-less with the antenna inside the can. But it could still send a signal to his computer or to his phone. "

"I know the police have Ed's computer so they must have found the videos," I said. When I saw the sly look on his face I knew I was wrong. He knew something else I didn't.

"Ed used a second small computer. I think he said it was in the attic or in the garage somewhere. He wouldn't show me where. It had a hard drive large enough to record hours and hours of video. Ed had access to the information any time he wanted through his phone," Dave said still smirking.

I just stood there puzzled, shocked and amazed. Dave gave me a smile and patted me on the back. "Hope you find it Mr. Investigator," and then he walked over and joined the others.

I followed him over to the group. People were visiting but I wasn't paying attention. My mind was on overload with what Dave had just shared with me.

I walked over to Donavan, thanked him for the use of the room and paid my part for dinner. It was time to go home.

My head was spinning and I wanted to stop by Ed's house immediately but thought better of it. I'd have to check things out in the morning. When I arrived home the guys were excited to see me and I gave them each a treat. I called Marti and we talked for about twenty minutes, but the call was cut short because she needed to get up early. We said our goodnights and "Love yous". I didn't mention what Dave had shared with me at tonight's gathering.

I went into the office and started making notes about what Dave had said about the hidden camera in Ed's garage. I still couldn't wrap my head around this new lead. I sure hoped the police hadn't found his hidden equipment. By the time I finished it was close to midnight. As I walked into the bedroom the guys were already settled in on their beds and as I slid between the sheets I thought to myself, "I might have the magic bullet to solve this case if I can only find the camera and computer setup."

Chapter 20

The sound of my phone pinging woke me up. Before I could reach it both Oz and Annie pounced wishing me a good morning. I was covered in doggie slobber when I was finally able to get them settled down. I reached for my phone and it was Rod. The message said, "Meet me at the coffee shop at nine."

I texted back, "See you there." I wondered if he was going to tell me the police had caught the murderer and the case was closed.

I fed the guys and was getting dressed, when my phone pinged again. This time it was Marti, "Good morning, traveling on the east coast today. I will bring you a surprise. Have a great day my love."

I texted back, "Miss you, wish you were here," and added a couple of frowny faces for emphasis.

I was almost out the door when my phone pinged again. This was starting off to be a busy day. It was the state letting me know they had a couple of new cases for me to investigate, as if I wasn't busy enough already.

Holy cow, I thought when my phone pinged a fourth time. This time it was Vern. "Cutting your grass today. Do you want me to do the other place too?"

I stood there looking at my phone. It was way too early for all this activity. I texted back, "Sounds great."

I had just gotten in Marti's car when, you know it, my phone pinged again. It read "K". What the hell does "K mean?" I had a feeling I was going to have to sit down with that kid one of these days and have him teach me his generation's language.

I had planned to be at Ed's early but now that would have to wait since I was meeting with Rod. I drove Marti's car so I wouldn't be recognized when I parked down the street from Ed's. Today I didn't want to alert Ronnie I was next door.

The coffee shop was busy, mostly because of a large group of retired men sitting around shooting the bull. I arrived before Rod and I ordered a cheese, bacon, sausage, and onion omelet with a cinnamon roll on the side. The waitress must've seen Rod walking in because she had his coffee on the table before he sat down.

He looked tired. His eyes were bloodshot and his clothes were wrinkled and looked like he had been living in them for days. "You look like shit!" I said.

He gave me a half smile and replied, "Go to hell!"

The waitress brought my food and a fresh pot of coffee. Rod took one look at my plate and ordered the same. I took a bite of my omelet when a fork from the other side of the table stabbed my cinnamon roll, "Why don't you help yourself?"

"Thanks, don't mind if I do." After a couple of sips of coffee Rod began, "I was up all night at a crime scene. There was a break-in on the west side of town and the owner of the house shot the intruder. Get this, with a bow and arrow."

"Ouch," I replied.

"Yea, when we arrived on the scene, the first thing I saw was that the front door had a bloody arrow sticking out of it. On the inside of the door was the intruder. The arrow had gone through his arm and into the door and he couldn't move. What a mess." The waitress brought Rod's breakfast and she saw he was eating my cinnamon roll so she placed his roll on my side of the table.

"So what do I owe the pleasure of this meeting? Let me guess you've solved the murder," I asked.

He finished off the last of my cinnamon roll and didn't answer my question. He started in with, "We found Ed's safety deposit box the other day. It wasn't at the branch where he worked. It was at a branch across town where he first worked." He took a bite of his omelet and looked at me. "Hey, this is pretty good. I didn't know you had such good taste." After a few more bites he proceeded telling me, "It had the usual stuff. We read his will and it listed you as one of his beneficiaries."

I just about dropped my fork, "Why in the hell would Ed list me as a beneficiary?"

Rod just smiled, "Relax hot shot, it says in the case of his death he wanted you and Marti to have Annie. He felt she would benefit from your good home."

I took a deep breath and smiled, "She's settled in nicely." I couldn't resist asking "Who's is going to get the Trailer Queen?"

He just smiled and stabbed at my second cinnamon roll, "For that you'll have to wait until the official reading of it. Oh, and that is going to be two p.m. Tuesday at Ed's lawyer's office. I'm sure you'll be getting a call soon. Act surprised when you hear the news about Annie. I really shouldn't have told you."

Hearing the will was being read on Tuesday told me I better get my last looks in at Ed's. I had to find the video equipment if the police hadn't already. I thought about asking Rod if they had but that would surely get their forensic team back out there and I didn't want that. I watched as he continued to shovel food into his mouth. "So are you close to finding the murderer?"

He just smiled, "We're getting there."

"Can't you give me a hint about who it might be?" I asked hoping he would share some information.

Rod just looked at me while taking the last bite of my cinnamon roll and smiled, "Thanks for the breakfast, I'll catch you later." He stood up and headed for the door.

Being Mr. Businessman that I am I picked up the check, anything for a tax write off. It was a little past ten when I parked down the street from Ed's. I was about to get out of the car when I saw Ronnie loading Lyle into her car. Soon Linda came out of the house and climbed in the front seat. They drove off in the opposite direction from where I was parked. I quickly walked toward the house and checked to see if Lois was watching out her front window. She wasn't. I locked the front door behind me so I wouldn't be disturbed. I checked the doggie door to see if anyone had gotten in. The tape had been loosened but there was no new mail on the table. Whoever was coming in the house was still looking for something. I opened the door into the garage and the lights came on as Dave said they would. Since there was plenty of light coming in through the side windows I turned off the overhead lights not wanting to attract any attention. I found Ed's drill and some screws and made sure the doggie door was secured this time. No one would be able to crawl through it again.

I walked over to the collection of old antique oil containers and there must've been at least a hundred of them. They all seemed undisturbed. There wasn't an empty space where one can might have been which told me the police hadn't found the camera. One by one I carefully examined each one and carefully made sure to put it back exactly where I found it. "The camera lens was the size of a ten penny nail," Dave had said.

After an hour of searching and having inspected about a third of the collection without finding anything, I figured with my luck it would be in the last can. Just then I heard a car door shut which caused me to freeze. I looked out the side window and saw Ronnie and her family had returned home. I watched as they unloaded the car from shopping and walked inside the house. I continued with my search. Some of these old oil cans were pretty cool and in great shape considering how old they were. I bet this collection would bring in some big bucks if sold on EBay. The next can I picked up was heavier than the others, it read "Quaker State". I looked closely at the logo and I could see a small reflection from the camera lens. Being very careful, I pried the lid off and there inside was the camera. "Bingo! I hit the mother lode!" I thought. Putting the lid back on I proceeded to move the other oils cans around to hide the fact that one was missing. Next was to find the computer.

I located a ladder in the storage room off the garage to access the attic which was in the hall closet. There was no light in the attic but after opening and closing almost all the kitchen draws I found a flashlight. I made a mental note next time to bring my own. I looked around in the attic but I came up blank. I wondered if the police had already found the computer. I closed the access panel and was starting to put the ladder away when I heard the side gate open.

I froze as to not let whoever it was know I was inside the house. They were trying to get in through the doggie door again. When they weren't able to open it they kicked the side of the house out of frustration. After a few choice words I knew it was Ronnie. She stormed off slamming the side gate behind her. I took a deep breath of relief. I now knew who had been bringing in the mail but I still needed to know why.

I returned the ladder to the storage room in the garage and started going through the cabinets one by one hoping to find where Ed had hidden his computer. After a thorough search and coming up empty, I had just one last cabinet to look through. I opened the door and saw a reflection of a red blinking light. Eureka!! I removed everything from the shelf so I was able to get a better view. There was a knob right next to the light and the back panel had hinges. I pulled on the knob and the panel slid open revealing a small electronic unit about the size of a cell phone. "Bingo!" I shouted. I unplugged the computer and put everything in the cabinet back almost the way I found it. Who would notice at this point where things belonged? I was so giddy about finding it I actually spoke out loud, "Yes, they call me Mister Investigator!"

I grabbed the can with the camera in it and made sure to turn the garage light switch back to on when I exited. I didn't want to risk being noticed leaving the house so I peeked out the front window first to see who might be around. Lois was looking out her window and Ronnie's car was gone from her driveway. I must have been so focused on trying to find the computer that I hadn't heard her leave. This was my opportunity to make a break for it.

As I opened the front door and was about to step outside I could see out of the corner of my eye Ronnie's car coming back down the street. Darn! I quickly closed the door and nervously waited for her to park and go inside. I was anxious to get home and find out what was on this computer. I took a deep breath and told myself to be patient. After a long ten minutes of waiting I looked out the window and saw that it was quiet next door. Time to go.

I opened the front door and just then here came Vern riding his bike and towing the lawnmower behind. Oh, great, I thought I as shut the door again. Was I ever going to get out of here? I watched from the front window as he pedaled past Marti's car and gave it a funny look. He seemed to recognize the car but shrugged it off and pedaled on. I made sure he didn't see me and watched as he unstrapped the lawnmower and pulled the cord to start cutting the grass. His phone must have rung because he stood there talking for twenty minutes before I heard the lawnmower start up again. I wished this time he would start in the back. Another delay, this waiting is killing me. I continued to pace back and forth, trapped in Ed's house. I really wanted to get home to see what was on this darn computer. My time was running out on solving this case.

Finally, Vern started mowing out back and it was time to attempt another escape. I slowly opened the front door but I heard Ronnie's voice. I shut the door and continued to wait. I listened to the sound of car doors closing and an engine starting and saw out the window of the front as Ronnie, Lyle and Linda drove past the house. Quickly I made my escape closing the front door behind me. I bolted for Marti's car before they came back. I looked up to see Lois was back her post and she waved at me and I waved back. She smiled and gave me a thumbs up.

I had just gotten into Marti's car when a black pickup pulled into Ronnie's drive. Nick got out and went inside their house. I thought about going over and having a talk with him but I wasn't packing Oz. No, it was probably best to get out of Dodge. I took a deep breath and thought my next stop should be to get some new pit juice. All the stress of this morning was too much for mine to do it's job.

The real challenge was ahead of me now. How was I going to retrieve the information from his computer? I returned home to two smiling faces. The guys were prancing and dancing with excitement. Annie was walking around with one of Oz's tennis balls in her mouth daring me to throw it. I gave them both a scribble behind their ears and headed for the kitchen. I made a peanut butter and jelly sandwich for me and they each got a chew stick. I hoped that would keep them out of my hair for a while. In my office I took out a USB cord and hooked up Ed's computer to mine. After an hour of trying to extract the information with no luck, I realized this kind of tech stuff was way above my pay grade. I was going to need an expert and there was only one person I could trust with such a task. Vern, besides being good at cutting grass he was also a computer genius.

I called his house and his mother answered, "Vern's gone to the water park with his friends. I can have him call you when he gets home." I thanked her and waited again.

The guys finished their treats and started to run around the house chasing each other. We all needed some exercise so I grabbed their leases and loaded them into the truck and off to the dog park we went.

There were plenty of friends for the guys to play with and I found a shady place to sit and try to make sense of everything.

I closed my eyes and pictured my notes. I should have brought them with me. Ronnie was the one I heard trying to gain access to Ed's house by way of the doggie door and she fought with Donna and was the one arrested. Was she the one who killed Ed? If so, for what reason? Maybe Ronnie had help; Nick, Linda, Donna, Mac, Joy and Mr. James Dean, anyone of them could have been Ronnie's accomplice. Crap, for all I know it might not have been Ronnie at all but one of them who killed Ed. But why? For now Ronnie had moved to the top of my list, she was now "Public Enemy Number One."

I looked up to see the guys running around chasing each other and having a good time. My mind was racing as I started thinking about who other than Ronnie might have had a motive to killed Ed.

There was Nick; both times I had met him he was distant, avoided eye contact and conversation. Then there was the time I caught him and Mr. James Dean together at the store and then at the bank. How did they know each other? I had to figure out how they were connected with this mess. Did they both conspire to murder Ed? But then who was the lady who tried to sell the Trailer Queen?

And what about Linda, Donna and Joy, they each had a motive for killing Ed. I couldn't get Linda to talk to me and possibly Donna wasn't telling me everything. She said she only knew Nick from the bank but was that true? She must've seen Nick when she was over visiting Ed. I'm not quite sure I believed her story or about not coming to the service. Maybe there was more to her story than she was letting on. I wondered if she and Ed had had a fight and in the heat of the moment she killed him. Then as for Joy, she had been all over the emotional scale. First cold toward me and then warm and then cold again. I knew there was more to her story too since she had a long history of hating her brother. Money and hatred could be her motive.

And what about Mr. James Dean? What was his part in this mess? I hadn't liked him from the first time we met at Joy's apartment. I really hadn't given him much thought until I saw him with Nick at the store the other day. Maybe it was the two of them together, but for what possible reason? What an interesting cast of characters they were. Which one or ones had murdered my friend?

I turned my attention to the guys, who were lapping up the water at the community water dish as if there was no tomorrow. It was time to head out and they both had the "I'm ready to go home" look on their faces.

We stopped for ice cream and once inside the house they both crashed on the sofa. Since I hadn't heard from Vern, I decided to call Joy to see if we could talk. I needed to get more information about her boyfriend. Her phone went straight to voicemail so I left her a message. About twenty minutes later she called back and told me her shift ended at midnight. She told me we could meet during her lunch break around eight if I wanted. I agreed which gave me enough time to grab a couple of winks. Since the guys had taken up all the room on the sofa I went into the bedroom.

My phone pinged waking me up. It was Vern saying he was home so I immediately called instead of texting. I explained I need his assistance accessing the information on Ed's hard drive. He agreed to take a look so I fed the guys and rushed right over to his house. It was seven thirty and I had just enough time to be at the truck stop by eight.

The traffic wasn't too bad even though the highway was full of campers trying to get out of the city for a weekend getaway. I pulled into the truck stop and noticed it was packed with customers getting last minute supplies and gas. The restaurant however, was pretty quiet. I walked in and saw Joy was busy waiting on customers so I took a seat by the window and waited. Here I was, waiting again.

She walked over when she saw me, "I'll be on my dinner break in ten minutes and we can go down the street to the burger place and talk."

While I waited, I kept myself entertained by watching the people outside coming and going. Joy walked up to me and said, "Let's go."

"Why did you want to come here?" I asked as we got to the burger place.

She smiled and replied, "I serve the same food all day. Do you really think I want to eat it?"   I nodded and smiled, we placed our order and I paid. We found a booth by the front window.

"So how are you holding up?" I asked, as she took a handful of fries and dipped them in ketchup.

"Okay, I guess."

"I still have the key to Ed's house if you want to go by and check it out again," I volunteered.

After downing another mouthful of fries, she replied, "Not really."

Her demeanor to me was neither cold or warm it was somewhere in the middle. It was like her mind was somewhere else. I could see it was going to be a challenge to get her to open up. I grabbed some fries and thought about what to say next when she offered, "Some lawyer called and said I was to meet with him on Tuesday. Most likely I'm going to get stuck with Ed's burial and legal expenses. It just keeps getting better and better." There was the frustration and anger I had heard before in her voice. She was one hard person to figure out. The last time we had met at the memorial she was crying and appreciative. I couldn't figure out if she was playing me or not?

"What makes you think you're going to have to pay for anything?" I asked.

"Because I'm his only living relative and they're going to want their money, money that I don't have." She stood up at this point and finished with a "why am I putting up with all this crap?" Then she walked out leaving most of her dinner still on the table. By the time I cleaned up our mess and chased after her she was on the street corner lighting up a cigarette.

"Joy, I would like to ask you some questions about your boyfriend."

A car horn sounded and we both looked toward that direction. She halfheartedly waved and then replied, "Why do you want to know about Rex?"

I started to answer when the horn blared two more times. She looked at me and said, "Shit! Gotta go," and stormed off toward the car. She got in the passenger's front seat and I watched as the car drove to the truck stop.

I was just about back to where I had parked my truck when Joy opened the door and got out. Before she slammed it she started yelling and screaming at the person inside. I was unable to see the driver's face because of the tinted windows but I could see the tears on her face. Her eye makeup created black streaks down her cheeks. The conversation was very much one sided and it was Joy doing all the shouting. She gave the driver the finger, slammed the door and stormed inside the truck stop crying.

The car peeled out of the parking lot and I decided to follow. Maybe their argument had been about Ed. Maybe this was the person who helped her with the murder and things were beginning to unravel in paradise. I followed the car back to Joy's apartment complex and watched as Rex, aka Mr. James Dean, got out of the car carrying a red bag with him. It was the same bag I had seen when he visited Nick the other day at the store. I was surprised when he knocked on the door of an apartment on the first floor in a different building of the same complex. A young lady opened the door and gave him a big kiss. She looked really excited to see he had the bag with him. She started to grab for it when he pulled it away. They stood there talking, then she gave him another kiss and they both went inside. Just before the door closed, Rex looked around to make sure no one was watching.

This was the second time I had seen him carrying the same red gym bag. I wondered what was inside. It must be important since he wouldn't let this lady take it from him. He also didn't want to get caught going into the apartment. I wondered if he had seen me follow him? I thought I did a pretty good job of not being noticed but couldn't be certain. It was some pretty suspicious behavior. The one thing I learned this evening was the first name of Joy's so called boyfriend the "James Dean wannabe", was Rex and he was kissing another woman. The plot thickened.

No wonder Joy was crying. This bastard was cheating on her. I considered going over and beating the crap out of him but I thought better of it. I didn't have Oz, and I didn't want to bruise my knuckles. It was his lucky day, besides the last time I saw him at Joy's apartment, he had a gun. A better idea would be to just leave and stop on my way home to get some food. I had only taken two bites while talking to Joy and by the sounds coming from my stomach my tank was still running on empty.

I was almost home when Vern called to tell me he was able to access the information off the hard drive and he downloaded it on some of discs for me. I stopped by his house picked up the equipment and the discs and gave him a fifty for his time. It was well earned. When I got home there were no smiling faces to greet me. I looked out into the backyard and they were chasing each other around and hadn't noticed me come in. I went into the kitchen and peeled a couple hard boiled eggs and quickly ate them so I could see what Vern had discovered. A thunderous crash rocked the house as both Oz and Annie tried to get through the doggie door at the same time. They must have heard me eating. They jumped on the sofa as if to say "You're home, and we missed you so much."

I spent hours watching the DVDs Vern had made for me but there wasn't much to see: Ed working on his car, Ed coming and going, Ed getting out his tools and so on. It was getting late and I was ready to call it quits when my phone pinged. It was a text from Marti, "In Ohio for the night". I called and we talked for about an hour. She told me stories about her flights and a couple of crazy passengers. I told her about taking the guys to the dog park. I felt it best I leave out the part of looking for Ed's camera equipment and meeting with Joy. Marti said she would be home Monday afternoon for two days and she had some good news to share. We said our ""Love yous"," and it was back to the DVDs.

I watched two more and still didn't have my smoking gun. I was getting tired and there were only three more discs to go through but I just couldn't keep my eyes open. I called it a night and went to bed.

I laid there trying to get to sleep, but my mind continuously ran through the information I had gathered. I found Ed's secret video camera and I met with Rod. Then there was my short meeting with Joy her emotions all over the scale. There was the lawyer who had called her and the fight in the parking lot with Rex. Did that have something to do with Ed's murder? For sure something bad had happened between them. He was her so called boyfriend. Did he have another woman on the side? And what was with him always carrying that same red bag? So many unanswered questions! The clock was ticking and time was running out on solving Ed's murder.

Chapter 21

It was dark except for the single light over our heads. The four of us stood there staring at the door. Chuck made the first move and walked up the steps, and I followed close behind. He rapped on the door a couple of times, "It's the police! Open up!"

We waited. The smells from the alley were making me nauseous. Chuck pushed the door open and took the first step inside. The three of us followed with our guns drawn. We heard voices coming from another room and saw a light shining from under the door. At first it was hard to make out what they were saying but as we stepped closer the voices became clearer. Chuck pulled the door open and there stood Ronnie, Linda, Joy, Rex, Mac, Donna and Nick. Mac was the first to turn toward us and the first to notice our drawn guns.

Chuck yelled, "Police! Everyone keep your hands where we can see them!"

Mac was the first to speak, "Hey, it's five thirty in the morning and it's going to be a great day in the city. A perfect day to visit the farmer's market downtown, starts at ten."

Suddenly, I was attacked and before I knew it I was on my back with my arms pinned. I struggled to get free but it was of no use. My attacker was breathing heavily in my face, his rotten breath made me want to puke.

Through the haze of dreaming I realized that hey, wait a minute, I know that smell. "Damn it Oz, get off of me!" I opened my eyes to see his nose inches from mine. He quickly started licking my face before I could protect myself.

The week had been full with both finishing up the state's case and working on Ed's murder. I hadn't had a chance to get the Bird ready for the today's show so I quickly got up, fed the guys, did a quick once over on the Bird with spray wax and wiped down the inside. At least it would presentable. With the chair, blankets for the guys and cooler loaded I still had time for quick a shower. Oz sensed we were going on a road trip and shadowed my every move with Annie close on his heels. We were just about out the door when my phone pinged. It was a text from Marti wishing us luck at the show today.

I texted back, "Will do, love you."

The guys picked their spots in the back seat and we cruised to Betty's Donuts, our pre-car show ritual. When I drove into her parking lot there were three cars from our group already parked out front. It looked as if Betty's had become a popular pre-show meeting place. I walked inside, took a deep breath and inhaled the smell of fried donut heaven. I said hello to everyone and placed my order.

Mike walked over, "I called everyone last night since I knew you would stop here first and told them to meet us here instead of the market on Broadway. This way we could get our sugar and caffeine fix and cruise to the show together."

I nodded and that's when I noticed more of our group pulling into the lot. Mike and I walked outside to greet them. I had my bag full of donuts for the guys and me.

After a short visit with the group I walked over and fed the guys their donuts. A loud musical horn blared as Donavan drove up in his Lincoln. It looked as if he had been working on it all night. There were a lot of whistles and hubba hubba's to go around. He kind of reminded me of Ed, the way he beamed like a proud papa showing off his baby. I bet he'd take home a trophy today. Mike led our caravan to the park. It was really cool to see a line of American Detroit Steel from days gone by cruising in a group. It always got my heart beating a little faster. We received a lot of "Thumbs Up" from people along the way. The park wasn't too far away but by the time we arrived there must have been at least one hundred cars already there. Doug and Doris had come early and had saved us parking spots under some tall shade trees which was great since it was going to be another hot day. I placed my chair in the usual conversation circle behind our cars followed by a quick once over with the spray wax. I mostly had to wipe off the dog slobber which had run down the doors.

Oz took his usual place out front guarding the Bird and Annie found a home on Jane's lap. Annie's eyes were closed and she had a smile of contentment on her face. It always amazed me that collies thought of themselves as lap dogs.

Cars kept arriving as the show got into full swing, and the band had started playing their first session. People were filing into the park to check out the rides and Donavan was busy showing off his baby. He was attracting quite the crowd. You almost couldn't see the car from the amount of people around it. This was his first show and all the car people stopped by to check it out. I walked over to visit but laughed at Donavan, the new car show guy and business man. He took this opportunity to market his pizza parlor and handed out coupons offering a free one topping pizza for today only.

Oz was also getting plenty of attention as people stopped to look at the Bird, but I think was it mostly because of his doggy charm.

People watching was one of my favorite past times. I even liked going out early on Black Friday, not to shop, but just to watch people fight, push, shove and hurry to be the first to get that prize gift for Christmas. But there was no better place to watch people than at a car show. People who walked by these car were mostly reliving their past with friends and family. The amateur and professional photographers took their time making sure to get the perfect shot and one day hoped their photos would be in a gallery, even if it was only on a gallery in their own homes. And then there were the car owners with their chest puffed out, guts sucked in, and egos inflated every time someone asked, "Is this your car? What cool a ride!" And let's not forget the dreamers who hoped one day they'd be part of this exclusive club, the classic car owner club. There was so much entertainment at these shows that people watching never got boring.

When it was time for me to take the guys for a walk I pulled Annie reluctantly off Jane's lap. We walked around looking at the cars and had almost completed the full circuit when Oz's nose picked up that familiar scent. Bill had burgers cooking and Oz was pulling me in that direction. It was a real struggle trying to walk back to the Bird to get money since both Oz and Annie were like a strong head wind pulling me in the opposite direction. I had just gotten my wallet when a load of pizzas showed up. Donavan had had one of his employees make the delivery. "What a great addition Donavan was going to make to our group," I thought to myself.

Donavan walked over to me with two small boxes and pointed to the guys, "I had these specially made for them." I asked him how he knew to make the guys their own pizzas and he just smiled and said, "Bruce." I thanked him and placed each individual ham and cheese pizza on the ground for the guys. Before I could even get a slice from the big people's pizza they had wolfed theirs down and were begging for more. The ladies gave each of them bits and pieces of their crust since it was hard for anyone to resist those sad brown eyes. Even Donavan caved and gave them some of his crust.

When the pizzas were finished Oz resumed his post at the front of the Bird and Annie had found a new lap to lie on. I said to Marsha jokingly, "You know she's not really a lap dog."

Marsha put her finger to her lips saying, "Quiet, she's asleep. She helps me not think about how much I miss Ed."

Dave showed up just in time for pizza and signaled for me to follow him over to his car, "Well, did you find the camera set-up?"

I played it cool not wanting to show my hand, "I haven't had time to go over to Ed's place yet. I've been busy working on cases for the state. I hope I can make it over there Monday."

Dave nodded and proceeded to show me what new features he had added to the engine of his car. When a classic car hood is up and two men are looking under it, all the car buffs have to come over and see what all the excitement is about. As the crowd grew around Dave's car I went back to sit down. Oz was still on guard and two young ladies were giving him their full attention. I saw a familiar smile on his face so I took some photos. It was a Kodak moment.

It was getting late in the day. It was about an hour before the trophy presentations but I was ready for the show to be over. I wanted to get back home and check out the rest of the discs Vern had burned for me. I was hoping to find something that would help me solve Ed's case. I impatiently sat with the others and talked and watched as the lookers started to thin out of the park. The group around Dave's car was gone and even Donavan was now taking a break from showing off his Lincoln. He joined us and we discussed the next show our group wanted to attend. It was in a neighboring state about a two-hour cruise away. The ladies were talking about the possibility of making it an overnight adventure. Fortunately, that would not be an issue for Marti and me since Vern was our house and dog sitter. He'd surely want to spend the night keeping Oz and Annie company. What teenager wouldn't love to get paid watching television, surfing the web, talking to their friends and eating all of our food. Oh, and playing with two fun loving dogs. It was the ideal job.

A voice suddenly broke the calm, "Hey, stop that guy! He just took my wife's purse!" Someone shouted.

I quickly stood up to see what was happening and that's when I saw a man running in our direction. When I took a closer look I recognized it was the same guy Oz had had issues with before. I quickly grabbed my camera and started taking pictures of the purse snatcher running our way. I hoped my pictures could be used as evidence in an arrest. He was being chased by a group of older men who didn't have a chance in hell of catching him. Suddenly, the thief stopped dead in his tracks. I saw a big black and white ball of fur lunged toward him. Oz had gone into attack mode and was on the purse snatcher before he knew what had hit him. Oz had the man pinned to the ground and was bearing his pearly whites. The thief covered his face with his arms fearful that Oz was about to take a bite. The men running after him quickly surrounded him as he was screamed, "Get him off of me! Get him off of me!"

I walked over and joined the circle surrounding the guy and whistled for Oz to come to me. The car owner vigilante group took over from there and made sure the guy didn't get away while they waited for the police. The crowd of men and even women were angry and there were a few kicks here and there and a smack or two across the guy's face. The purse snatcher just laid there in the fetal position trying to protect his body.

The police arrived and took control. Statements were given and the purse was returned to its owner. Oz was the hero of the day and he knew it. He was getting attention from all directions and I knew it was going to be hard living with him now.

I was anxious to get home and check out all the pictures I had taken of Oz stopping the purse snatcher but that would have to wait until after the award ceremony. We walked over as a group to see who the winners would be. Hopeful someone in our group would win. Donavan's name was called and he took home the "People's Choice" award. He beamed from ear to ear. We all snickered under our breaths, "Bet he bought his trophy with free pizzas." Dave won a trophy for "Best Engine". It was a good representation for our group since there were a lot of amazing looking cars.

We waited with anticipation to see who had won the "Best in Show" because this meant bragging rights. It would be water cooler talk Monday at work, kind of like fish stories but for classic cars. There was a hush in the crowd when the announcer walked over and presented the trophy to Oz. Oz! Really? I stood there and said, "What the hell?"

At first there was a look of bewilderment on many faces, but it was soon replaced by laughter and cheers as they all clapped for Oz. The announcer said, "Since Oz caught the car show thief it has been decided among the judges and a few car owners that he should be awarded 'The Best in Show Trophy'." Oz sat there proudly, looking at his prize and gave it an approving nose nuzzle. People one by one walked over and gave Oz a pat on his head and took pictures of him sitting proudly by his prize. Annie walked over and gave him a nose nudge of approval and I just stood there stunned. I bet he was the first dog to have ever won a "Best in Show" at a car show. I took his picture and texted it to Marti. She'd get a good laugh out of this.

We walked back to our cars and Donavan placed the trophy on the Lincoln's hood like a proud papa. He made sure we took plenty of pictures so cell phones and cameras were clicking right and left. I bet the next time we have our meeting at his pizza place the trophy will be on display. It was time to head home. Oz sat in the back next to his trophy while Annie sat up front with me. I looked in the rearview mirror and just chuckled, no one is going to believe this.

The first thing I did when we got home was to place Oz's trophy on the mantel. It would be the topic of conversation at many car shows to come. I wondered if Oz was going to expect me to bring it to all the shows from then on. "It's not going to happen," I said to him as I placed their dinners in front of them.

I made myself a peanut butter and jelly sandwich and settled in to watch the next DVD from Ed's garage. Since it had been a busy day it was hard to keep my eyes open watching these discs. They weren't very entertaining.

I was in the middle of the second disc of the night when Marti called, "So you won a trophy?" She said with shock in her voice.

"No, Oz won a trophy for catching a bad guy," I replied.

There was silence, so I proceeded to tell her the whole story. Once I was done she was laughing so hard I bet tears were running down her cheeks. I knew this would be breakfast conversation with her flight crew. We ended our call with ""Love yous"," and I went back to watching the DVDs. It was getting late so I decided to get up early and finish the last two. I locked up the house and by the time I had gotten in bed the guys were asleep in theirs. My hopes of finding that smoking gun were fading fast.

Chapter 22

It felt good to get up and start my day with an early morning walk. Oz took point leading the way with both Annie and I following. I had tossed and turned all night trying to sleep but my mind worked overtime try to process all the facts I had gathered. The neighborhood was quiet at 5:30 a.m. on a Sunday morning so I was able to be productive in gathering my thoughts. When we returned home the guys emptied their water dish and went outside to sleep in the warm sun. I was almost ready to settle in and finish watching the last of the DVDs.

I walked passed Oz's trophy on the mantle and chuckled to myself. In all my years of going to car shows the only thing I had ever won was a measly plaque. Now we had this giant trophy on display in our house and I would have to explain to our friends it belonged to Oz. It was embarrassing. With the sound of the can opener buzzing the guys came running. I put down their breakfast and watched as they inhaled it. As for me I made my famous oatmeal with walnuts, brown sugar and lots of butter. I called it my breakfast of champions. There were two more discs to watch. I inserted the first DVD in the player and settled on the sofa and hoped I could stay awake. It was no different than the previous ones, very long, very slow and very boring. I had one more chance, I put the last disc in the player.

About ten minutes into watching it I about dropped my half eaten bowl of oatmeal. I couldn't believe what I was seeing! I pressed the rewind button on the remote and replayed the scene over and over. I now had proof of who had taken the Trailer Queen! I had my silver bullet!

I went into my office and made a couple of extra copies of the disc just to be safe. I would give one to Rod along with the camera and computer. I still couldn't believe what I had just seen. I sat there looking off into space. I now had the "who", the "how" and the "where", but the last puzzle piece, the "why" was still missing.

I needed to visit with Lois and Eric to see if they were able to accomplish the task I had asked of them. It was around one in the afternoon when I called and we made plans to meet around four. Lois sounded excited when she told me they had been successful with their assignment.

I had some free hours before meeting with them so I grabbed the guy's leases and yelled out the back door, "Who wants to go to the dog park?" They came running all excited. I was not sure they understood what I said but the sound of their leashes meant something good.

I stood by the dog park gate and watched as they started playing with the other dogs. I found my shady spot under a tree and closed my eyes. My mind was running in high gear as I played over and over what I had seen on the DVD. I was startled when I heard a familiar voice call out my name.

It was Carrie, my next door neighbor and she had her dog Dolly with her. "I didn't know you came over to the dog park," I said.

"Hey, we girls have a life too. You never know what kind of stud you might run into here for the taking unless you get out and see the world," she replied with a chuckle.

She walked over and let Dolly in the play area with the other dogs and Oz ran over to her. He stood by her like a big brother making sure the other dogs didn't move in on her. Carrie joined me in the shade, "So what's going on? When I walked up you looked as if you were in deep thought."

I told her about my friend Ed and how he had been murdered. I explained that I was working on trying to solve the case and put the murderer behind bars.

"Okay detective, you tell me everything you got and let me help. I am pretty good at figuring out who committed the murder on *Matlock* even before he does." I thought it might be helpful to share my findings with Carrie so we spent the next hour working through the details of the case. Every now and then I would look up to check on the guys and Dolly.

"You know on *Matlock* I've discovered that most of the murders have to do with some kind of love triangle. From what you've told me this looks exactly like that," Carrie guessed.

She looked at her watch and got up, "Gotta run, it's time for our daily dose of *Columbo* and *Law and Order*. If you need any more of my advice you know where to reach me," she said with a wink.

I watched her struggle to get Dolly out of the gate since she wasn't quite ready to leave. I smiled and thought she might have a point. It could be a love triangle.

My stomach alarm was going off so I rounded up the guys and we drove straight to Bennie's to get some burgers. At the drive-thru the guys always got a couple of treats from the lady behind the window. The drive home was a blur as I tried to figure what my next move should be. Unlike me, the guys were only interested in the smell of burgers coming from the front seat. By the time we got home the back seat was covered in dog slobber and more dog hair. Sometime tomorrow I'd be making another trip to the car wash. It didn't take them long to wolf down their burgers and turned their attention to mine.

"Sorry guys but you already had yours so back off," I said while taking another bite. They both just sat there with sad looks hoping I would change my mind and give in.

It was time to meet up with Lois and Eric so I left the guys asleep on the sofa. As I backed out of the driveway, Marti sent me a text, "Hope you're having a relaxing day. We just landed and are finished for the day and are going to the beach. Love you."

I texted back, "Yep, crashed on the sofa watching cars going around in circles and taking it easy," I didn't want her to worry.

I decided to drive Marti's car because my truck was so recognizable. This time instead of parking in front of Ed's house I parked in Eric and Lois's driveway. As I shut the car door I could hear what sounded like Ronnie, Linda and Lyle playing out in their backyard. Luckily Nick's truck was not there so and I assumed he was at work.

Lois greeted me at the door and ushered me inside as Eric walked over and shook my hand. We walked into the kitchen where the smell of fresh baked brownies filled the room. "I thought it would be good to have a treat while we tell you about our adventure and findings," Lois said.

I took a seat at the table and couldn't resist one of the brownies. Eric brought over a container of milk, "Can't have a brownie without milk," he said.

I couldn't have agreed more and poured myself a glass and reached for a second one. For the next hour I listened intently as they described their adventure, making it sound like they were spies working for the government. They both smiled the entire time.

Once finished, Lois got up and returned with a stack of mail they had pilfered from Ed's mailbox. Lois made sure to point out one envelope in particular, one she thought was important. I looked at it and put it on top of the other mail. She looked disappointed that I didn't open it in front of them.

Before I knew it I had polished off at least six brownies. Eric changed the subject and wanted me to come out and see his car.

"He has been waiting all day for you to show up so he could show you his prized possession, next to me of course," Lois said as we left the table.

Out in the garage was Eric's pride and joy. It looked as if it had just come off the showroom floor. It was a black, four door Model A. I wasn't sure the year but it looked amazing. For the next hour I listened to him and walked around the car as he told me all about it. Little did he know I was not the car genius he thought I was. He kind of reminded me of Ed.

It was getting late and time for me to get home and feed the guys. I started to leave when I saw Ronnie and her family getting into their car so I quickly ducked back inside. Lois looked out to see what was going on and smiled. She walked outside and waved to them which prompted Ronnie to come over and visit. I heard her asking about the car in the driveway. "Boy, everyone in this neighborhood was always spying on each other," I thought.

"Oh, it's a friend of Eric's. They're out in the garage working on Eric's old car. You know men and their toys," Lois replied.

The two of them talked for a minute or two and then Ronnie returned to her family and Lois returned inside with a big smile on her face, "They're going out for pizza. The coast will be clear soon."

We all watched from the front window as they drove down the street. Once I knew it was safe to leave I headed to my car but before I was to the sidewalk Lois came out and handed me a plate of brownies. Who was I to refuse such a generous offering? I thanked them both for their efforts and told them I would let them know what I found out.

The guys were happy to see me but even more excited when I put their dinner down in front of them. I went next door to Carrie's and delivered a couple of brownies to her and thanked her again for her help during the afternoon. When I got back to my office my phone rang. It was Marti and we talked for about an hour. She told me about how much fun she had at the beach but how it would have been more fun if I had been there. I told her about meeting Carrie at the dog park and sitting around watching DVDS and eating brownies. I stretched the truth but there was no need for her to worry. We said our "Love yous" and promised to text before bed.

I worked putting all my findings from today together while they were fresh in my mind. By the time I was finished it was dark and it was time to call it a night. As I stood, I glanced over the stack of mail Lois had recovered from Ed's mailbox. I still hadn't opened the envelope Lois thought might be important. I decided to open it and see if it might have something to do with Ed's murder. I read it and re-read it before putting it back on the stack. I stood and said to myself, "Sherlock, by Jove I think you just solved this case!"

I gloated to myself the whole time I locked up and got ready for bed. The guys were already asleep on their beds when I settled into mine. I texted Marti, "Good-night," and she texted back, "See you tomorrow."

"Oh my God!" I still could not believe how things had come together. With any luck Ed's murderer would be behind bars by tomorrow night.

Chapter 23

Chuck was the first to go through the door and I followed close behind. The two backup officers were so close that I felt one of them literally breathing down the back of my neck. He needed a breath mint in the worst possible way but since the whole alley stank it was a moot point. The room was dark except for a light illuminating from under a door in back. We walked toward the door and heard voices on the other side. Chuck opened the door and started to say, Police…," when I saw a figure running toward us. I raised my gun and yelled, "Freeze! Police!" but this didn't stop him.

Chuck and I both knew this was our killer and we weren't going to let him get away. I recognized the face and could see his determination. This wasn't going to be an easy arrest. I had seen this look this morning when we interviewed him down at the precinct.

We had a fight on our hands, but Chuck still tried a "Hey buddy, why don't you make it easy on yourself and come quietly?"

The first blow was to my face and then the next to my body. I tried to block each with my arms but didn't have much success. Chuck took a swing at our suspect and accidently knocked my arm causing my gun to drop to the floor. There was a lot of pushing and shoving and I crashed to the floor falling on my gun. It pressed into my back as the killer jumped on top of me.

I screamed, "Get him off of me, get him off me!" He was spitting in my face and then for some strange reason he started licking me and that's when I opened my eyes and yelled, "Damn it, Oz! You've got to stop doing this!"

I thought this might be a good time to stop watching Charles Bronson movies at night and maybe try something a little less intense like the *Three Stooges*. My yelling hadn't persuaded Oz to get off my chest and now Annie had my right arm pinned to the bed. There was a sharp pain resonating in my back. I looked into their eyes and said, "You know guys, you're not as dainty as you think you are," and with that I pushed them aside. I rolled over to find the television remote pressing against my back.

A quick glance at the clock revealed 5:00 a.m. and it was still dark out. Crap! I was wide awake now and my mind was busy mulling over the results of the information I had gathered. I began sorting out my day and looking forward to Marti to being home this afternoon. Rod, however was first on my list and I wanted to meet with him early. I hoped it would be enough to put Ed's killer behind bars.

I fed the guys and reviewed my notes one more time. It was only 6:00 a.m. and I reached for my cell phone to call

Rod but thought better of it. For the next twenty minutes I tried concentrating on the state's case but after reading the same words over and over I knew I needed to burn off some of this pent-up stress. I grabbed the guy's leases and out we went. The sun had just crested the mountains and was beginning to light up the city. I watched as my neighbors got into their cars and headed out for another week of the eight to five grind. I figured our walk must have been about four miles long and as soon as we got home we all went straight for water. I grabbed a bottle of water and headed to my office.

I was so focused on reviewing my notes that when my phone rang I nearly jumped out of my seat. It was Lucy from the state letting me know they had a couple more cases for me. I told her I would be in the following day to pick them up. I looked at the clock and figured I had waited long enough to call Rod. As the phone rang I hoped he would be in his office by now. I was in luck! I told him I that had a present for him and we planned to meet at Ed's around noon.

He asked, "So what kind of present?"

I just replied, "It's a surprise. You'll love it."

"Okay hot shot, I'll be there."

I made sure I had my mini video camera's battery charged. I wanted to make a video of Ed's antique oil can collection. Hopefully whoever inherited the estate would allow me to purchase the collection. I would show them my video when we meet tomorrow at the lawyer's office to show them what I was interested in. The collection would look great on a wall in my office. My stomach grumbled and reminded me it was time for breakfast. I was too anxious to make something so I decided to try one of Marti's diet shakes. Yuck! I wouldn't ever do that again. I couldn't get the funky after taste out of my mouth.

I loaded the guys in the truck along with my mini video camera, Ed's camera equipment, the discs, and the mail Lois and Eric had collected. We pulled up in front of Ed's house and sadness overwhelmed me again. This would most likely be my last visit here since the reading of Ed's will would be tomorrow. I was sure the new owners wouldn't like me coming and going as I pleased. As we got out of the truck I made sure to slam the truck door hard. I wanted Ronnie to hear and see my truck parked out front. I needed her to be here when Rod arrived.

I opened the front door and stood there for a moment looking down at where I had found Ed's body. "What a tragedy," I thought to myself. I then unbolted the doggie door and the guys raced out into the backyard. I placed the mail on the table in plain sight, making sure the official looking envelope was on top. I had just started filming the antique oil can collection in the garage when I heard Ronnie walking through the front door.

"Hey, I just thought I would stop by and say I'm sorry for the way I acted the other day. It was very rude of me. Please accept my apology."

I walked back into the kitchen and set my camera on the kitchen counter and before I could reply she walked over to the mail on the table. She stared at the official looking envelope on top. After what I had read inside I knew this was what she had been looking for all the time. Luckily I had found it first. Looking directly into her eyes I replied, "Not a problem."

"Have the police told you anything more about Ed's murder?" she asked.

"No, but I get the feeling they are close to making an arrest. I think it may be very soon."

These words caused her to sink into a chair at the dining room table. She was now within arm's reach of the mail. I could see the panic look on her face when she saw the one on top had been opened. She picked up the entire stack and started flipping through the envelopes.

"Are you looking for something?" I asked.

She replied nervously, "No, just being nosey I guess." She then put the stack of mail back on the table.

We sat there not saying a word. She had a blank look on her face and just starred at the walls. I walked over to the table and picked up the large envelope.

"I bet this is what you were looking for when you were going through all of Ed's mail."

Her eyes widened showing fear that I had found it before her. She quickly reached for it but before she could grab it I pulled it away. "I'm saving this for the police and they're going to be very interested about the contents."

Her body began to shake and her face went white and tears flowed freely down her cheeks. I took the envelope with me as I got her a glass of water and a towel to wipe her eyes. After a couple of sips she looked at me and completely lost it. She became hysterical and her body violently shook. She sobbed uncontrollably. I just sat and waited. I was certainly not feeling any sympathy for her today. After a couple of minutes, she regained her composure and started to talk.

"Yes, I was the one trying to find that letter. I knew Ed had sent off a request for some information and I wanted to intercept it before anyone else got ahold of it. I wanted to read it before anyone else did. It all started a long time ago. You see, Nick and I were going through tough times. One night we got into a big fight. He packed a bag and moved in with one of his buddies just to get away from me. I was so angry and I hated him for leaving. I was depressed so a few of my girlfriends decided I needed time to forget about him and have some fun. One night we went on a bar stroll downtown."

"Let me guess, that's when you hooked up with Ed?" The look on her face told me I was right.

"Yes, how did you know?" She asked in disbelief.

"I put two and two together and got four."

She gave me a puzzled look and continued, "Yes, I met Ed at the bar in one of the downtown hotels. He was by himself sitting there drinking a beer watching some crazy car race on the television. My girlfriends wanted to go somewhere else but I had had enough socializing, I just wanted to be alone and give myself a pity party. I sat at the bar and ordered a gin and tonic. I was so frustrated with my life that I began to cry. The next thing I knew I had another drink in front of me. The bartender indicated it was from the man sitting a couple stools down. I was lonely and depressed and wanted someone to talk to so I moved over next to him. For the next couple of hours I did most of the talking and he sat there and listened." Ronnie got up and went into the kitchen and got another glass of water.

I waited for her to continue her story. She took a deep breath, "It was getting late and the bar was closing. Ed walked me out into the lobby and before I knew it he kissed me on the lips. The kiss melted me and I wrapped my arms around his neck and pulled him in close for another. We stood there in the middle of the hotel lobby kissing like a pair of teenagers. I didn't want to let go of him. He was giving me the comfort I needed so badly. Like a gentleman he offered to take me home but I suggested we get a room. I needed someone close to me that night. I needed to feel loved again. After that magical night we started secretly seeing each other. I was giddy that I had a man in my life that loved me. Our time together was amazing but there was a problem."

I said, "I know. You were still married to Nick, right?"

She looked at me confused, how did you know." she asked.

"It's public record, remember I am an investigator. I bet you never told Ed you were married."

"No, I didn't tell him. I was so venerable that I couldn't control my emotions or tell him. Nick and I hardly talked or saw each other after our fight and Ed made me feel special. He gave me what I needed at the time. I suppose deep down I was hoping being with Ed would make Nick jealous and he would want me back. Ed would book a hotel suite for long weekends together. We would go to the movies and dinner and he treated me like a queen.

After we made love I would fall asleep in his arms knowing he loved me. I thought I loved him, too. I even thought about divorcing Nick and moving in with Ed but when it came right down to it, I couldn't. I realized I was still in love with Nick so I broke it off with Ed. I started doing whatever I could to get Nick back into my life."

"When did you realize you were pregnant?" I asked. She replied with that "deer in the headlights" look.

"It was about three months after I moved back in with Nick. I was so scared. I started having nightmares that Ed was the father of my child. I never said anything to Nick about my time with Ed. I knew if I did I would lose him forever. I've been keeping this secret inside of me all this time and it's been tearing me up. I hoped Lyle was Nick's child but deep down inside I felt he was actually Ed's. When he was born Nick and I were happy. He was so happy to have a son. I just couldn't tell him he might not be the father and break up our then happy family." She took a deep breath. I could tell this was the first time she had ever told anyone about her affair with Ed.

"If you were unsure who the father was why not have a DNA test to find out?"

"I really never thought about it or maybe I was afraid Nick might find out. I didn't want to be one of those single moms try to make a living and raise my son alone."

"So what made you decide to move next door to Ed?" I asked. "Why would you put your family into that situation?"

"After Lyle was born, Nick and I decided it was time to move out of our apartment and buy a house. We were even thinking about having another child so we started house hunting. One day I saw the house next door was on the market. It was my dream home and Nick liked it too. We bought it and the first day we started moving in was when I saw Ed walking out of his front door. I couldn't believe it, you see when we had our affair he had never told or showed me where he lived. This was a total surprise. We both stood there in total shock staring at each other. Since the purchase had gone through it was too late to back out of the sale. We now owned our home. I wished I'd had never seen it! We were happy when we lived in the apartment and we should have stayed there. What a frick'n nightmare this has been."

She stopped talking and the house went silent. I got up to check on the guys who were asleep in the sun. "I bet Ed was shocked to have you move in next door?" I said returning to the kitchen table.

She looked around the room and said, "Yes, there was some tension between us at first but when he saw Lyle things seemed to change and we became good friends."

"So you never told Ed there was a possibility that Lyle was his child?" I asked.

"No, I never told him. There were many times I wanted to but I didn't want to break up my marriage. As time passed Lyle and Ed became buddies. He would come over and play with Ed and he even called him "Uncle Ed." There were even times when Ed would offer to watch him when Nick and I would go out."

I looked at her, "That explains the basket of toys I found in the garage along with the picture Ed had of the two of them on his desk at work. So if you were such good friends why were you always spying on him?"

Ronnie took a deep breath, "At first, Nick and I were in a good place in our marriage and we were happy but things started to change. We started to have money problems. Nick said that the store was struggling due to lack of business and so to keep his job he had to take a pay cut. This put a financial strain on us. There were times when we thought we were going to lose our house. Nick even took a second part time job. I offered to get a job but he wouldn't hear of it. I would look over the fence and was jealous of Ed's easy going life and stability. At one point I started fantasizing about rekindling our relationship but then he started dating Linda. I had a real hard time with her always coming over here and I didn't want them dating at all. I tried a couple of times to break them up but with no luck. I was so relieved when Linda came crying to me one afternoon and told me Ed had broken off their relationship."

"So what changed between you and Ed that made you want to bring up the subject that Lyle was his child?" I asked.

"It was when Ed started dating that other woman. I knew things were getting serious between the two of them. I could hear them laughing and kissing in the back yard and I was so jealous. My marriage was in shambles and I wanted what she had, Ed. One night I snapped and got into a big fight with them. The police were called and I was arrested. From that time on I was required to keep my distance because of the restraining order. One night I overheard them talking about getting married and moving away together. If they did that then Ed wouldn't be able to see Lyle and the possibility of us hooking up again would be gone. I was also tired of carrying this secret alone. Money was getting tighter and tighter for us and my sister was spending most of her time living with us. Nick and I were constantly fighting, and my life was a mess."

After catching her breath, she continued, " One day I approached Ed about Lyle being his son, and he was shocked. He became very upset with me and he paced back and forth yelling at me for not telling him sooner.

After a few minutes he calmed down but then he kicked me out of his house and slammed the door behind me. Over the next couple of days I tried to reason with him but he wouldn't even talk to me."

How long ago was this"? I asked.

"It was a couple of weeks prior of his death. He told me that he had sent off a DNA test to make sure Lyle was truly his son. He had taken a swab from Lyle one day when he came over to play. The results hadn't come back before he was murdered and yes, I'm the one who has been bringing in his mail. I was waiting for the results and wanted to destroy them before anyone else had a chance to find out."

There was a break in her story when a booming voice broke the quiet and startled us both. "You stinkin' bitch. I knew something was up with the two of you!" Nick shouted.

We turned and saw him standing in the hallway.

"Nick, how long have you been standing there?" Ronnie asked with terror in her voice.

"Long enough to hear it all," and with that he pointed his gun at her. "I knew something funny was going on after you got into that big fight with Ed's bitch and I had to bail your sorry ass out of jail. After that night I figured it out.

You were always looking out our living room window and you were over here more than you were at home. And my darling, soon to be ex-wife, it's hard to keep secrets when you talk in your sleep. I bet while I was working long hours at two jobs you were over here screwing the guy! Well you stupid bitch, you no longer have your sugar daddy."

"No! Nick, it wasn't like that. I never had sex with him after that time...." her voice trailed off.

"I knew something was up. There were the times when I wanted sex, but you were too tired or just not in the mood. You must have been worn out from being with your sugar daddy all afternoon," Nick yelled at Ronnie as she sat there quivering.

She was visibly shaken. Tears were running down her face and her body was trembling uncontrollably. I prayed Rod would come walking through the door any moment because this was getting way out of hand. IT wasn't even close to how I had planned this meeting. It was getting very ugly and I wanted out.

Just then my phone rang and the house became strangely quiet and they both looked at me. It sent shivers down my back. By the ring tone I knew it was Marti and I also knew it would be in my best interest not to answer it. I let it go to voice mail and took a deep breath.

Nick continued to scream at Ronnie. I started to stand when Nick shouted, "Where the hell do you think you're going? Just sit your ass back in that seat and shut up." I sat back in the chair and watched this family drama unfold before my eyes. My phone rang again with Marti's three blind mice ringtone. I just looked at both of them and let it continue to ring.

Nick shoved the gun in my face. His hand was shaking and sweat covered his face. His eyes had that same glassed over look like the first day we met. "Give me your goddamn phone." I took it out of my pocket slowly, being careful not to make any sudden moves and handed it to him as if I was handing him the butt of a gun. My hand was shaking like crazy and I almost dropped it. He threw it on the floor and stomped the hell out of it.

"Hey, I just got that! I have almost two more years before it's paid off," then realized I should have kept my mouth shut.

Nick turned back to me, "You son of a bitch! You just couldn't leave things alone. You had to keep coming around and asking questions. I saw you across the street talking to that nosey lady who is always spying out her window. You even came to the store and tried to talk to me like we were best buddies," he snapped at me.

He looked over at Ronnie, "Look at me you stupid bitch! I bet every time this guy was here you came over, right? Were you screwing him, too?"

All I could her was Ronnie's sobs as Nick stood there silently waiting for her to answer. Out of the corner of my eye I saw my camera on the counter. The red light was still on. I must have forgotten to turn it off when Ronnie came in the house. I hoped the battery didn't run out soon as it was recording this confrontation. It might end up being my dying declaration if the police found it before Nick saw it.

"So, big sister, were you screwing Ed while I was dating him?" Linda shouted as she barged into the room. "Oh Linda, no!" Ronnie shouted in disbelief when she heard her sister's voice. Linda wrapped her arms around Nick and gave him a kiss on the cheek. "Well, surprise I was screwing your husband, too. How do you like that?" "Could things get any worse?" I thought to myself. I couldn't believe what I was hearing. This was one really messed up family. Where in the hell was Rod?

"So, Honey, what should we do with these two? I'm sure they've figured out our little secret," Linda asked Nick.

Ronnie looked at both of them in total shock. She had no idea that her sister had been sleeping with her husband. Linda looked back at her and gave her a little girl cute look and said, "Nick needed someone to love and I filled the void. Besides, he said I was a better lover."

"Shut up and let me think! This has gotten all messed up!" Nick yelled. "This has gotten way out of hand. What a goddamn mess. Shit, it was never meant to go this far. "

I decided there was no point sitting here watching this daytime soap opera unfold before my eyes without trying to get some evidence on tape. I needed to know about Ed. "So Nick, why did you kill Ed?"

At first he looked puzzled and my voice brought him out of his trance. "Shut up before I do something you're going to regret." He pointed the gun again in my direction.

For some reason I didn't follow his advice, "So when did you decide to confront Ed?"

"That son of a bitch laughed at me when I told him I knew Lyle was his son. I told him that he owed me back child support and I was going to get the money one way or another."

"Let me guess, Linda became your partner in crime because she was pissed off at him too for dumping her. I bet she was pissed that Ed liked Ronnie better than her," I said adding fuel to the fire to get a confession.

That's when I saw the true hatred in Linda's eyes. "That bastard didn't dump me! I dumped him! One day when

Nick and I were in bed he told me about what Ronnie had done. I wanted both of them to pay! And now look what happened. Ed paid with his life," she said with a haunting laugh. "Now it's my big sister's turn to pay! Hey, Sis, I now know why you didn't like me dating Ed. Because you wanted him all to yourself you stupid little bitch. Well, pretty soon you'll have your wish and the two of you will be together forever." Linda's laugh sent chills down my back. "Boy did he pay. Come on Nicky, let's hurry up and get rid of these two. All this talk about killing them is making me horny."

"Linda was freaking nuts! No wonder Ed broke it off," I thought to myself. She was getting out of control and the thought that I might not ever see Marti again terrified me. Both Nick and especially Linda had a few screws loose. Since they killed Ed then what were two more bodies? It was not looking good for yours truly. I glanced at my camera and it was still recording. I had to get a confession before it was too late.

"Let me see if I get this straight. Ed was not going to pay you any money and so you killed him and stole his Caddy. How am I doing so far?"

"You think you're so damn smart jackass, but you've only got it half right. After I found out about him and my wife I came over and told him I was taking his car as collateral until he paid me the back child support he owed. I started to walk into the garage and he took a swing at me. I swung back and knocked him flat on the ground. I opened the garage door and started for the car when I heard the gunshot. I turned and Linda was there with a gun in her hand. Smoke coming out of the barrel and she had a big smile on her face. Ed just laid there in a puddle of blood. Hell, she's the one who pulled the trigger."

"I told you I would make him pay," she said smugly. "Come on Nick! Give me the gun. If you can't do it I will!"

I had the whole picture now. Poor Ronnie was sitting there in shock. She kept repeating, "Oh, no! God no!"

"Let me guess. So after Linda shot Ed, you both rummaged through the house looking for any valuables. You got the title to the car and just left Ed in the hallway to die. Then you stole his Caddy," I said.

"Well, jackass you figured it out. Too bad you're not going to be able to tell anyone," Nick snapped. "Now I just have to figure out how to make this look like a lover's quarrel. Then police won't need to look any further. Yea, we'll make it look like it was you who killed Ed. Then you and Ronnie had a lover's quarrel and you killed her. Out of guilt you then took your own life." I couldn't believe what I was hearing. He was going to try to pin this on me? "What an asshole," I thought.

Linda started goading Nick on, "Kill them, kill them, hurry up and kill them!"

I began to see my life flash before my eyes as Ronnie kept shouting, "No Nick! What are you doing? Stop this madness and put the gun down." All this yelling had alerted Annie. She suddenly appeared from the backyard and started growling at Nick. "Get away you stupid mutt! All you ever did was bark and keep me from napping. Maybe I should put a bullet in you too," he threatened as he tried to kick her.

She moved out of his way but kept on barking. On the second try Nick connected and kicked hard into her side. She let out a loud scream of pain and collapsed to the floor. Nick pointed the gun at her and I thought to myself, "Nick you stupid fool, you just made a huge mistake."

A loud crash came from the kitchen and before Nick knew what had hit him there was eighty plus pounds of Oz all over him. He launched himself so violently on to Nick his teeth found their way clear to bone. Nick struggled to free himself from Oz's grip, but his teeth continued to rip into Nick's flesh. There was blood everywhere. Nick could no longer hold onto to the gun and it dropped to the floor. Linda and Ronnie watched in horror as Oz kept up his attack. Nick tried with all his strength to get Oz off of him but Oz was having no part of it.

Oz wrestled a screaming Nick to the ground and was about to sink his teeth into his throat. "Get him off, get him off of me! Someone do something! Get this goddamn mutt off of me!"

I watched Nick get what he deserved. As Oz went for his throat I knew he had had enough. I tried to get Oz to let go, but he was on a mission. As I tried to pull him off I saw Linda standing there with the gun in her hand. She pointed it at Ronnie, then me, then Oz and then back at me.

"You bastard! You messed up everything and now you're going to pay just like Ed did. Get that goddamn dog off Nick or I'll kill him and you both!"

An ear shattering bang filled the room. We jumped as blood spewed from Linda's mouth. Her eyes glassed over and her body crashed to the floor. Rod stood there, his gun smoking. He had an unsettled smile on his face.

"Some party you're having," he said.

Ronnie was dumbstruck and had yet to realize what had just happened. I sat down as my legs turned to rubber. Nick was on the floor bleeding and afraid to move for fear Oz would tighten his grip. Linda's body lay motionless next to him. Dead. I closed my eyes not wanting to believe the horror of what had just happened. My head was spinning.

It took me a while before I realized Rod was talking to me. He grabbed my arm and escorted me out of the room and onto the patio. Oz released his grip on Nick, he and Annie followed us outside. I looked back to see two police officers guarding Nick and Ronnie. I wondered where they had come from.

I sat down and sucked in some air to get focused. Both of the guys were by my side, Oz not letting anyone get near me. He was on guard. Rod returned with some water. "You okay buddy? Take a minute to catch your breath and then tell me what the hell just happened in there."

I just looked at him not sure where to start. I had remembered the video camera. I told him about it and that it had been running during the entire time. He smiled and walked into the house to retrieve it. He returned with the camera the red light was still on. "Could you just give me a quick rundown in your own words?"

I told him everything I could remember. I explained how it had all started last year. Ed was so concerned about protecting the Trailer Queen that he set up a computer to record any and all of the activity in the garage. On one Disc was the video of who drove off with the Queen. Boy, I could have sworn it was Ronnie, but it turned out to be Linda. They looked so much alike from a distance. I figured it was Ronnie under the big garden hat and the large sunglasses. I really needed to brush up on my investigative skills. I told Rod he would find the disc and equipment out in my truck. He sent an officer out to retrieve the evidence.

He had me repeat my story one more time and then told me to go home. As I got up to leave he said he would be in touch. It took a couple of steps before I was able to steady my legs enough to walk without shaking.

I left through the side gate since the police had roped off the house. Oz and Annie were both by my side. Oz was on full alert ready to pounce again at a moment's notice if he felt either one of us were in any danger. I tried to miss all the police and their activity, but there were a lot of them. It was like busy bees buzzing around a hive. I noticed Ronnie was sitting on the back of an ambulance being attended to by a medic. I walked over and gave her a pat on the shoulder.

"Just so you know, Ed was not Lyle's father. The test results proved it."

She looked up at me and started crying as I walked to my truck. Lois and Eric were standing out in their front yard.

Eric said, "This is a three ring circus. It's better than a *Blue Bloods* episode on television. Are you alright?"

Lois looked up at me and asked, "How did we do?"

I just halfheartedly smiled and replied, "You guys did great! You helped catch the killers."

The guys and I walked to the truck and just sat there for a while watching the circus continue to unfold. There were police cars, ambulances and firetrucks lining the street all with their lights flashing.

I looked in the rearview mirror and I let my tears flow. "Rest in peace my friend, rest in peace." I was suddenly exhausted.

The drive home was a blur. I think I fed the guys and then crashed on the sofa. My mind was trying to make sense of what had just happened. Marti came through the front door and slammed it behind her. "Thanks for picking me up like you were supposed to," she said annoyed.

I thought to myself, "Oh crap! How am I going to explain this to her?" I started to speak but she took one look into my eyes and saw my pain. She knew something was wrong. She sat down next to me and put her arms around me. All four of us sat there in silence. I hugged her tightly not wanting to let her go and just closed my eyes and tried to get my body to relax.

A loud knock at the front door jolted us. The guys immediately went into attack mode and charged the door. I opened the door and there stood Rod.

"I thought I would stop by and check up on you. Hey there, how's it going Marti?"

She looked at him and replied, "You tell me!"

I invited him in and the two of us explained to Marti what had happened. She sat there in horror. Her head kept moving back and forth from Rod to me as we told our stories. Her hands gripped my arm so hard it hurt.

Rod ended with, "It was one crazy afternoon. Nick has been screaming lawsuit saying it was all Linda's idea, however, when we showed him the video he shut up and asked for a lawyer."

I said, "I bet it's still a mess at the house."

He replied, "Yes, the neighborhood won't be the same for quite a while."

Rod stood, "I better get back to work." He started out the front door and turned to Marti, "Look after this guy. He's had a pretty rough day." He then patted Oz on the head, "You would make one heck of a police dog."

Marti nodded and then put her arms around me. "You bet I'll take good care of him but you can't have Oz! He's our protector and hero."

Rod was almost to his car when I asked him, "I was expecting you to meet me at Ed's, but why the back up? I mean how did you know to bring extra help?"

He replied "It wasn't me. I was just as shocked to see them there as you were. It was your guardian angels or should I say the nosey neighbors across the street that called 911. They saw the whole thing unfold through their window and when Nick and Linda showed up they knew there was going to be trouble, so they called."

I just chuckled, "They are quite the characters, I must admit. I'll take them out to dinner one of these nights to say thanks."

Rod finished by saying, "Be at my office at eight in the morning."

I walked back inside and Marti walked over and she hugged me tight.

I looked into her eyes and said, "I love you more than you will ever know."

She smiled, "I love you more than you will ever know."

Chapter 24

The guys and I were up early and out for our morning walk. After the events of yesterday I needed some time to clear my mind and burn off some of the calories from last night's dinner. Marti had ordered in bar-b-que, and I stuffed myself. I started to question myself as to why I thought it was Ronnie who had murdered Ed. I was surprised when it actually turned out to be Nick and Linda. I chuckled as I thought, "Boy, that's one messed up family!" I wondered what was going to happen to Ronnie. Her husband would most likely spend the rest of his life behind bars for being involved with the murder and her sister was dead.

It felt as if we had walked at least five miles by the time we returned home. As soon as I opened the front door the guys with their tongues hanging out rushed over and emptied their water dish. The smell of bacon and blueberry pancakes filled the house. There stood Marti with just an apron on flipping pancakes. I walked over and gave her a hug and kiss, "So what is the special occasion?"

"I just thought for once in this decade I would make you breakfast," she replied then shoved a piece of bacon in my mouth.

Marti had the guys' breakfast ready for them and she added a couple of pancakes in each of their dishes. Seeing the pancakes and their food dishes full, they went straight to scarfing down their breakfast.

"Go take a hot shower and I'll have breakfast on the table when you get back," she said. I kissed her again and went to take my shower.

While I was in the shower Marti had gotten dressed and was waiting for me at the patio table. She had prepared: bacon, pancakes, eggs and fried potatoes.

I took my first bite of pancake and said with a cheesy grin, "When you go to this much trouble to cook you usually want something."

She replied, "Well, I thought if it was okay with you, I'd go with you to the police station."

She gave me her sad puppy dog look, like the one the guys always gave me when they begged for snacks. How could I resist? Besides I could use the moral support. We finished breakfast, gave the guys goodbye hugs and headed out to meet with Rod.

This was going to be a first for me, having to give an official statement to the police. The traffic was bumper to bumper and moving at a snail's pace. I now wished Rod had asked me to come down to the station around ten instead of eight. The station was located in the center of town in the city hall building. I said to Marti, "Glad I don't have to drive this every day." She agreed.

While we were stuck in traffic we listened to the radio news. They were reporting about the arrests in Ed's murder case and how the police had solved the case. We both laughed. I circled the downtown three times before I was able to find a parking spot and it still ended up being five blocks away from city hall.

A police officer from the front desk escorted us to Rod's office. Rod explained to Marti she wouldn't be able join us in the interview but she could wait in his office if she liked.

She was disappointed but understood, "I'll go for a walk but please call me when you guys finish doing your thing."

Rod directed me to a small conference room down the hall from his office where three other people were waiting for us. He made the introductions and then started the video recording from yesterday. We all watched the whole drama unfold. It was my first time watching the video and I found it to be very unnerving. My stomach was doing flip flops as I watched. I shouldn't have stuffed myself with pancakes and bacon this morning. I sat reliving the horror as the scene unfolded before my eyes. I had relived the events in my mind many times but seeing the video was almost too much for me to handle. Once the video was over Rod and the three other police officers looked at me and smiled.

I must've had a puzzled look on my face because Rod's superior, Captain Ross, explained, "This is the first time we have all the evidence needed on a video card for a clear conviction. I just have one question. What prompted you to bring your video camera in the first place?"

"I took my camera to video tape Ed's antique oil can collection. I was interested in purchasing the collection if it went up for sale. I also figured since the reading of the will would be later today it was my last chance to have access to Ed's home."

Captain Ross continued, "Rod told me you're an independent investigator for the State Insurance Department. After solving this case for us I think you should consider working for the police department, we could use a good investigator. From the information Rod had given us we were actually looking in the wrong direction. We were thinking the victim's sister Joy and her boyfriend were the murderers. We hadn't even considered the neighbors as suspects."

I smiled, thanked him for the job offer and declined, "No thanks! Are you nuts? After yesterday, the kind of stuff you guys investigate is way too dangerous for me. I'll stick to the fraud cases. Besides, I don't like guns and that's why I pack Oz with me."

Captain Ross stood, shook my hand and thanked me again before walking out of the room. This left me in the room with Rod and the other two officers. Rod explained to me that Nick had confessed and that they considered this case to be closed. He went on to say that Nick told them that his family was having financial trouble because he was addicted to cocaine. He said nobody in the family knew. He had kept this secret from everyone, especially Ronnie. His supplier was Rex, Joy's boyfriend. Rod went on to tell me the narcotics squad had gone to arrest him but he was nowhere to be found but they were confident that they'd eventually catch up with him.

I spent the next couple of hours retelling my story and signing papers. I was finished for now but would probably have to testify if this case ever went to court. However, Rod and the other two officers didn't think it would go to trial.

Rod walked me out of the building, "I owe you lunch one of these days for solving the case but first let me give you some advice. Next time you find a body, leave the investigating to the pros. You almost got yourself killed."

"No problemo. Once was enough for me," I assured him.

Just then a beautiful lady wrapped her arm around mine. "Hey sailor, going my way?" she asked and followed the question with a kiss.

Rod smiled and said, "Hey, Marti do you think I should use your husband's investigative skills on my next case?"

She just chucked and replied, "Once is enough. No more murder cases for him."

"Okay, if you insist. See you love birds later," and with that Rod walked back inside the building.

As we started toward the truck Marti asked if we could go somewhere to talk. We went to the coffee shop around the corner and I found a table by the front window and waited for Marti to get her coffee. When she joined me she had a big smile on her face and handed me a bag. "I got you a present," she said and then took a sip.

I looked into the bag and saw a new cell phone. "I always want to be able to get ahold of you," she said as a loving smile crossed her face.

I took the bright red neon covered phone out of the bag and turned it on. It immediately started pinging as messages began coming in. We spent the next hour reading texts and replying. They were mostly from our car group. They were all asking for details about what had happened. After texting my story a couple times it would be easier to tell it to the whole group at once. I sent out a community text to everyone in our little car group to meet us at Donavan's around six this evening to get the whole story. Within seconds my phone lit up with a barrage of text replying in one form or another they will be there.

As we walked to the truck, Marti's arm in mine, she whispered in my ear, "Hey stud do we have any plans for the rest of the week?"

"No, nothing pressing at this time. What do you have in mind?"

"While you were in the station, I made some calls. I'm all yours for the rest of the week or should I say you're all mine."

I started to say something when she put her finger to my lips. "I don't have to be to work until a week from Wednesday and so we're going on a road trip."

"A road trip?" I said with a puzzled look on my face.

"Yes, a road trip. You know me and how I hate to fly," she said laughing.

We both started to laugh and I asked, "What about the guys? Are they going with us?"

She shook her head no, "I've already made arrangements for Vern to keep them company."

"So, when do we leave?" I asked.

"First thing in the morning. Just point the truck east and I will be the navigator."

We had some time before meeting with Ed's lawyer for the reading of his will. We stopped by the flower shop and picked up a bouquet of flowers and drove to Ed's. The police tape around his house was still up warning everyone to stay away. When Marti got out of the truck she stopped and stared at his house for a moment. I grabbed her hand and we walked across the street to visit with my so called guardian angels. We started up their driveway and the front door opened and there stood Lois and Eric. I smiled, handed Lois the flowers and she gave me a great big hug. I introduced Marti to them and they invited us inside. We listened to Lois as she told us their side of the story. I invited them for pizza and to tell our car group all about it. They accepted our invitation and Eric was especially excited when I told him to bring his Model A.

After leaving their home with a plate full of her sugar cookies, we had just enough time to get a quick bite before meeting with the lawyer. We stopped at a place called U-Stackum Burgers and Brew. We liked going there because you got to design your own burger. I had a double bacon cheeseburger with mayo, tomato and lettuce. I also ordered a large side of onion rings, knowing from past experience I would just get a couple and Marti would eat the rest. Marti ordered a turkey club and a side salad. While waiting for our food I tried to use my super investigative skills to pry information out of Marti about our upcoming road trip, but with zero success. On one of the televisions the local news station was streaming at the bottom of the screen how the murderer had been killed and an accomplice arrested. The waitress brought our lunches and offered her two cents, "What a mess. I heard some private investigator and his dog solved the crime not the police. I bet the cops were too busy eating donuts and drinking coffee."

Marti took an onion ring and said, "You and Oz are famous. Now I'll have two men in the house with big egos."

I just smiled, "What's the problem? You knew that when you married us."

We arrived at the lawyer's office and were seated inside a luxurious conference room. Joy was already there and looked very nervous. She and Marti hugged and cried together. I asked if she was okay and she looked at me and replied, "No."

The reading of the will was short and sweet. It stated that Marti and I were to look after and take care of Annie. Joy was to receive the house along with what was left of two hundred thousand dollars after the burial, legal fees and taxes were paid. She just sat there staring out into space. I had a feeling she was having a hard time comprehending what had just happened. She looked at the attorney and said, "So I don't have to pay anything for the funeral? It's all taken care of, and I get the house and the money?"

The attorney replied, "That is correct. I just have some papers for you to sign and you're good to go."

Marti and I started to walk out of the office when I turned, "What about Ed's Trailer Queen, I mean his Caddy? He was so proud of it and I didn't hear mention of it in the will."

"Ah, yes, the caddy. The car is to be given to the local children's hospital and raffled off. The monies will be used to help the children."

We all smiled. That was perfect. Some car buff would continue to give the Trailer Queen the life it deserved. We invited Joy to dinner with the gang and she told us that she would think about it. I told her I would be interested in purchasing Ed's antique oil can collection. She said she would get back to me about it once her head cleared.

We had just gotten to the truck when Joy came running, "I thought about it and for helping me and Ed, the collection is yours."

I hugged and thanked her. We made tentative arrangements for me to pick them up after I got back from our trip.

We stopped by the house to feed the guys and pick up the Bird. When I backed out of the garage Marti had changed clothes and walked out wearing a sexy summer dress.

"Hey, how about we skip dinner and go back inside," I said whistling at her.

"There will be time for that later," she said as she got into the car.

As usual the traffic was hell but we listened to the oldies on the radio and sang along with our favorites.

Donavan's lot was full of classic cars and sure enough there was Eric's Model A. All the car buffs were standing around oohing and awing. Once we parked Marti walked over to where the ladies were talking. I joined the men and they shook my hand and patted me on the back and congratulated me for solving the case.

Bruce said, "This old dude here," pointing to Eric, "and his very fine looking lady over there, said they know you."

Eric stood there with a big smile and I replied, "Never saw him before in my life." We all laughed and joined the ladies.

Just then Dave, his sister Jane and Joy arrived in their 57 Chevy. As they started walking toward us, Dave took Joy's hand and they smiled at each other. I wondered if they were now going to be a couple.

As we headed inside the pizza parlor Joy walked over to Marti. "You have a good man. He helped me realize how very special my brother was."

Marti nodded and replied, "Yea, I know, I think I'll keep him. Besides, it was Oz I wanted in the first place. They were a package deal." They both laughed and Marti winked at me.

We formally introduced Eric and Lois to the group and while we ate I told my tale of crime, passion, and murder. I concluded by saying, "But the real heroes of the day are Lois and Eric."

Everyone stood up and cheered. It was Bruce who, with little convincing got Lois to tell their side of the story. It was fun watching her tell every little detail and a big smile never left her face. Every now and then when Eric tried to say something she would give him the evil eye and he would shut up. I thought to myself, "They will make a great addition to the group."

Bruce stood, "Everyone let's stand and let's give a round of applause to Wes, Lois and Eric for finding the killers of our friend."

I interjected, "Let's not forget Oz. He saved my bacon."

We all laughed. I raised my glass and the others followed, "To Ed."

A NOTE FROM THE AUTHOR

Thank you so much for reading *"Death of a Trailer Queen."* I hope you were entertained and will recommend this fun and exciting mystery to your family, friends and co-workers. Since I am a self-published author, I would greatly appreciate it if you would write a review on Kindle Books.

I would also like to give you, my readers, a heads up on the second in the series which I hope to have out on the market by the middle of 2019. It's another exciting adventure of Wes and OZ titled *"A Mechanic's Worst Nightmare."*

Check out the great selection of memorabilia at the Wes and Oz Mysteries online store. Twenty five percent of the profits will go to one of Oz's local animal shelters. You will be helping other animals in need and show everyone you're a member of the Wes and Oz fan club.
https://www.cafepress.com/WesandOzMysteries

If you would like to reach out to me on a personal note, please feel free to write me at the email address below.

WesandOzMysteries@yahoo.com

Again, I want to thank you for reading *"Death of a Trailer Queen."*

Stephen B.

Made in the USA
San Bernardino, CA
23 April 2019